# SHARK'S
## *Edge*

SHARK'S EDGE: BOOK ONE

# ANGEL PAYNE & VICTORIA BLUE

# SHARK'S
## *Edge*

### SHARK'S EDGE: BOOK ONE

## ANGEL PAYNE & VICTORIA BLUE

WATERHOUSE PRESS

*David Duck, on our twenty-fifth anniversary,
how appropriate to write a book with the very
name you playfully gave me one summer night,
long, long ago? We're the proof that love stories do
exist. That real lives have colorful characters,
black moments, and happily ever afters.
Join me for another twenty-five?*

*XOXO SHNSHRK*

*—Victoria*

*For the man who swims all the depths with me . . .
and always protects the dolphin in me.
My beautiful hero, Thomas.
I am so grateful for you.*

*—Angel*

*Special Dedication*

*In loving memory of our dear friend
Ceej Chargualaf, who gave us so much of her heart
and generous, loving, kind spirit each time she beta
read for us. She's left an empty place in our lives
and our hearts, and we will carry a part of her
with us every day, especially when we need to
feel brave or sassy about something we're not
particularly confident doing. Ceej would
encourage us to move on that way.*

# CHAPTER ONE

## ABBI

I was hot.

Sweaty. Aching. Breathless.

Just how a girl should feel after being jolted awake in the middle of a naughty dream.

"Uhhh." I shut off my phone's alarm, fell back into my pillow, and glared at the time display through squinting eyelids.

Getting up at four thirty in the morning just wasn't sane. Wasn't. Sane.

My screen flared to life with a text message from a sender whose profile picture was a skull-and-crossbones Chuck Taylor high-top.

Rio.

I couldn't help but grin. My sister-in-law and right-hand woman loved to message me when she knew I should be getting up. She usually offered some bullshit reason for the predawn communiqué, but I saw right through her game. I had a terrible habit of oversleeping, and everyone in my family knew it.

*Did I interrupt a good dream?*

I forced my eyes open enough to tap back a reply.

*As a matter of fact, yes.*

I hit Send, hurled the phone into the covers, and draped the crook of my elbow over my face. "Oh, God."

The entirety of my dream crashed over me.

It had been another one of those dreams.

A dream in which I really had been hot and gasping, sweaty and stripped...

With Sebastian Shark.

Sebastian. Freaking. Shark.

The CEO of my catering company's biggest account. He who sat in his penthouse high in the Los Angeles skyline, ruling his kingdom with the subtlety of a Mack Truck. He with the body of a modern-day pharaoh—and the allure of one too.

That dark, dangerous allure.

Another moan tore up my throat. *Shark.* He was the last person on the planet I should've been harboring these cravings for, but he was the one my subconscious refused to forget. I couldn't ignore his hypnotic sensuality, his raw animal attraction.

If only my dream mind would listen to my awake mind.

Sebastian Shark liked the fact that he shared his name with a predator, and he made damn sure the entire world knew it, each and every day. And today would be no different.

"No different," I repeated to ensure my psyche got the message—and to prepare myself for the ordeal.

And yes, that was the right word. Though I was only going to be delivering lunch to him, the experience was always an ordeal. On good days, he'd give me an obligatory nod from behind his computer monitors. On the rare occasions when he decided I deserved a hello—never an actual smile, though—I relied on the breathe-deeply-and-count-to-ten method to deal with the war in my senses. And yes, that was the right word too.

It was a war in there. My raging libido versus my frustrated logic.

Because I knew I wasn't imagining the way the air thickened between us. An unmistakable call of his body to mine like mating animals in the springtime sun. Invisible strings pulled between us. And from the way he tracked my every movement with fixed attention while I set up his lunch each day, I knew he felt it too.

It was insanity.

"No." I brought my feet down on the rug next to my bed, but this morning the trendy shag pile was useless. The polished concrete floor of my "Bohemian Charm" condo felt like an ice block. Right now, that was a good thing.

"You're a glacier with that man, Abbigail Gibson," I growled at my reflection in the bathroom mirror. "Glacier. Cold. Glacier. Calm."

*No more letting Sebastian Shark under your skin.*

*No more letting Sebastian Shark into your damn dreams.*

After quickly showering and dressing for the day, I threw my long hair into a high ponytail and headed out the door for the large commercial-grade kitchen I rented in Inglewood. Fifteen minutes later, I parked my F-150 next to the van we used for deliveries—but stopped short when a distinct smell hit my senses. Savory. Earthy. Cheesy.

I hurried toward the door adorned with the words *Abstract Catering*, noticing the prep area lights were already on. Inside, a petite woman was folding serving containers and humming along to the radio.

"Morning." My greeting was lifeless but accomplished the job.

"Morning, sister friend!" Rio called out in return.

I rolled my eyes. "Don't you mean slacker?"

The whiskey of her irises flashed to gold. "Abs, you're a lot of things—but a slacker isn't one of them."

"Says the woman who probably sent me a wake-up text from here."

She smirked. "I couldn't sleep. Big deal."

*Again?*

I kept my question to myself for two reasons. One, it wouldn't get me anywhere. Rio had her demons, and she made it clear the one time she told me about them that it would also be the last. Two, we had an insane morning ahead of us. On top of our regular lunch-order routine, we had to prep for a private party tonight in Brentwood.

"You're crazy," I said.

"But you love me."

"Yeah, well . . . nobody turns veggie loaves into an art form like you. They're my biggest seller on the lunch runs."

"I don't think art has anything to do with it," Rio said. "More like all those health nuts in the skyscrapers would kill their own mother for something that tasted anything like meat."

"Which is why I love what you do with those." I nodded toward the row of loaves she'd just pulled from the oven. Their smell was savory to the point of mouthwatering.

"Yeah, well . . ." She moved to transfer the cakes to the individual serving containers, working to preserve as much of their heat as possible. "I know my meat, even when it's the fake stuff."

I spilled a wry giggle. "Not sure you want me touching that one."

She scooped up a bottle of Abstract Catering's secret

sauce and swirled the amber goo over the boxed loaves. If there was anything customers loved more than Rio's veggie loaves, it was that damn sauce. Never would I reveal that the special recipe was a simple mixture of ketchup, mustard, and— gasp—garlic mayonnaise.

"So . . ." The woman's suggestive tone put me on high alert. "It's Wednesday, which means your route includes Viktor Blake's office, yes?"

*Clang, clang, clang.* And there went the alarms.

"You know it does. But that means nothing more than my delivering his yummy veggie loaf promptly at eleven thirty, and that's it."

And it really was. Rio knew this drill already. I'd never be more than the lunch delivery girl to any of the high-powered executives on my downtown route, and that was by my design.

"Abbi—"

"Rio."

"We need to talk about this."

"We've already talked about this, which means you know how the conversation is going to end."

"Jesus Christ on cornbread." She capped her retort with a frustrated tilt of her head. "Unfortunately, I do. Also unfortunately, it won't be with you and that beautiful hunk getting horizontal."

While I let out an awkward laugh, Rio folded her arms and pouted. The woman was a force of nature when it came to scheming for everyone's Happily Ever After.

The idea of Viktor Blake wasn't horrific. Quite the opposite. He was a blond-haired, blue-eyed hottie who honored his sinewy Russian heritage so well, he'd been offered a promo deal with Stone Global's fitness supplement division.

If getting horny and horizontal with someone were my main goal right now, the man would be in the top three on the list. But still third. One of the spots would always be filled with Chris Hemsworth's name. And the other?

Sebastian Shark.

Viktor Blake was no Sebastian Shark.

A fact that neither man mourned, if the rumors about their professional rivalry were true.

"Come on. Getting horizontal with Viktor the Golden God has to have crossed your mind, Abbi. No disrespect to your brother, my amazing husband, but it crossed *my* mind when I covered for you that afternoon last month."

I raised a firm hand. "See it and talk to it, Rio. Shit like that is not going down between Viktor Blake and me."

"But—"

"Leave it."

"But—"

"Leave. It." I could hear the next *but* already churning in her throat. "You know my rules, okay? I didn't just make them up for my health. Or even for . . . How do you always say it?"

"Misplaced nobility." Her tone was wry but incisive.

"Ahhh, yes. My misplaced nobility."

My own tease earned me a huff from my sister-in-law. She folded her arms, facing me like a lawyer in cross-exam mode. "Why don't we just call it what it really is?"

"And why am I scared to ask what it really is?"

"Because you know what I'm about to say." She filled the air with tinny clangs as she tapped a fingernail against the table. "They're self-erected walls between you and humanity."

"Self-erected wa— I don't erect anything!"

Rio turned her hand over with splayed fingers. "Dropping

the mic. My work here is done."

I pressed my lips together, holding in a retort. All right, fine. Maybe I was fond of walls. But sometimes—a lot of times—the world needed walls. They kept life organized. Created boundaries where they were needed.

I wasn't indifferent and unfeeling. I was ambitious and focused. Separating professional and personal relationships was good business. And good business led to great business. And great business was the measure of my success.

And success—the resounding, undisputed kind—was where I was bound. No matter what it took. Including lifelong celibacy.

Since arriving here four years ago, just a month after high school graduation, I'd worked to build my name in a city where every other person owned a restaurant or catering outfit. Some of LA's most prominent companies—and with their notable leaders—relied on me. Crossing the line with any of those clients would be killing my dream before it began.

Speaking of that dream . . .

"Not so fast, dear sister. Your work here also means prepping the appetizers for the private party tonight." I smacked my hands together. *Back to the grind.* Best subject change in the world. "Chop-chop. We're running behind on the pesto."

"And you're running behind on the erections."

"Burning daylight, girlfriend," I hollered while turning and punching the button for the roll-up door, preparing to load the van with the lunch delivery boxes.

"Wasting your va—"

"Don't you dare finish that sentence, Rio!"

I looked back into the kitchen from the loading dock and

saw a glazed stare overtake Rio's face. I thought it was my threat that brought her crass retort to a grinding halt, but I was mistaken.

"Holy shit," she muttered as I got closer. Eyes riveted to the TV in the corner.

I rushed back into the prep area as fast as I could. Though the verbal expression was one of Rio's favorites, there was something extra in it that jolted every hair on my neck. "Holy shit *what*?"

We'd typically watch the local morning news during our meal prep hours to stay informed about weather and traffic conditions, but it wasn't Cy the Commute Guy on the screen. Rio was staring at a fresh-faced blonde, newly arrived from Omaha, who'd clearly never had to deliver difficult news. But she had to now, as the word *suicide* scrolled across the bottom of the screen, accompanied by video footage depicting emergency responder trucks next to a large expanse of water and a massive suspension bridge.

"Oh my God. Is that the Vincent Thomas?"

"Yeah," Rio rasped.

"Holy crap. Did someone—"

Rio finally located the remote and turned up the volume. "The woman, identified as twenty-seven-year-old Tawny Mansfield from Inglewood, leaped off the iconic bridge in San Pedro during the early morning hours. A dock worker who witnessed the event called 9-1-1. Her body was recovered from the water within hours."

The newscaster paused to take a drink of water. I didn't blame the woman. At last, she set down the water bottle and continued.

"The woman, wearing jeans and a sweat shirt, had an

airtight plastic bag wrapped around her torso, in which the police located a suicide note with details about Mansfield's recent breakup with local businessman Sebastian Shark."

And suddenly I was the one craving a drink.

Maybe two or three.

Within seconds, I was overheated. Aching and agitated. Unable to find the rhythm of my heart, the cadence of my thoughts, or the feeling in my toes.

Because that was what a single mention of Sebastian Shark did to me.

*Oh, God.* That had to make me the most messed-up person in this city. This state. Maybe in the entire world.

It changed nothing.

"Oh, hell. Sebastian Shark. Why am I not surprised?" Rio said.

Her comment, a bizarre mix of fascination and irritation, affected me like a fist to the gut. I was compelled to defend him. Demand she be fair and not accuse him of something we knew nothing about. All I could think about was how the news must have hit him.

Who the hell was I kidding?

He'd likely hit back even harder. Like he always did. With fire in his eyes, thunder in his swing, and ambition that'd likely be called inspirational in some future news piece.

"Shark, the enigmatic owner and CEO of Shark Enterprises, amassed his substantial fortune in worldwide logistics and shipping." Cindy was clearly more comfortable with these details of the story. "However, his business portfolio has expanded throughout the years. Recently, he announced plans to construct Shark's Edge, on target to be the tallest and most luxurious skyscraper in the LA skyline.

"Through our exclusive sources, Spotlight News has learned that Miss Mansfield's note made references to Shark's obsession with breaking ground on the building as soon as possible. There were several other items found in the airtight pouch, but as this is an ongoing investigation, those items have been collected as evidence and are confidential at this time."

Rio sniffed. "Oh, I can imagine what that's about."

I backhanded her shoulder. "Stop. Someone's dead."

"Exactly. Most likely after that man tossed her out of his life like rotten coleslaw."

"Coleslaw?"

"Clearly you haven't had to toss out an old batch lately."

"For which I'm grateful."

I wrapped an arm around her shoulders and tugged her close. She returned the embrace, but as we pulled apart, she hurled her next blow to my gut. "So how long do we wait before dropping Shark Enterprises?"

I laughed. Then scowled. Then laughed again. "Uhhh... none."

"Abs." Her stare turned to fire. "You're not seriously thinking—"

"Of continuing to serve the biggest client we have right now?"

She re-crossed her arms. "And because of that, you're automatically taking his side?"

"Whoa." I raised both hands. "How are there suddenly sides?"

"You don't realize the media is already creating them?"

"That woman jumped on her own. He wasn't up on that bridge with her."

While she openly fumed about that, I grabbed the chance

to neutralize my own features. My argument to retain Shark Enterprises as a customer made a ton of sense, but no way could I reveal it was based on anything except business. No way could Rio—or anyone else—discern what a mess Sebastian Shark made of my nerves, my senses, my sex drive.

"Look, I know the guy seems like a real douche sometimes. But we don't have to be in bed with him for—"

Rio cut in with a cute snort. "Luckily, we don't have to be in bed with him at all."

With an eye roll, I said, "You know what I'm talking about. The checks I'm collecting from Shark Enterprises are the surplus revenue we need to make headway on the dream."

I didn't elaborate past that because I knew Rio got it. My whole family did. Ever since the day my mom was suddenly supine on the kitchen floor, breathing her last breaths due to a massive coronary, making me promise I'd never give up on our vision. Ever since that morning, when I swore to her I'd one day own and operate a full restaurant and not a piddly food-delivery service.

Rio's huff saved me from diving down that heartache hole. "I get that. But you can get someone else as big as him, Abs. There are hundreds of huge corporations downtown."

"Yeah? And tell me how many of them are planning to break ground on a skyscraper that'll be a hundred stories high? That'll have both professional occupants and personal residents? That'll have hundreds, maybe thousands of people not just wanting lunch at noon but something easy to cook up for dinner that night? That'll be one of the largest exclusive catering contracts to ever be landed in the city?"

She hauled out a headstrong pout. "I hate it when you're right."

I preened—but just a little—and said nothing else. We were wasting time, and it was going to be a scorcher of a day. So instead, I refocused on loading the sandwiches and entrées for the day's runs.

Our new silence meant we could hear Cindy again. "LAPD has stated they'll be reaching out to Mr. Shark today, hoping he'll be able to provide more clues about Miss Mansfield's actions. But at this time, no foul play is suspected, and Mr. Shark is not under criminal investigation."

"Not a suspect." Rio harrumphed. "Too bad shattering a woman's heart isn't a criminal offense."

I had no idea whether to laugh, scream, or both. "The prison system would have an even bigger overcrowding problem then, wouldn't it?" I walked toward the delivery van. "Text if you have any issues with the pinwheels."

"Only if you promise to text back with pics of the circus at Shark's office."

I halted in my tracks. "Huh?"

She stared back, lips quirking, before drawling, "The... media circus?"

"*Pffft.*" I shook my head. "Not going to happen."

Her grin grew into a full giggle. "How do you call yourself an Angelino?"

I shot her a narrowed glare. "There's not going to be a circus, Rio."

"I predict at least a dozen rings, honey." She brightened and raised a finger in the air. "Hey, if you see TMZ, can you snag a selfie with their cute ginger reporter for me?"

"Oh my God."

"No, just little ol' me." She shrugged and gave me a playful wink. "The one you love with the passion of a thousand suns."

I spread my arms heavenward and turned to leave as Rio pumped a victory fist into the air.

"Pesto pinwheels!" I yelled over my shoulder.

"Cute ginger!"

"I'm doomed," I muttered for my ears alone while climbing into the driver's seat.

★ ★ ★

The frantic energy in the air was palpable the second I turned onto Hill Street. It was the same vibe that emanated from crowds gathering to ogle film or TV shoots, except worse.

Traffic crawled for several blocks before reaching the turnout where I normally kept the van while making deliveries in the building Shark Enterprises occupied. Not happening today. Four bulky vans were parked bumper-to-bumper in the spot, with a fifth attempting to be part of the mayhem.

"Dream on, asshole," I growled at the van, its back end trapping me in place while the honking cars behind me tried to merge into the next lane over.

I was getting ready for some head-slams onto the steering wheel when a bright spot in the chaos appeared. A cutie with a lanky physique and big hair jogged out to the curb. I pressed the switch to lower the van's passenger-side window, and Maddon leaned in.

"Yo, sandwich goddess," he said in a relaxed drawl. "So what's the sitch, right?" He gestured toward the media mob with a dazed look.

"Hey, Mads." I gave him a friendly smile. I admired how hard the guy worked but always made it look like fun. "Guess it's a slow news day."

I'd have to admit to Rio how right she was about all this. *Damn it.*

"Truth. And there's more of them inside. This is just the overflow." He dragged a hand through his wild auburn locks. "Apologies about your spot. I set cones out, but CBS flattened them. Crazy, right?"

"Right. Crazy." But that wasn't going to help me unload sixty prepaid lunch orders... Most notably, the meal for the man everyone was here to see.

The man in the penthouse.

The same man who hardly stopped to look at what I brought anyway.

Still, as I considered the likelihood of going a day without Sebastian Shark's menacing glory, there was an undeniable sensation in the pit of my stomach. The feeling seemed to swell until it lodged between my breasts, causing every inhalation to be a physical ache.

What the hell was this?

The answer wasn't reassuring.

*Disappointment.*

Unfounded. Unexplainable. But there all the same.

Maybe I really should have let someone pop my cherry at some point over the years. Maybe I wouldn't be sitting here in a funk over a man who barely knew I existed.

"I know it's not a perfect fix, but I called back to the loading dock." Maddon grinned, as if that alone was an accomplishment and a half. "They have a place for you to park back there if you promise not to take more than an hour."

And just like that, my frustration turned into jubilation. "Mads, I could freaking kiss you."

The poor kid looked instantly conflicted. "Or I could have

a turkey and tomato on rye instead?"

I swooped the sandwich out with eager speed—and a hell of a lot of gratitude.

Which was the last sensation I should've had as I drove the van to the rear of the building, now making my load in twice as difficult.

I unpacked the delivery coolers and ordered myself to take in calming breaths, begging the extra oxygen to ease my anticipation. The same ritual I practiced every time I arrived at this building.

No use, though. Apparently changing how I entered the building didn't change the emotional riot inside me once I did. My nerves got no relief. The torque in my stomach became the pressure in my chest—and there wasn't a damn thing I could do about it until I was up in the penthouse.

And why was that? I'd be lucky to get a hello, yet I craved his attention like a forgotten middle child. But my body had become addicted to the physical reaction he induced. The chemical high I got from the excitement of knowing he watched me. I caught him enough times by then to know it was a part of our regular routine. He was getting bolder, though, and no longer bothered to look away when our eyes met. I was usually the one who would quickly avert my gaze back to my approved task.

Did that make me a coward? Maybe. But at least things would be in their proper place, business as usual. Everything that was expected to happen would. Right on cue. Rules followed. Lines colored within. Everyone knowing their roles.

*Walls erected.*

Whatever. So what if Rio was right? It wasn't a bad thing to keep professional lines very clear. Even if I wasn't the only one blurring them. All this nonsense just served as a reminder. A reminder to approach this whole ordeal like tossing out bad coleslaw. Just like Rio said. It would be unpleasant for a little bit, but I'd be better off in the end.

"Coleslaw." I turned it into a whispered mantra while disembarking the elevator at the penthouse level. "Coleslaw. Coleslaw. Coleslaw."

But there was just one hitch with that plan now.

Damn it...

I really liked coleslaw.

# CHAPTER TWO

## SEBASTIAN

Two hours. Two goddamn hours into the day and my brain felt like it was splitting along the corpus callosum into its two equal halves.

The collection of oversize monitors on my desk displayed different news channels' coverage from outside my own building. Overly dramatic talking heads were spouting facts and less-than-facts about a woman who threw herself from the Vincent Thomas Bridge in San Pedro before dawn. Somehow, my name was being dragged into the fiasco, and now the bloodhounds were sniffing and yipping at my front door, looking for an exclusive scoop.

A sharp knock on my office door barely sounded above the helicopters that droned overhead.

"Terryn! I told you, I don't want to talk to anyone."

I had to give my assistant a bit of credit. She'd lasted longer than all the others. We might even see the full turn of a calendar at this pace.

"Sorry to let you down, boss man. Not Terryn." Grant Twombley strode into my office and quietly closed the door behind him. My best friend—hell, my only friend—had a grin on his face that was completely out of place considering the media hailstorm swirling around the building.

"I hate when you call me that." I stabbed at the keyboard to bring up a different news outlet on one of the screens.

"Precisely why I say it." He chuckled, his grin growing impossibly wider.

"What can I do for you, Grant? I'm a little busy, in case you haven't noticed." I motioned with a huff toward the monitors on my desk and then to the floor-to-ceiling windows lining the far side of my expansive penthouse office.

"You'd have to be unconscious not to notice the chaos in here today, my man. What have you gotten yourself into this time?" He rubbed at his chin with his thumb and index finger, looking at me with open skepticism.

"This is complete bullshit. I didn't even know this... this..." I thought better of calling a recently deceased woman the derogatory term that came to mind. Even a bastard like me knew that would be in poor taste.

"Way to rein it in, Bas. Charm school is finally paying off." Of course Grant didn't miss my self-edit.

"Fuck off," I muttered again, not bothering to spare him my true feelings. He'd seen me at my highest highs and my lowest lows. We'd grown up together on the streets of the east side of LA and had each other's backs more times than either of us cared to remember. Our friendship was beyond brother-deep.

"Seriously though, my friend. What's the story here? Before the legal team assembles. You must have really done a number on this one." He flopped down onto one of three black leather sofas that were arranged in a perfect U shape in the sitting area of my suite.

Just as he stretched his long legs out to prop them on the table in front of him, I stood and scolded, "Keep your nasty feet off my furniture. Do you do that at your own house?"

"Actually, I do. Why do we go through this every time I'm in here? You're worse than a nagging wife." He planted his feet on the floor and sat farther back into the deep cushion. At six feet six, it was hard for the man to sit comfortably on most furniture, but that was hardly my concern.

"Because if Pia saw you putting your feet on that table or sofa"—I stabbed my finger at each piece as I lectured—"or anything other than the floor, she would serve us both our balls for lunch."

Grant held up his hands in surrender. "Enough said. Enough said. But speaking of lunch, when does the little redhead scurry by? I'm starving."

"Those are Terryn things. Not Shark things."

"Nice try. And we're talking about ourselves in the third person now? How dictatorial asshole of you."

I leveled my stare at him to convey *explain*.

"I see the way you sneak in gawks at that catering girl's ass."

"I do no such—"

"Cut the shit." Only Grant could get away with such rudeness and live to do it a second time. He stood and walked over to my desk. "This is me you're talking to. The same guy you confessed your crush on Miss Dandelion to when we were in the third grade, remember?"

"Yeah." I let out a sigh, remembering our heavenly third-grade teacher. "But her tits . . ."

"They were stellar tits."

"I wonder whatever happened to Miss Dandelion." I let myself drift to the past, away from the disaster of the present. Life was so much simpler then—even if my father was a neglectful drunk and I was already taking care of myself and Pia.

Grant's voice interrupted my memories. "Every boy in the class sported their first boner for that doe-eyed teacher."

I shook my head hard before snapping, "Yeah, well, some douchebag probably plucked her pretty flower and then she became old and bitter, just like the rest of the teachers at that school."

I smacked the top of my desk with my palms, making Grant jump.

"So jaded." Sadness clouded his normally lively eyes. "Always so jaded."

"It's called reality, Grant." I walked over to the wall of windows while I spoke. "And you know it's the truth. Look at the bullshit going on right now if you think it's anything else."

This was my usual thinking spot. Mid-room, staring out from the top floor of my downtown building over the City of Angels. I crossed my arms over my chest and faced the extraordinary view, this bird's-eye vantage point of my empire. I owned a good portion of this city and made deals by the hour to acquire more.

A king.

My kingdom.

I'd earned every bit of it.

Every. Single. Bit.

But now someone was messing with me, and they wouldn't get away with it. I barely recalled the woman's name, even though it kept popping up on the news reports. *Tawny Mansfield.* But really, in a sea of Candys and Sugars and the occasional Minx or Jinx, Tawny didn't seem all that special.

I wasn't doing much better with her face in the grainy

photo that flashed across the screen repeatedly. Dancers and escorts had a certain look in common. A little too much makeup, a little too much hair product, clothes that were worn a little too tight. Nothing really stood out about her appearance either.

What did it matter?

What did they matter?

Well, of course they mattered, but not to me. That was my issue. Mine. I wasn't interested in getting attached. I didn't have time for relationships, and I certainly didn't have time for emotions. I stuck to secure sexual transactions. Uncomplicated arrangements where both parties knew exactly what was—and wasn't—expected.

"Do you think she was one of LuLu's girls?" my best friend asked, as if he had a direct link into my thoughts.

"I don't think so. I imagine LuLu would've already been breathing down my neck by this point if she were. She's fiercely protective of her assets." It wouldn't hurt to confirm the thought, though.

"Siri, page Terryn."

"Do you mean fucking Terryn?" the disembodied voice volleyed back.

"Yes!"

Grant's face split in two with a wide grin.

"Yes, Mr. Shark?" Terryn's voice came over the intercom speaker.

"Get Louise Chancellor on the phone." I didn't bother with "can you" or "please." Just merely stated what I needed and expected my assistant to make it happen.

"I can, but I may be able to save you a call. Ms. Chancellor left a message about fifteen minutes ago. I'm sorry I haven't been able to give it to you before now, sir. It's been a bit hectic out here."

"Cry me a river, Terryn. Just tell me what she said." I scrubbed my hand down my face, hoping to hell Tawny Mansfield hadn't worked for the high-end madam I regularly used.

"Ms. Chancellor said, and I'm quoting..." Terryn inserted a dramatic beat. "'She wasn't one of mine.'" She paused again before adding, "Uhh, I'm guessing that makes sense to you?"

"Terryn?" I queried, impatience oozing from my voice.

"Sir?"

"Is it your job to play superspy decoder ring or just give me my phone messages?"

"Uhh. I was just trying to make sure—"

"Terryn?" I cut her off before she could stammer any longer, wasting my valuable time.

"Yes?" she answered timidly. *Christ.* I'd break this one too. It was just a matter of time.

"Just answer the question so we can both get back to work."

"To give you your phone messages, sir." Her voice had gained strength as she repeated the answer option verbatim.

"Perfect. Now where's my lunch?" I switched topics, ready to move on to the next item.

A soft knock sounded on the door, and just like that, my dick twitched in my slacks. It was like my goddamned body sensed the young redhead was within a fifty-foot radius.

"Never mind," I said, disconnecting the intercom. "Enter!" I shouted toward the door, the way I always did when Little Red Riding Hood came by with my lunch.

Most days, I attempted to appear occupied with my work

as she set up my meal, but since I was already standing in the middle of the room, there'd be no way to avoid her today. Maybe that was a good thing. It just meant I could sneak in a few glances of her glorious, lithe body from a new angle. I'd been getting more obvious with my staring lately, but it couldn't be helped. The air thickened between us the moment she walked through my door. The thrill of the hunt, maybe?

"Oh. Well. Hi. Hello," she stammered, taking in my looming form from head to toe as she came into my penthouse office. Gazes locked. Breaths stuttered. Cheeks flamed.

And then my annoying COO cleared his throat, tramping through our moment like a wayward puppy through a newly planted flower bed. I gave him a sideways glance, and Ms. Gibson slipped past me while asking her daily inquiry.

"Where would you like me to set up lunch today, Mr. Shark?"

*On your flat stomach. Between your milky thighs.*

"Here, let me help you with that." Grant, a warm smile on his face, all but tripped over himself to take the large tray from her.

"Sit down, Twombley. Let the girl do her job." *Because you're spoiling my view.*

He glared at me over his shoulder and continued taking the burden off Little Red, ignoring me completely. "This looks fantastic," he said, giving her the full force of his pussy-slayer grin.

"Thanks. I tried something new with the dressing today. We've been working on a few new recipes." She gave an impish shrug toward the food before looking back up to Grant. "Are you having lunch in this office today, Mr. Twombley? I can get your tray off the cart and set it up in here as well." As they moved deeper into the penthouse to the area I used for meetings, they continued chatting. She tilted her head way back since he towered over her by a solid twelve inches. Then they both swung their gazes to me.

"Well, shit, don't let me interrupt." I threw my hands up, unexplainably pissed after watching their exchange.

Who was I trying to kid? It was completely explainable.

*It's called jealousy, motherfucker. The good old-fashioned green-eyed monster.*

But what the hell was that about?

I didn't experience jealousy. I inspired it.

I narrowed my eyes at the young caterer and then shifted my stare to Grant. "We need to strategize about this Mansfield situation. More specifically, how it might delay progress on the Edge. We can do that while we eat."

Grant pivoted smoothly back toward Abbigail. "If it wouldn't be too much trouble, then . . . I'm sorry. I don't think I've ever caught your name." He set the tray down on my sleek stainless-steel conference table and offered his hand. "Grant Twombley."

I continued to stare in borderline fury while my chief operating officer gently caressed the inside wrist of the intriguing redheaded sandwich girl. Her lips parted slightly while she stuttered to form her own name, wholly affected by his attention.

"Abbigail Gibson. Abstract Catering. It's very nice to meet you, umm, Mr. Twombley." She smiled shyly, causing me to suck in air sharply. The woman yanked her hand from Grant's at once, darting her eyes in my direction as if caught doing something she shouldn't be doing.

Grant leaned down, sharing a conspiratorial murmur.

"Ignore him. Nearly everyone does."

"I find that hard to believe," she replied quietly. I almost thought I misheard her but trusted my senses. I also had help from the sexy red flush spreading like wildfire up her neck and cheeks.

What the hell was it about this girl that had my balls pulling up so tight?

Literally.

She was young. Very young. Something that generally had me running the other way quicker than a wedding band on a flirtatious woman's finger. But there was an unmistakable pull from her that rendered the complete opposite effect. And that bastard Twombley—who knew me better than anyone—was playing me like a fiddle and using her as the bow.

"So, Mansfield wasn't from LuLu's stable. Are you using anyone else?" Grant asked as we sat down to eat. Anyone who had access to this room had signed a nondisclosure agreement, so we didn't have to censor our conversation.

I watched the sandwich girl walk out of my office to get his food, finding it impossible not to focus on her tight ass as she went. Christ, I'd love to dig my fingers into the flesh of those perfectly round cheeks while she bounced on my lap and I gave her the best ride of her life.

"Dude."

I shook my head slightly. "No, but I've been thinking; maybe she was from Club Delilah. That's the only other place I may have met her—if I ever met her at all. I'm still not convinced I did. She doesn't look familiar. This whole thing could be a setup." I shifted in my seat, trying to adjust myself in my suddenly too tight slacks.

Abbigail came bustling back in with another tray of food for Grant.

"This smells like that Russian bastard if you ask me."

Grant scoffed. "I think you're giving Blake more credit than he deserves. How would he manage details of this magnitude? Finding a woman you slept with, a damaged one at that, and then planting a suicide note that implicates you? Think about it. Just saying it all out loud"—Grant shook his head slowly—"do you hear how ridiculous it sounds?" He leaned back in his chair to make room for Abbigail to place his food in front of him.

"I don't know," I said, unrolling my utensils from the tidy rolled linen napkin that always accompanied my lunch. "I wouldn't put anything past him. He's a bitter, ruthless cocksucker. Vengeance drives men to do unhinged things."

"Excuse me, gentlemen." The caterer stood off to the side, waiting for a break in our conversation.

We both looked to Little Red. Grant smiled, but I was mid-chew, just about to swallow the first bite of my lunch.

"Forgive my interruption… I just wanted to see if you needed anything else before I left."

"Did we ask for anything else?" I tilted my chin in her direction.

Her already large green eyes widened farther.

Grant quickly interjected. "This looks great. Thank you so much, Ms. Gibson."

My God. Her eyes. Green like emeralds. Emerald City in *The Wizard of Oz* emerald. They were mesmerizing.

She slid her head back as if ready to launch into some sort of tirade or comeback. Likely about my lack of civility. With a rough swallow, she tamped down the inclination.

Without another word but with the unmistakable welling of tears in her huge green eyes, Abbigail Gibson bolted from the room. Complete with a slight—and sexy as hell—stumble right before she reached the door. She caught herself on the ornate knob and then let herself out. My ears vibrated, catching the buzz of her mumbled comments as she frantically exited.

"My God, you can be an asshole." Grant stared at me in disbelief.

"What?" I said around a second forkful of greens, making the delivery something more like "*Whuu?*"

"You made that girl cry." He pointed toward the door with his fork.

I chewed slowly and then wiped my mouth with the linen napkin. Today it was sky blue. A different color every day. Yes, I'd noticed.

"I didn't make her cry, Grant." I grinned from behind the napkin. "But now I have a hard-on, too. This day just keeps getting better."

"Her crying made you hard?"

"I'm an asshole, Grant. Why are you acting like it's breaking news?"

"You're going to die a lonely old man."

"Again, breaking news? And to clarify, I don't enjoy making women cry. But something about seeing her cry . . ." I shook my head, bewildered. "I don't really understand it myself. She just looked so fragile and vulnerable. Like she needs someone." My voice had gotten unusually quiet as I pictured the tears filling Abbigail's eyes. "Someone to be her everything."

Wonder of wonders, I'd finally rendered my best friend speechless. There really was a first time for everything. But I'd also succeeded in coating the room with a heavy shroud of intense emotion. An environment in which neither of us were particularly comfortable.

So I shrugged and took another bite of my salad. "And really, she should've left the dressing recipe alone. This one sucks." I pushed the plate to the side. "Why can't she just serve an old favorite like coleslaw? Everyone loves coleslaw. My mom made the best coleslaw ever, and we'd always bring it to family reunions. When we went to those sorts of things."

Enough of Abbigail Gibson talk for the time being. I had real problems to deal with, as I was reminded by Terryn's familiar knock on the door.

"What?" I called from the far end of the room.

"Sir? Your twelve fifteen is here." Her mousy voice sounded from the other side of the panel.

"Damn it!" I thought for a second. "Terryn, get in here."

She opened the door slowly, looking like she was ready to duck and take cover in case I threw something. Which, for the record, I had never actually done. The woman was as overdramatic as Grant.

"Clear this out of here." I made a sweeping gesture to the lunch spread on the table. "I need to take the meeting here."

She looked down at the barely touched lunch. "Do you want me to wrap it for later? You'll probably be here late; your schedule is pretty full today."

I knew I should be touched—or some shit like that—that she was thinking of my well-being and planning for the entire day, not just appointment by appointment. I admired that about this assistant, but I wasn't about to dole out compliments and risk her getting full of herself.

"No. It wasn't good the first go-around. I can't imagine it reheated." I grimaced.

Grant stood. "Terryn, please wrap the plate for Mr. Shark. It's a sandwich, for Christ's sake. It won't need to be reheated.

He's just being his usual pleasant self. If he doesn't eat it, I will."

She smiled up at him while he helped her consolidate the leftovers from both our lunches onto one tray and stack the empty plate beneath, and then he held the door open while she scurried out with the food. But not before she gave him another imploring smile and a quickly mouthed *thank you*.

"You're such a pushover."

"Next to you, everyone looks like a pushover. Ebenezer Scrooge would look like a doormat next to you, Bas."

"Meh." I shrugged. "Dude was a cuck. What can I say?"

★ ★ ★

The meeting with the soils engineer was dragging on for the longest thirty minutes of my life. The spreadsheet in front of me showed seismic fault evaluations, color-coded by date and lot number, for most of the downtown corridor where my new building would be constructed. But between the tedious nature of the material being discussed and the constant nagging reminders of what was going on with the media outside the front doors, focusing on any of it was challenging.

The project had been named Shark's Edge years ago when I'd first announced my dream to the team I'd assembled to turn my lifelong vision into reality. The marketing gurus I had paid ungodly amounts of money felt like the name reflected both my corporation's mission statement and my personality's strong attributes all while mirroring the architectural design elements of the edifice itself.

"Is any of this going to delay the forward momentum? I'm committed to staying on schedule." I looked pointedly at Jonathan Brookside, the man sitting across from me, expecting a straightforward answer.

"Well, that's hard to say." Brookside shifted in his seat.

"*Booooonnnnkkkk*," I blared obnoxiously, imitating the quarter-ending horn at a basketball game. Grant scowled in my peripheral view. "Wrong answer, my man."

Taking a fortifying breath, Jonathan launched into an explanation of why he was, indeed, giving the right answer. By the time he was finished, I was both annoyed that he'd challenged me and impressed because the man really knew what he was talking about.

"It's a complicated process, Mr. Shark." He set down his pen and spun it from the center. "As we outlined in our initial proposal, many factors are at play here. They come together to form our final report for the architect and structural engineer. Both entities need our report for sign-offs with the city's inspectors. We sent you images when we did the on-site boring to obtain soil samples several weeks ago." He looked up to make sure I was still listening. "Did you get that email?"

"Yes, I did, and I appreciate you keeping me in the loop. This project is of the utmost importance to me. Despite what the circus out front may imply." I settled back in my chair and waited for him to continue.

Brookside nodded once and continued. "The lab is wrapping up their testing of those samples. I'd like to schedule another meeting next week to present our final package. Your team will be able to see the three-dimensional geometry of the underlying earth materials, the lab results from the soil samples, the seismic fault evaluations and predictions, similar to what you have in front of you here." He tapped his neatly manicured finger on the spreadsheet in front of me. The man dealt with dirt all day but apparently didn't touch much of it himself.

"Lastly, we will recommend foundation and sewage disposal options for your project based on the compiled data. The only issue we've had up to this point is obtaining public records for the property itself and the surrounding lots. This information is vital in forming a complete picture."

Keeping his eyes fixed on me, he asked bluntly, "Have you pissed someone off at City Hall?"

Grant chuffed from the seat beside me. "You'd probably be better off asking who he hasn't pissed off. Anywhere. Ever."

"That's what I was afraid of. I realize you don't know me from Adam. I also get the distinct impression you aren't the sort of man who takes advice easily. But I'm going to give you some anyway." He held up his hand to stop me from spouting off before I could say a word.

"I've built a lot of buildings in this city, Mr. Shark. Start playing nice with the suits up there. They can make this project a real headache for you if they want to. And figuring out what the holdup is can be nearly impossible. If someone owes you a favor, hold on to it. You'll probably have to call it in."

He efficiently shuffled his papers together and stood to leave. We shook hands and agreed he would set up a follow-up meeting with Terryn on his way out. When he cleared the door and closed it securely, Grant heaved into the sofa, much as he had earlier.

"I knew we were going to run into trouble at the city."

"Anything worth having is worth fighting for, my friend."

He sat forward, rubbing the back of his neck. "God, my neck is stiff already. I need a massage. What's next?" He slumped down lower on the couch to rest his head on the low back cushion.

I scrolled through the calendar app on the monitor that

displayed my dashboard—the hub of the inner workings of my life.

"I thought I had a meeting with Pia, but that's been moved to dinner." Frustrated, I activated the computer's virtual assistant. "Siri, page Terryn."

"Do you mean fucking Terryn?" the voice asked from the built-in speakers.

"Yes!" I turned to Grant. "How am I ever going to retrain that thing?"

He laughed. "I think you're stuck with it like that. I hope she never hears it, though."

"Yes, Mr. Shark?"

"Why has my appointment with my sister been moved to dinner?"

"Because the police are here to speak with you. I called to reschedule with Pia, and the first thing she had open was at six. She said if it doesn't work, you can see her Sunday at Vela's game."

"Fine."

Dead silence.

Then finally, "Sir?"

"What?" I snapped.

"Shall I send in the detectives?"

"Give me three minutes and then send them in." I mashed my fist onto the keyboard to disconnect the conversation, launching an unwanted web browser window and opening a new email message all at the same time. Muttering a string of profanity, I began quitting the unnecessary applications I'd opened in my frustration.

"You're going to blow a gasket if you don't settle down," Grant mumbled, rubbing his sore neck. I didn't miss the tension he was holding himself.

"Thank you, wise and healthy one." I checked my email and spotted an incoming message from my amazing, smart, and sassy niece, Vela. She was only eight, but she already showed her mother's take-charge temperament.

*Dear Uncle Sebastian,*

*I can't wait to see you at my soccer game tomorrow. My number is four so you can look for me on the field. Mom says your eyesight isn't that great because you are so old. She was laughing when she said that, so I think she was just teasing you like she likes to do. After the game we have snacks and juice, but I will share mine with you if you want.*

*See you tomorrow!*

*Love,*

*Vela*

That child was one of the few things that brought light into my life. A genuine smile spread across my lips but vanished as Terryn knocked on the door. The escape was nice for the two minutes it lasted.

"Email from Vela again? That's the only time I see that peaceful look on your face." Grant stood and slid on his suit jacket.

I quickly did the same, buttoning up and pulling the cuffs of my shirt into place.

"Yeah." I sighed heavily. "She's so precious. Innocent. I want to protect her from everything. All the bad shit in the world. All the bad people. My sister gave humankind the best gift when she created that little girl. On the other hand, if I ever find the loser who fathered her and then abandoned her..."

With that unpleasant thought, I strode across the room to greet the two police detectives, hoping to convince them I had nothing to do with Tawny Mansfield's alleged suicide.

"Well, I'll be damned." I shook my head, hand outstretched to greet the two detectives.

Terryn looked crestfallen that she'd missed the opportunity to do some sort of dramatic introduction, but when the taller of the two cops clasped my hand heartily and grinned from ear to ear, it became clear to her that introductions wouldn't be necessary.

Grant stepped in to slap the man's back in hello. "Josh Peters, how long has it been, man?"

"Too long. Too long. You both look good." The blond detective looked Grant and me over from head to toe a couple of times and then took a quick turn around the penthouse. "I should've stuck with the two of you back in the day. Apparently whatever you're doing for a paycheck beats the hell out of the police force."

"Let's sit down, please. Can I get either of you something to drink?" I offered, reminding Josh of the partner standing beside him.

"Shit, sorry, man. This is my partner, Detective Branson Hale."

I shook the stout man's hand, introducing myself. "Sebastian Shark. This is my chief of operations, Grant Twombley." Grant leaned in to shake Detective Hale's hand too.

"Drinks? Anyone?" Grant asked, heading toward the refrigerator as I motioned to the sofas for the detectives to get comfortable.

"No, thank you," they answered in unison. Josh chuckled but Branson winced.

"We won't take up much of your time, Mr. Shark. We have a few routine questions regarding an incident that took place this morning on the Vincent Thomas Bridge in San Pedro."

Grant rejoined us while Detective Hale spoke, and I made eye contact with my old friend, Josh. I could already tell his partner was a completely by-the-book kind of police officer.

*Good.* I had nothing to hide, and the sooner any suspicion surrounding my name was cleared, the better.

"Judging by the chaos in front of your building, I assume you're familiar with the incident in question. Or do you always have that many reporters and groupies with signs hanging out near the entrance of your office?" Josh asked, more lighthearted than his partner.

"No," I said, forcing a laugh. "That's a new development."

"So how did you know Ms. Mansfield?" he asked, brows raised.

"I'm not sure I do. Or did, rather."

"You never met the woman?" Hale twisted his mouth with doubt. "Odd, since she claimed you were dating. And that you broke her heart."

"We definitely weren't dating. I don't date."

Hale went on as if I never spoke. "She went through great lengths to secure a suicide note, detailing the whole thing, to her body before jumping off that bridge."

"I don't know how else to word it, Detective. I don't date women. I fuck them. Usually once. That's it." I shrugged. Seemed pretty cut and dry to me. I looked at Grant, and he gave a matching shrug.

*See? He understands where I'm coming from.*

"Why do you think this woman, Ms. Mansfield, would say that you broke her heart, then? That seems a bit extreme if you only slept with her one time."

I pushed Josh's knee so it knocked into his other one, playing up our friendship. "You know how women can get after you sleep with them—all starry-eyed. Add in my money and shit, maybe she thought I was going to be her next sugar daddy? I don't know."

But Hale was like a dog with a bone. Question after question until I finally stood up, calling an end to the interrogation. "I think I should probably have my attorney present if you gentlemen need to ask me anything else."

"I think we have everything we need for now. Here's my card—"

Hale made to offer his card, but I held my hand up to stop him. "I don't need your card, man. You can leave it with my assistant if you feel like you need to, but I won't be using it. Guaranteed."

"Sebastian." Josh shook my hand, giving me a solid smack on the shoulder while doing so.

"Grant." He repeated the gesture with my best friend while I showed them to the door. "Thanks for taking the time to chat with us. It was great to see you two."

"Same here, Josh. Take care," Grant said as he closed the door and faced me.

"What in the actual fuck is going on?" I asked him, rubbing my throbbing forehead.

"I was just going to ask you the same thing."

# CHAPTER THREE

**ABBI**

My lungs screamed and my thighs burned, but I pushed myself to finish strong on the final leg of my sunset jogging loop along Venice Beach.

Though I usually avoided the shorefront trail at this time of summer—when runners and cyclists were joined by tourists, street performers, and the owner of every sculpted body in Southern California—the chaos was a welcome distraction for my mind right now.

Ever since the bizarre turn of events on Monday, I'd refused to return to the Shark Enterprises building.

Clarification. I'd pulled myself out of the picture, not Abstract Catering. I was shaken, not stupid. Rio, like the superstar she was, had jumped in on covering the downtown route after I'd sneaked in a sentence about the media mob freaking me out—not completely the truth, though not a lie—but now it was Thursday, and the reporters were tiring of Shark's information blackout regarding what had happened to Tawny Mansfield.

Not that he gave a crap that they all needed to make a living too—or that some people in this city might care about what had driven a woman to take her own life. A woman he didn't even remember, if I was correctly interpreting the snippets I'd heard during his chat with Grant Twombley on Monday.

Yeah. A freaking chat. As if they were shooting the breeze about the Dodgers' winning streak or a fluctuation in the stock market, not a woman who'd been dead for less than twenty-four hours.

I forced my eyes open, grimacing into the wind as I paced in a circle, hoping to walk off a cramp. The pain didn't dissipate. Neither did my memories of those unbearable, unnerving, utterly arousing moments.

"No."

I plopped onto a bench and dropped my head onto my crossed arms.

I couldn't take it back. I'd finally admitted the truth. I'd been standing in Sebastian Shark's office, aroused as hell and trembling like Red Riding Hood in the middle of a wolf pack.

All while being assessed by the pack's alpha himself.

At least he'd come all the way out from the computer monitor man cave. For the first time, I'd discovered Sebastian Shark actually had legs—and they were glorious. And of course, they were topped by an ass that belonged on some graceful angel, not a devil with ice-blue eyes and a steel-angled jawline.

By the time I realized we weren't alone in the room, his right-hand man had witnessed our mutual gawk fest. Not that it bothered Shark—in the least. After all, what was another lascivious leer of another pair of breasts and thighs to the man? Hell, they probably had a good laugh at my expense after I tripped out the door in frustration. Just thinking about it now made me wince with residual mortification.

The alarm from my calendar app cut through the playlist still filling my ears. I needed to get across town for a hair appointment I'd scheduled weeks ago after Rio encouraged me to try something new for summer.

Who was I kidding?

"Something new" could be as simple as a two-inch trim instead of the half inch I normally went with. Rio teased me mercilessly that I acted more like a steadfast sixty-two-year-old woman instead of the twenty-two-year-old I actually was. Rio thought I should be footloose and fancy-free—her words, not mine—and I couldn't even come up with a valid excuse not to be. Because she wasn't wrong.

When I got to my truck in the public lot, I whipped my sweaty T-shirt over my head and grabbed a fresh one out of the bag on the passenger seat. Just as I was plugging my phone into the charger, I received a text.

> *Hello Abbigail. It's Viktor Blake. Pardon the note on your personal device, but your sister-in-law was just here delivering lunch and said it would be fine to contact you. Hope you are feeling better and will soon be back to brightening our days.*

I sighed, watching the dots bounce from his end as if he had more to say, but after I started the engine and my phone connected to the truck's Bluetooth, they were gone.

*Thank God.*

I didn't want to wake my cell back up from sleep mode, for fear of what the screen would bring from my "friend," so I put the truck in drive and headed toward my hairdresser.

No matter what Rio was attempting to spin, the man wasn't my friend. Honestly, I wondered how many friends Viktor Blake actually had. There was something off about the way he handled himself, always ready to greet me like some housewife from a forgotten era.

It was creepy.

Which made his text *really* creepy.

Amber, my hair girl, had a shop located about half the distance between the beach and my condo in Torrance, and the late-afternoon traffic gods smiled down on me. I made the journey in about forty-five minutes, which also gave me enough time to check in with Rio while I drove to my appointment.

"Greetings, savior of my sanity," I said into the open cab of my truck when the phone call connected. It wasn't the first time, especially in the last few days, that I'd given Rio an honorific greeting of one type or another. I owed her—big-time—for taking the heat around Shark's offices, but she was so much better at handling stressful situations than I was. Plus, there was the whole *obsessed with the man and the way he looks at me* situation that I was secretly dealing with and had no intention of sharing with Rio.

"Mmm, I don't know, Abs. You might want to go light on the savior awards today." She cleared her throat nervously.

"Why? What happened?" I forced myself to sound easy. Didn't think I was fooling her, though.

"I just want you to understand that I didn't start it, Abbigail." Rio sounded like a schoolgirl hurrying in from recess to tattle on a classmate.

"Shit." *Did we lose the contract at Shark Enterprises?*

"I did *not* do a thing, Abs," Rio insisted.

"I heard you the first time, Rio, and I believe you. Just tell me what—"

"I walked into his office, dropped the tray on the table in front of the couches, and then left." She let out a deep sigh. "Well, I tried to leave."

"What happened?" And why was I so torn between being worried for her and being jealous of her?

"At first, it was just like every other day."

"A few growls from the wall of computer monitors?"

"Bull's-eye."

"Okay . . ." Just the thought of Rio in the same room with the devil from my fantasies infected me with more dark envy—and a swath of shame. "So what was the problem?"

"Well . . . he was the problem."

"In what way?" I was trying to not sound too curious. And again . . . didn't think I was fooling her.

"He ordered me to stop. Like . . . in my tracks. And I wasn't bothering him at all. I didn't say a damn word to him, Abbi. I promise."

"Rio. I believe you. He can be very demanding. He's like that to everyone," I said conspiratorially to ensure Rio knew I was sympathizing with her. "Routinely."

I rubbed at the ache in my belly. "So why did he order you, as you called it, to wait?"

"Well . . ." Her pause was strange because my sister-in-law was never at a loss for words. Ever. "It was because of . . . you."

"Me?" I stopped rubbing. It wasn't going to help. "Why me?"

*And tell me everything he said. And how he said it. And what he looked like while he was saying it.*

"I think his opener was, 'Where is Little Red Riding Hood?'"

Against every logical bone in my body, a giggle burst free. Maybe it was all the tension that had built up while I'd been waiting to hear her big reveal a moment ago. "Okay, that's pretty funny."

"Funny? Why?" Rio demanded, still frustrated from the

day's events.

"In my mind, I always compare him to a wolf. The way he stalks around. Silently. You know?"

"Lovely. You have a nickname for him." Her tone shifted to accusatory. "What exactly goes on in that penthouse when you deliver his lunch?"

"You can't tell me you don't see the wolf analogy!" I ignored her second comment altogether. Her imagination was at least twenty-three times more active than mine. "Don't you think?"

After a few seconds, she conceded. "Okay, fine, I get the wolf thing. But getting back to the bigger point, please?"

"Which is? I don't think you've gotten to it yet, sister dearest."

"He asked about you, Abbi. Demanded, actually."

"Shut. *Up*."

"He knew exactly how many days you'd been gone and wanted me to tell him why."

My stomach was done aching. The whole thing flipped now, plunging my psyche into trepidation. "You didn't... I mean... Wh-What did you tell him?"

"That it was none of his damn business."

I gasped.

"What? That was the most tasteful thing I could come up with. He has the superpower of getting under a person's skin in record time. Haven't you noticed that?"

Silence. I was still trying to digest the fact that she told Sebastian Shark it was none of his damn business.

"Or is that just me?" Rio asked hurriedly. She never could stand quietude.

A laugh burst out before I could stop it. "Superpower for

sure. I think that might be one of the reasons his business is so successful. People just give in and do what he wants."

"Hmm. Well, anyhow, that was all the explanation he got from me regarding your absence."

That, along with my laugh, helped me take a normal breath again. "Sorry, girl, but seriously, to have been a fly on that expensive wallpaper . . ."

Her mirror of a chuckle had me wondering whether to be heartened or worried. "Well, I'm glad to hear that longing."

"Do I even want to know what you're talking about, Rio?" Suddenly, the stomachache I'd dropped a few exits back on the 405 was back.

"Pretty simple, Abs. If Abstract Catering wants to keep Shark's business, you will be delivering his lunch tomorrow. Not me. You." She pushed out a final defined breath in emphasis. "Tomorrow."

"Are you messing with me, Rio? This isn't funny. I don't joke about business, and you know that." My voice grew louder as I finished my sentence.

"Wish I were, *mami*—but no. Shark insisted I bring his decree back to you. Word for word." She sucked in a breath so sharply, I feared something might have happened to her.

"And, Abbigail," she breathed more than spoke.

"Rio, you're freaking me out! What? What is it?"

"If you saw the look on that man's face when he was telling me all that? Holy. Mother. Of. God. I'm pretty sure I've never been so scared and turned on and confused . . . and turned on." She drifted off for a few seconds and then, as if catching herself, said, "Shit, I said that already—but yeah . . . just from a look. Why doesn't he have a wife? Or a girlfriend at the very least? My guess is he's lethal in bed with all that game."

I really didn't need the syllable-by-syllable breakdown. My imagination was already at work just from what Rio had supplied, hearing every note of his lush baritone ... and seeing it roll off his broad, full lips ...

"I'm sorry, honey. I know you needed space from him, even if the media circus wasn't the real reason"—her defined drop in tone betrayed how she knew that part this whole time— "but he told me that if you're not the one delivering his lunch tomorrow, with the silverware wrapped in a dark-red linen, he will terminate our current contract and reject your bid for the Edge as well."

I sat up so high and stiff, I bounced up off the seat. "He'll do what?"

Rio cleared her throat. "You really need me to repeat it?"

I answered with the defined *thwonk* of my hand against the steering wheel. "Damn it! Sparkle City Catering is probably waiting for his call."

"Well, of course they are. On their knees with their mouths open."

"I really want to laugh at that."

Rio's shrug was evident in her comeback. "Well, you know what they say."

"If you're not laughing, you're crying?"

"Yep. And if you're not crying, you're not sucking hard enough."

This time I did laugh. "Christ, you're impossible."

"And you love me this way." She meshed her good-natured chuckle to mine. "Just tell me this isn't going to be impossible for you."

"Impossible?" I countered. "What do you mean by—"

"It's really none of my business, okay? But the truth is,

I'm worried about you, Abs. I mean, about you and him. About Shark."

"Huh?" I hated how I had to bring out my Oscar contender skills to play innocent about her words. "Why? I ... I mean, what are you worried about?"

"What am I not worried about?" she rebutted. "That man ... he's a real hunter. I don't know, and don't want to know, all the things that make him tick. But that shark celebrates the smell of blood. Rejoices in it."

"And your boy Blake doesn't?"

"Point for the redhead. But—I don't know how to explain this." She hummed in the back of her throat. "There was a gleam in Shark's eyes when he talked about you ..."

Somehow, I managed a dismissive *pffft*—for myself as much as her. "He's like that about everyone, Rio. He's passionate."

She *pffft* right back. "You can say that again. But not about everyone."

"I'm serious."

"I am too." She subjected me to her exasperated sighs as she banged around in the background. "All right, just tell me this, then. Why don't we have all this extra drama when servicing Viktor Blake's office?"

I started my incensed groan before she was finished. "Are you even kidding me right—"

"What? They're in the same business, they're about the same age, and their offices are only three blocks from each other."

"And one of them is starting to creep me out."

"Huh? What?"

"Not important."

I didn't want to think about explaining myself right now. I was already obsessed with steeling myself for the return to downtown—and handling the dread that was mounting along with it.

★ ★ ★

My anxiety got worse during the night and then doubled down on itself during the next morning's meal prep at the kitchen. It got three times worse as I rolled up in front of the sleek lobby of the building I'd last entered four days ago.

Days that felt like centuries.

I'd traversed enough emotional ground to justify that feeling, too. Accepted the fact that I was a damn schizophrenic about Sebastian Shark. That my mental aggravation by him existed weirdly next to my sexual attraction to him. I couldn't control how my instincts were hardwired or how they were drawn to the man's pheromones, harmonic vibrations, stallion legs, or chakras. *Whatever.* I didn't care what it was. I was just grateful to be aware of it.

That meant I was a huge step closer to controlling it.

Which led to my ultimate decision about how to work him.

I'd simply stay on neutral ground.

Enlightened but not engaged. Diplomatic but not subservient. Friendly but fair.

Which was why I rode the elevator to the penthouse of the skyscraper with my head held high. My loaded cart was in front of me. Sebastian Shark's lunch was already prepared and on top. Next to it was his silverware.

Rolled in white linen.

# CHAPTER FOUR

## SEBASTIAN

I pushed back from my desk and rechecked the time. Only twelve minutes had passed since I'd last checked. While I should've been disgusted with my schoolboy behavior, the grin on my face told a different story altogether. The dueling reasons for the grin were at such odds, I wasn't sure which I'd hoped to see come out on top.

Firstly, my cock needed some relief.

Desperately.

It had been too many days since I'd seen Little Red Riding Hood tremble and stumble through my office, giving my spank bank fodder. While at the same time, I hoped like hell she wouldn't show. Because the uneven footing I felt beneath my soles because of her, just the thought of her, was so unfamiliar, exorcizing her seemed like the smartest option.

"Get a grip, man," I muttered to myself, standing to pace another lap around the penthouse. A light path could be seen in the pile of the carpet, and even that grated on my nerves. Nerves that were akin to live wires the past few days. All the bullshit with the Mansfield case, the stress of running a business the magnitude of Shark Enterprises, and the launch of a project the size of Shark's Edge were starting to wear me down. Not that I would ever admit weakness of any sort. To anyone.

Maybe I needed to give LuLu a call and set something up with one of my regulars. Who was I kidding? None of her girls would come close to taking the edge off my need now that the green-eyed pixie was so deeply under my skin. There was only one red length of hair I needed to wrap around my fist now.

A knock on my door pulled me up short as I paced along the far side of the office near the conference room table. The very same table I'd presided over the last time I'd seen Abbigail dash out of my office.

"What?" I barked toward the closed door.

Grant poked his head in cautiously.

Wisely.

"She still hasn't come by?" He closed the door quietly behind him, as he always did. The man moved like a panther for his tall size.

I scowled at him, willing him to let it be. But he had never been one to bend to my will. Probably the one person who hadn't—and the precise trait that made me respect him enough to consider him a friend.

When he went to take his usual spot on my black leather sofa, I stopped him. "Don't get comfortable. You aren't staying. If you need something, spit it out." I paused for a beat. "And then get out."

"Do you really think you should be alone with her?" He eyed me skeptically.

"What is that supposed to mean? I'm not some sort of monster, Twombley. You've been watching too many gossip shows after work. You need to get out more." I smacked his rock-hard abdomen with the back of my hand as I ushered him toward the door. "Maybe hit the gym or something. You're getting a little soft, doughboy." I grinned as I said it, my knuckles still stinging from the contact.

"Yeah, okay. Keep telling yourself that. On both counts. I'm not the one who sprung a woody seeing a girl in tears at the beginning of the week."

"Out." I held the door open impatiently and then closed it with a *whoosh* as soon as he was clear of the jamb. When there was a knock just a few short moments later, I swung it open in a fury, ready to rip his head off and shit down his open throat.

"Fucking Grant, this is your last—"

Abbigail Gibson stood in the hallway, emerald eyes as breathtaking as Benbulben Mountain. I watched the rise and fall of her chest under her crisp white apron, the small, colorful logo moving in an enchanting rhythm with the heaving of her rib cage. Every jab and insult I'd carefully planned over the past few days fell away, and instead, for some unexplainable reason, I blurted, "Have you been to Ireland?"

"Wha—what? No. I mean, my family, my ancestors, are from there. Obviously." She made a careless gesture toward her red mane. "I've seen pictures. But I've never actually been."

Clearly my question had taken her off guard.

Hell, it had taken me off guard.

We stared at one another for unmeasured moments, people moving around us in the hall while we stayed locked in the force field of one another's gaze. Someone cleared their throat behind her, and the spell was broken.

"I see you got my message." I turned on my heel to move back into the safe confines of my office suite. I didn't bother to look back. I just assumed she'd follow.

But my asshole routine didn't override common courteousness with the fairer gender this time. Especially since Grant wasn't around to play the part. I turned abruptly and asked, "Do you need help with that?" I gestured with my chin to the tray of food she carried.

"I can manage." All signs of uneasiness from my initial question in the doorway dissolved. "Where would you like lunch today?" She seemed to have a bit of sass in her tone today. If I wasn't mistaken, she might even be spoiling for a bit of a fight. I had become an expert at reading people's body language from my years in business, and hers was telling a whole new tale today.

And why did my dick surge in my slacks at the thought of that? I couldn't remember the last time a woman challenged me. In the boardroom or the bedroom. But I had a feeling Abbigail Gibson could be the one to do just that.

"The coffee table is fine."

And wasn't that a kick in the balls? Here stood this sexy-as-sin young thing. And I mean young. As in *are you old enough to legally buy alcohol?* young, and all I could think of was pushing her up against the wall and pushing her for more.

Inch by naughty inch.

Jesus Christ. I needed to get a handle on myself.

"How old are you?" Again, just blurted out the random question that came to mind while I stared at her ass in the black whatever-the-heck sort of pants she wore under her prim little apron.

She turned slowly from the coffee table to face me, a sly grin on her pink lips. "Pardon?"

"Just curious. You seem young to own a business." I leaned my weight back against the edge of my desk, crossing my long legs out in front of me.

She turned back to the food, carefully unwrapping the salad and then the dressing.

"Don't put that dressing on my salad," I said while she was mid-pour. "Not if it's the same as Monday's."

"You didn't like it?" She looked at me. Was that hurt in her eyes?

"No. I didn't." *Too bad. Suck it up, darling. Criticism is part of the big bad business world. It's how you get better. Stronger.*

"Interesting," she said, carefully and methodically covering the salad and putting it back on the tray.

Why were my feet walking toward her? I wasn't going to apologize for not liking the damn dressing. No, that wasn't it. It was curiosity. Were there tears again? Seriously? Over salad dressing?

"Are you crying, Ms. Gibson? Again?" My voice was rough and low in register.

Her head snapped back, fury burning in her eyes. Tears hadn't been there when she first met my stare, but now they were brimming while I stood and watched in fascination.

And moved closer.

Closer.

*What is happening?*

She was like a tractor beam. Pulling me. Sucking me in. Those eyes. Those tears. Tugging me closer. Then her bottom lip trembled—ever so slightly—but I was close enough then, I couldn't miss it.

"What's this about? Salad dressing?" I growled.

"I changed that recipe." Her voice, on the other hand, was barely a whisper.

"You shouldn't have."

"You're an asshole." Now she gained some spine back.

"Hashtag truth." I shrugged, channeling my eight-year-old niece and remaining unaffected by her remark.

"I can't believe you just said that." She raised her hand to wipe away the free-falling tears.

I caught her by the wrist and lowered her arm back to her side. Her stare, filled with indignation, was fixed to mine while I watched the tears track down the apples of her cheeks in single-file lines. Slowly, I caught one of the watery soldiers with the pad of my thumb and lifted it to my mouth, holding her gaze while I did so.

"That's just the tip of the iceberg, Little Red." The salty drop exploded on my tongue, making me want to taste more of her.

"What?" Disbelief and arousal strangled the word in her throat.

I tilted my head in question while moving another step closer.

"What did you just call me?" she rasped, cheeks nearly the same scarlet as her hair.

"Little Red. Like Little Red Riding Hood. I've thought that since the first day you came in here. All this." I reached out and fingered the flame tresses that framed her doll-like face. Her eyes slid closed and her nostrils flared. Clearly she liked when I touched her.

"You have no right to touch me." Her hoarse whisper was barely audible in the silent suite.

"Tell me to stop. Just say the word." My own voice was as low and rumbly as one of the famous performers whose names graced the marquee on the Pantages Theatre.

Her eyes popped open, seeming even wider than they were just moments before.

"Because I really don't want to stop."

Her bottom lip trembled again, making me want to bite

her there. Then soothe the wound with my tongue.

"How old did you say you were?" I risked touching her again. This time, I swiped a tear from her cheek and painted her swollen bottom lip with the wetness, making the pink shade darker.

"I didn't."

"You didn't what?" The last tear. Captured. Painted.

"Say"—she inhaled shakily—"how old I am."

"Tell me." I took one more step. Our toes touched, and she had to tilt her head back to keep her gaze locked with mine. "Tell me, Little Red."

I bent forward, almost brushing my lips to hers.

Waiting.

Waiting for her answer.

"Twenty-two. I turned twenty-two at the beginning of January."

"Jeeeessssus Christ." I pulled back, scrubbing my palm down my face and around to the back of my neck, where I squeezed tightly, trying to get a handle on my lust-addled brain.

"What just happened? What did I miss?" Her confused look wasn't unexpected.

"Momentary loss of my better judgment. Forgive me."

"For what? I would've told you to stop." She met my stare straight on. Ballsy girl. *Sexy girl.* "But I didn't want you to stop."

"You don't know what you're saying." I stepped back from her slightly.

She quickly closed the space between us. "I know exactly what I'm saying."

"I find that hard to believe. You're barely old enough to order a drink at a bar, let alone tangle with a bastard like me."

"Don't overestimate yourself, Mr. Shark."

I couldn't help but grin at the flash of boldness. "Maybe you shouldn't underestimate me, Ms. Gibson. Ask my assistant what an overbearing asshole I am. She probably has a story to match every minute of the day. Although if she were honest with herself, she's no picnic to be around either."

"She seems quite nice to me." Abbigail shrugged, something I noticed she did routinely. "She even allows me to keep my trolley in the alcove by her printer while I service the offices on this floor. She wouldn't do that if she weren't kind."

She looked triumphant that she proved me wrong in one simple sentence. Then a slow smile spread across her heart-shaped lips. "I'd guess you're probably more like a Chihuahua than a shark, as your name suggests, Sebastian. All bark, no bite."

Boy, she really thought she had me figured out, didn't she? Time to put this pup back in her crate.

I pressed against her body with my own, thrusting her against the wall behind her. The semi-erect cock lazing in my boxers surged to full attention from the heat radiating through our layers of clothing.

"I wouldn't mind sinking my teeth into you, Little Red," I said softly beside her ear as I tucked a wayward strand of silky hair behind it. "In fact, I'd like to sink a couple other body parts of mine"—I pushed my hips against her belly in punctuation—"into yours." Slowly, I pulled back to get lost in her kelly-colored eyes.

"But?" Her voice was tinged with impatience. Not the reaction I was going for, but maybe the cat-and-mouse game was growing old?

I leaned my head far to the side, lewdly surveying the

curve of her backside.

"It is a stellar ass, Abbigail. But I can't say I expected you to jump right into that arena. You're full of surprises today." I suspected my eyes were glittering with mischief.

She gave me a *be serious* glower. "I'm not even going to dignify that with a response."

"You just did." I arched a brow in challenge.

She huffed before getting back to her original point. "I was sensing you had an objection to your own comment."

"My objection is to several things." I lifted my hand to hold it directly between our faces, ticking off the problems as I voiced them.

"First…" My index finger popped tall, making me imagine drawing a line from her bottom lip, down her neck, and around the back to untie the apron's knot and then watching it fall to the floor between us. My eyes skittered to the ground, observing the imaginary fabric crumple to a heap and then flashed back to hers as I made my point. "You're much too young to be sullied by a scoundrel such as me."

She quirked her brow at my use of such archaic terms, but I wasted no time adding a second finger to my first.

Now my brain gave me thoughts of two fingers deftly working the moorings free on her button-down shirt and then spreading the two halves wide to discover what type of lingerie she hid beneath her sensible work clothes. Was she a utilitarian girl all the way down to her creamy white skin? Or was there a little bit of vixen underneath the layers of cotton? A sexy siren waiting to be uncovered and appreciated—stroked and petted by my skillful hands.

I dashed out the second reason. "You work for me. Vendors make messy bedfellows."

"Messy?" she asked, her voice pitching high with the insult.

*Messy,* I mouthed, no sound accompanying my lips' movement.

"And lastly," I said, adding my long middle finger to the grouping of extremities between us, losing all coherent train of thought. Dirty, dirty fantasies replaced reasonable remarks. In my mind, I stroked the inside of Abbi's pussy with the very finger that stood tallest between us. With that digital soldier, I'd reach in and find the secret spot that made her writhe and moan beneath my touch. The unique bull's-eye that would encourage her to call my name in a raspy moan as she rode my hand to her completion.

A low groan escaped from deep in my throat and vibrated across my lips as I dropped my chin to my chest with arousal overload.

"What?" she whispered, seeming to have followed my thoughts down the naughty, naughty rabbit hole.

"What, what?" I squinted at her with unfocused eyes.

"What were you thinking? Your eyes ... You just looked a million miles away." She reached up to touch my face with splayed fingers but quickly let her hand fall away as if thinking better of it.

"Oh, some things are better left unsaid, Little Red." A grin played on my lips, still imagining her tight pussy milking and coating my fingers.

"Better for who?" Rigidity returned to her spine. Frustration? Embarrassment?

"For you." I sucked in a deep breath through my nose, definitely picking up the scent of woman on the air. "In this instance, definitely better for you."

"That's mighty high-handed of you." All traces of arousal were gone from her voice.

"What is?" I turned away and headed over to where my lunch was spread out, needing to get physical distance from her before I did something I'd regret.

Like kiss her.

And not being able to stop kissing her until she was naked beneath me, chanting my name.

"Deciding what's best for me," she snapped. "You don't even know me."

"My point exactly." I unrolled the *white* napkin from around the silverware on the tray.

She was quiet, and then moved to stand near the grouping of sofas where I sat. "You can be very obtuse. But I suppose that's intentional. I don't take you for a man who does anything willy-nilly."

"I could say the same for you." I looked pointedly at the white napkin. "For a woman who claims to be serious about a very large future contract, I find it interesting that you wouldn't follow the customer's specifications, just to prove some immature point. Again, though, perfectly illustrating the first of my earlier arguments."

Silence blanketed the penthouse. However, the rise and fall of her chest broadcasted her growing agitation.

*Come on, Little Red Riding Hood. Cry. Do it.*

"Jesus Christ," she muttered under her breath while a rosy flush spread up her neck. "Well, if you don't need anything else here—"

"Déjà vu, anyone?" I smirked, knowing she'd gotten the message. Loud and clear.

"I'll pass, thanks, though." She pivoted on her heel and

headed to the door, proverbial tail tucked between her legs.

I shot to my feet, rushing up behind her to slam my hand to the door above her head, effectively preventing her from opening it.

Without turning to face me, she seethed, "Excuse me. I'm leaving now."

"Is this how you handle yourself in a tough situation, Ms. Gibson?" I clucked my tongue in disappointment while she still faced the door. "When the going gets tough, you bolt?" I increased the cadence of my words but kept the tone antagonistic. "If you land the exclusive catering contract for the Edge, is this the level of professionalism I can expect from you?" I provoked her further. "If we had a black-tie event in-house—oh, I don't know... let's say international dignitaries for a seven-course meal—will my caterer leave in a huff because her feelings were hurt due to someone not liking the goddamn salad dressing?"

Slowly, she turned to face me, schooling her features so I couldn't predict what was about to come.

"Mr. Shark, I don't 'bolt' when things become difficult. Quite frankly, nothing could be further from the truth. There's a lot you don't know about me, and I can admit my behavior takes unusual turns when I'm in this particular office. And as much as I hate to overinflate your ego more than it already is, that seems to have everything to do with you specifically. Not my job nor my ability to handle it. Rest assured, I am the best person to handle the exclusive contract for your new building."

"Why the tears again, then?" I demanded but then inexplicably shifted to a softer mien. "What's this about?"

"Unfortunately," she sighed, inspecting her shoes before continuing, "when I get angry, I well up. I've been this way my entire life. It's very frustrating, trust me. It makes me look fragile to outsiders, which only makes me more mad and then more tears and so on."

"I have a theory about anger, Ms. Gibson."

"Please, enlighten me." She swiped her cheek with the back of her hand. One quick wipe on each side while she glared at me.

"Anger is fear's alter ego."

"That's absurd."

"Are you sure?"

"I'm not afraid of you, Mr. Shark."

"Maybe not of me, necessarily. But of the situation? This situation?" I couldn't stop myself from wiping the last tear that rolled down her flame-red cheek. It evaporated from the heat of her skin as quickly as it was shed.

"Fear, anger, excitement...no matter what you call it, Abbigail, they're all forms of passion. And to be good at something? Whether it's feeding people, housing people, or hell"—I chuckled—"even moving freight across the ocean. To be the king of your kingdom, you have to do it with passion. That's what gives you the edge."

I stepped away from the door and pulled the large panel back, holding it open while the captivating girl gathered her bearings and realized she was being dismissed.

"I hope you have a productive weekend, Ms. Gibson," I said in place of goodbye.

"Uhhh, yeah, you too." She shook her head slightly, still seeming to be working out what had just happened as she went.

The door closed, and I sat down to eat the lunch she made for me, grinning from the knowledge that her careful hands created my meal. Her sexy fingers manipulated the ingredients along with her intelligent mind that combined flavors and textures to assemble—honest to Christ—one of the best sandwiches I'd ever eaten.

To the extent that I was inspired enough to pull out my phone, snap a quick picture of the empty plate, and send it to Little Red along with a text message. How I had her cell phone number was inconsequential. I was a very resourceful man when properly motivated.

*Lunch was outstanding. Thank you.*

The throbbing ellipses appeared almost instantly, signaling her impending reply.

*My pleasure. I aim to be king.*

★ ★ ★

"Uuugghh." I groaned loudly. The wrenching pain in my abdomen had gone from uncomfortable to unbearable in an hour. I dialed my sister's cell phone for the fourth time only to end the call quickly, rush to the bathroom, and drop to my knees in front of the sleek porcelain bowl.

Dry heaves. Nothing was left. I'd lost all the contents of my stomach over the past forty-five minutes. But the sensation to retch continued. My guts felt like they were turning inside out and trying to make a break for it through my esophagus.

Food poisoning. It was the only thing that made sense. I felt fine otherwise. No fever, no chills or body aches.

As if cursing the gastro-gods, my lower intestinal area gurgled and cramped. "Jesus Christ," I muttered, wiping the sweat beads from my brow. I hadn't had "the spinners" since my frat days. Another gurgle rumbled through my bowel, and then sixty more minutes of just trying to stay out of the bathroom long enough to call my sister for help.

What had I eaten? Typical oatmeal for breakfast. The food service I had delivered to my home left portioned servings, marked with color-coded labels for each day. I'd felt fine after eating it.

For lunch, I had the fantastic turkey club Abbigail Gibson brought in. I ate every last crumb of the sandwich and didn't touch the salad. She took the offensive dressing out with her. I was all about eating healthy, but I wasn't a damn rabbit. Who the hell ate dry lettuce? I was so swamped the second half of the day; I hadn't even indulged in an afternoon pick-me-up.

*It had to have been the sandwich.*

I redialed Pia. I was going to need to go to Urgent Care at the very least, and I'd already sent my driver home for the night. I knew I was becoming dehydrated, though, and there was no way I could get behind the wheel.

The line rang twice before she answered. "Hey, brother. What's going on? You okay? It's pretty late for you to be calling, no?"

"Hey. Yeah, need some help." I groaned, trying to tone down my reaction to the pain.

"Dude..." Nope, she saw right through me. "Are you okay?" Her voice rose with concern.

"I think I have food poisoning. I need to get to the ER or Urgent Care—ugh! I don't know. Something." I was whining as only I could do in the safety of her presence.

"All right, all right. Calm down. Let me see if Millie can come stay with Vela, and I'll be over. Sit tight. No pun intended.

Okay," she snickered. "Maybe a little bit intended."

"Piiiiaaaa!"

"Sorry, Bas, couldn't be helped. I'm on my way, brother. I'll call you if I can't manage for some reason."

"You're a lifesaver, Dub." Cassiopeia, her birth given name, represented the W-shaped constellation in the night sky. Hence the "dub" moniker. My sister hated the childhood nickname, so I used it precisely for that reason. Brothers reserved the right to do annoying things like that.

"See you soon," she said, her voice gentle as she ended the call.

*God, please be soon.*

As soon as I felt well enough, I'd have a bone to pick with one Abbigail Gibson.

# CHAPTER FIVE

### ABBI

"Okay, how many more of these little buggers are there?"

Rio's sarcasm, blending with the sea-salted morning air, was another layer of a much-needed balm on my tattered senses.

Yes. Needed.

Especially because I was still recovering from my latest run-in with Sebastian Shark.

Run-in? More like run-over. In every startling, wrenching way.

Not that I could speak with authority about it or anything—after reliving it five hundred times in my mind's eye.

*Oh, God.*

The man wasn't considered the world's most dangerous billionaire because he'd signed a deal with Lucifer. He *was* Lucifer. And heaven help me, even now, I longed to strip naked and swim in his lake of fire—a fantasy only given more juice by the satellite radio station Rio had picked for our bag-stuffing party on her and Sean's front porch. The sensual European instrumentals had sound effects that came way too close to unraveling my composure. The memories of being pressed up against his office door . . . my body molded by his, my groans blending with his . . .

*Damn it.*

*No more.*

*Please . . . no more.*

The *Queen Mary's* ten a.m. horn drifted down the coast from Long Beach, supporting my effort with its distinct bellow. The sound traveled on balmy breezes through a crystalline sky, which provided a perfect backdrop for Rio's tinkling laugh.

"Okay, wow." She raked a stunned stare over the piles of goodies intended for the bags we were stuffing. "There's more stuff here than a trip to the goodie room at the Oscars."

I added my chuckle to hers. "And you know that . . . how?"

"Hmmm. I have my ways." She winked impishly.

I bet Sebastian Shark went to the Oscars every year. His was the kind of recognizable face that would actually make the *how we tally the votes* part bearable. And he'd accomplish it in a tux that fit him to a T, accentuating that carved face, that tapered torso, and those ungodly long legs.

The same legs that had pinned mine to the back of his office door yesterday.

"We're making forty total," I said, despite every tender inch of my pussy pleading me to take it home and take care of this fresh ache. Like I hadn't done just that this morning. "But officially, we only have thirty-two girls in this chapter of the Intrepids. The extras are for top performers with this quarter's fundraiser—running the snack stand at the Westside Junior Soccer League."

Rio tilted her head, her version of an affirming nod. If she discerned how desperately I was fighting off wicked fantasies of Shark beneath my chipper shell, she didn't show it. *Thank God.* That meant my effort of keeping it all stuffed down was a success.

"Success" being relative.

Did I want to tell her everything that had happened yesterday? More than anything. But I was still too damn upside down about it right now, and a Rio-style grilling would make it worse. Right now, Abbigail's Walls were the better choice.

"The Intrepids." Her echo was my saving goat hook out of that emotional mire. "That's short for what again?"

"The Intrepid Entrepreneurs." I supplied it while reaching for another empty goodie bag. I had to admit, she was right. We'd secured a generous haul of donations from local bookstores, beauty shops, and office supply warehouses. "The program is designed to hook up local female business owners and community leaders with middle and high school girls interested in the same. We're there to motivate and encourage but also to mentor and advise."

"So these teenagers learn valuable lessons from your mistakes?"

A wry snicker. "Something like that, yes."

"Hey, your misery now serves a purpose!"

"Gee, thanks for pointing that out," I answered with a generous helping of side-eye.

She flung back an equally droll smirk. "And all the girls are from different schools in the region, right?"

"Right. All the cities from Santa Monica down to Long Beach are included, and east of the 405 too."

I slid some neon-colored pencils into my bag, along with a copy of Thom Shea's *Unbreakable*. In the stack from the bookstore, there were also copies of *The 7 Habits of Highly Effective People*, *Tools of Titans*, and *Awaken the Giant Within*. We were distributing the copies evenly, with the plan that each group of girls who got a title would present the information to the others at upcoming meetings. I already smiled in anticipation of the concepts they'd be sharing from the reads.

"It's cool because they come from all walks of life and demographics. They're all learning that the real world"—I used my fingers to gesture air quotes around the words—"is a little different from what they might be experiencing in school. That there are lots of different kinds of people and that quite a few of them aren't selfish monsters or entitled bitches."

"Wait. What?" Rio flashed a bugged-out gaze. "Are you talking about groups of girls in puberty? Being mean and cruel and judgmental toward one another? Unheard of!"

A spurted laughter. "Don't faint on me, please."

"Who's fainting?"

The disruption came from inside the house, startling both of us. Sean, returning from his morning run, had obviously dashed in via the rear alley and then the bungalow's back door. My oldest brother—and Rio's husband—appeared just inside the screen door, the mesh distorting his handsome face.

"Babe, are you sick? You need me to scoot to the drugstore and get you something?"

I rolled my eyes. "You'd probably swim to that drugstore even if it were across the channel on Catalina, wouldn't you?"

"Of course he would." Rio preened and purposely magnified the look when I added an I'm-going-to-barf groan. "Beauty always slays the beast," she drawled. "Words to live by."

As she finished doling the advice, Sean unfurled a savoring growl. "I'll be your beast any day, princess."

"Oh, God." I doubled down on the groan. "Just no with the princess stuff, brother." Cradling my face in my hands, I whined, "My brothers are such dorks."

"And to think I longed for a big brother when I was little."

"Doomed yourself. You ended up with three by marriage."

She swept a look up at Sean, who had joined us on the patio. "Not complaining."

"Thanks, Abs." Then he added, "That reminds me. I gotta call Zander."

"Why?" I flinched a second time. "Does he need bail money again?"

A nod from Sean wouldn't have come as a surprise. Though I was the youngest in the birth order, Zander behaved like it more than the rest of us combined. The guy was a trouble magnet. Not all of it was his doing, but a big chunk was.

"Fortunately, nothing like that this time," Sean offered while scrolling through screens on his phone. "He's coming out for a visit and wanted to confirm some dates."

Sliding his phone into his pocket, he surveyed our work. "What the hell is all this?"

"Your sister's latest pet project," Rio said just as I was about to launch into the elevator pitch about the Intrepids.

My brother wrapped his wife in his arms while she answered his follow-up questions about her plans for the day, each new answer earning her a kiss or a squeeze, his adoration glowing like the Hollywood sign on a clear night.

*Jealous.* I was jealous of what they had because I wanted that too. And the worst part? The man I was pining for would never hold me in his arms in front of other people and pepper my cheeks with proud kisses. He would never take interest in simple things like household chores and weekly errands.

I was a damn fool, and I needed to stop wasting my time hoping for the impossible.

I had to curb my contact with Sebastian Shark.

Professional manners and culinary transactions only. Food on his damn table, wrapped in whatever linen he dictated. No more rocking his boat on purpose. I couldn't care about his boat anymore. He certainly didn't care about mine.

*Didn't care. Couldn't care.*

A few million more repeats, and maybe it would sink in.

In the meantime, I was thankful for the footsteps and throat clearings that filled the bungalow's tiny front yard, giving me an excuse to forget how my brother's PDA was tearing me apart inside.

I turned toward the source, ready to smile at whatever neighbor had chosen to come by and exchange greetings with Sean and Rio. My brother and his wife knew everyone who lived within a six-block radius.

I was completely surprised to turn and find two police officers instead of the usual surfers or retirees that dropped by. The first officer was fitted in an LA County Sheriff's Department uniform, and the second was wearing the colors of the Orange County Sheriff's force. Both were beefy guys who could've been fitness models, their biceps bulging from their short sleeves as they hooked their thumbs into waist-level loops.

"Oh." Rio's little peep, which she delivered while stepping back from her husband, echoed my astonishment. My gut tightened with the instinct that these fine public servants were the bearers of disturbing news. Because, really, how often did cops just stop by to say hello?

"Good morning," said Officer OC, adding a smile that dazzled like halogen in contrast to his dark sienna skin.

"Good morning, officers. Is there...some way we can help you?"

"My name is Deputy Silva, and this is my colleague from the Los Angeles Sheriff's Department, Deputy Bourne."

"Morning." Bourne, who resembled his famous spy-film counterpart, ticked a fast nod.

Silva flashed his brilliant teeth again. I might have actually smiled back if I wasn't so focused on maintaining my composure.

He walked forward a couple of steps while offering, "Sorry for disturbing your morning, but we're hoping you can help us. Are you Sean Gibson?"

"I am," my brother answered. "What can we do for you?"

Silva's nod was a clear acknowledgment of my sibling's acquiescence. "Deputy Bourne reached out for our help in locating a Miss Abbigail Gibson. He attempted to contact her at her home address in Torrance, but a neighbor informed us she might be at this address instead."

"I'm Abbigail Gibson, officers. What can I do for you today?"

"Seriously?" Rio swung around, grabbing my elbow with her free hand. "Don't you dare speak to them without an attorney present."

Bourne clenched his jaw, though he softened the action by taking off his glasses in a smooth swoop. "We're not here to take her into custody, ma'am." He spread his hands out, palms down. "This is a fact-finding visit only. Mr. Shark insisted that we—"

"Damn it," Rio muttered.

My pulse rate spiked. It was twisted and wrong, but hearing this burly alpha refer to my most trying client with such veneration... I liked it.

"He insisted on what?" I stepped closer to the cops, not

hiding my intense interest in their reply.

Bourne pierced me with his gaze. "You really don't know?"

Which was crap as far as explanations went. I told him so with my confused glower. "Know...what?"

"Mr. Shark spent several hours in the West Hills Hospital Emergency Room last night." He narrowed his gaze even tighter in response to my stark gasp. "This is the first you're hearing this?"

I gulped hard. "Is— Is he all right?" I stammered. "Wait. Is he hurt? What happened?"

"Did he trip over his own ego?"

"*Rio.*" I shot her a warning glare.

"What?" She gave innocence a solid attempt before Sean squeezed her hand.

Sebastian Shark consumed every inch of my imagination, but picturing him lying on a hospital gurney...

Impossible.

And unbearable.

"He was admitted for symptoms concurrent with food poisoning," Bourne said. "Likely because of something he ingested yesterday."

"Food poi—" I cut myself off with a shocked cough. I couldn't even finish the phrase. It was every caterer's worst nightmare—and now I was living it.

*Symptoms. Illness. Yesterday.*

"What are you saying?" Sean asked, face twisted in bewilderment. "He got sick from something he ate?"

"That's exactly what he's saying," Rio said. "And judging from all this"—she waved a frustrated hand toward the officers—"he's also saying our food was the culprit."

"Only alleging." Silva actually spoke up then, though

his mellow mediator smile had vanished. "Nobody's being accused of anything."

"Not yet," Rio mumbled.

"Babe." Another mental thank-you to Sean as he cinched his wife to his side, speaking directly into her ear. "Dial it down, beautiful. You're making things harder for Abbi right now."

But while I was grateful for my brother's intervention, his action didn't deter Bourne from funneling an intense stare at Rio. "You said *our* food? What's that all about?"

"It's about nothing. This is my sister-in-law, Rio Gibson, and she's an employee of Abstract Catering."

Bourne pulled out a small pad and started jotting everything I relayed. In terse clips, he added, "An employee with clear-cut views regarding Mr. Shark."

"An employee," I said, "who performs her job according to my strict standards of hygiene and food preparation."

Rio squirmed again, clearly wanting to add to that, but Sean checked her. I shot him a new look of gratitude.

"Mr. Shark states that his schedule was so packed yesterday, he only had time to eat lunch," Bourne went on. "And that the meal was hand-delivered to his office from Abstract Catering."

I swallowed hard again, despite how it felt like every river stone in their garden was in my throat. "I was the one who delivered Mr. Shark's sandwich," I said. "It was in a sealed container before I brought it into his office, but he enjoys his meals on actual china, so I set it up for him. He watched me the entire time."

"Fair enough," Silva said. "And where was the container before you delivered it into his office?"

"On my cart, where I keep all the preordered meals for each building."

"And you're with that cart at all times?" Bourne pressed. "It stays at your side?"

I tottered my head back and forth. "Yes and no. I mean, I don't abandon it or anything."

"Not even to use the ladies' room?"

"If that's necessary, I do it in the building lobby before loading the cart. Once I'm up on delivery floors, I only leave the cart for snips at a time." Which was technically already a lie—since my snip behind Shark's closed doors was more than that. Holy crap, so much more. Snips were what someone did to stray threads. Being with him had been like tangling in a whole bolt of fabric. Probably velvet. Soft on one side, rough and ruthless on the other.

I ordered myself to remember that—ruthless. Because it had led to this. Being scrutinized under the late-morning sun, which felt more and more like the heat lamp in an interrogation room. Making me wonder if this weekend was going to end with my ass behind bars, awaiting arraignment for poisoning LA's most prominent businessman.

"Snips." I wasn't sure if the quirk of Bourne's lips should make me hopeful or more nervous. "Since you set up Mr. Shark's meal for him, did that qualify as a snip too?"

"No." I shored up my posture. "It was longer than a snip. But I already had his lunch with me when I entered his office. Additionally, Mr. Shark's floor is always my first delivery for that building."

This time, Silva was the one to tilt his head in curiosity. "Isn't he in the penthouse?"

"From the top down," Rio cut in. "That's how we usually work it. Start at the top floor and work our way back down and then right out to the van."

Silva nodded. "Yeah, that makes perfect sense. The VIPs first." His shrug gave away how thoroughly he disagreed with such policies, but he wasn't the alpha dog on this interrogation—or whatever the hell it was.

Bourne was still clearly zeroed in on one prerogative. "Ms. Gibson, from the time you loaded your cart to the time you took Mr. Shark's lunch off of it, that conveyance wasn't out of your sight for even—what? How long would you say? Five minutes?"

I looked away, focusing my study on the modern statue occupying the yard across the street. I'd never been able to tell if it was an elegant pelican or a bizarre mermaid. Par for the course today, since the entire world seemed to be based solely on perception.

"Not even that," I replied. "Before I arrived at Mr. Shark's office, there were only a handful of other orders for the floor, and all of them approached me for their food."

Silva frowned. "Don't you think that's a little odd?"

"Have you ever tasted Abstract's sandwiches and salads?" Sean's comment, while dunked in pride, was the best and worst line right now.

The next question was once again Bourne's. "So there was no time for anyone else to have tampered with the boxes on the cart?" he pressed.

"No. Those containers are noisy. Even if I'd turned to talk to someone, I would've heard the plastic crackles." I shook my head, more defined about it this time. "I don't understand any of this. Seriously, who would want to do this to Sebastian?"

A choke tumbled from Rio. "*Sebastian?*"

"Leave it," Sean said, but I couldn't thank him this time. All my energy was fixed on Bourne and Silva, resulting in my racing heart and clammy palms.

"Unless . . . Mr. Shark wasn't the only one in that building who reported something?"

My question was awful but necessary. I'd delivered hundreds of lunches yesterday. Even if half of them had somehow gotten tainted and neither Rio nor I caught it, my business insurance company would never underwrite me again. I'd be finished before I ever started.

"He's the only one who came forward."

My shoulders sagged beneath my rush of relief. On the other hand, it was Sebastian Shark who'd come forward and told these guys to go specifically for me. But now that I was reasonably sure I wouldn't lose my business, a new sensation took the place of my dread. A full fire bursting to life inside me.

Fury.

Imagine *that*. I longed so badly to borrow from Bourne's stoicism, but that was not the natural inclination of my personality. I had the hot Irish temper bred into me from generation upon generation, and I felt insulted and infuriated. And, as everyone close to me knew, that meant tears.

Perfect. Goddamn tears pricked and burned, unwelcomed guests to this little patio party we were having, and I sucked in air through my nose, trying to get a hold of my emotions.

"Abs, it's okay. We'll get to the bottom of it. I'm sure there's an explanation." My brother stepped away from his wife to comfort me instead, and I couldn't be strong enough to turn him away. His arms felt so good wrapped around my shoulders, his chest a comfort I needed.

Rio stepped in behind me and rubbed circles on my back while the deputies stood awkwardly by and said nothing. No one needed to know the tears weren't just from the stress of this debacle. No one needed to know the tears weren't just from the fear of my hard work being flushed down the john with a client's food poisoning remains.

No. These tears were the culmination of a week of frustration and confusion and mixed-up feelings and emotions that I was so unfamiliar with having. I missed my mom and my other brothers, and I missed having someone to confide in when I had questions that only a girl's mother could answer with complete honesty and without judgment.

I pulled back from Sean's embrace after only a minute.

"Okay?" he asked, ducking down to be level with my eyes.

"Yes." I nodded, swiping at my cheeks. "I'm fine now. Sorry about that." I brushed hastily at his T-shirt where there were creases and light swipes of makeup.

He grasped both of my wrists to halt my fussing. "It's fine, Abs. It's fine. You needed that. I wish you'd lean on us more, actually." His voice was tender and protective, and his big brotherliness swaddled me in a cocoon of love and compassion. It was the exact balm I needed.

"Outstanding, then," Silva announced awkwardly, snapping my family out of the tender moment we were sharing. "I think we have all we need for now. I'd like to leave our information with you, Ms. Gibson. If you think of anything or have any questions—"

"That reminds me!" I interrupted excitedly as a memory flipped to the forefront of my mind.

"When you said 'outstanding,' it reminded me that I have this on my phone." I dug in the pocket of the hoodie hanging on the back of the chair to get my cell phone. "A text message I received from Mr. Shark yesterday afternoon after he enjoyed the lunch I made for him. And no, it's not something I casually interpreted." I pointed to my phone. "The evidence is right there. I'll be saving his words for posterity. Or a court of law. Whichever comes first."

I had to admit, Silva's answering grin was a blast to enjoy.

Bourne's was even better.

I gave in to an easy smile. "If you don't mind, gentlemen, I have to get back to what I was doing here." I waved at the goodie bags still strewn about the patio. "I will definitely give you a call if I have any questions."

We said goodbye to the officers, and Rio went inside to mix up a big batch of margaritas. It was definitely five o'clock somewhere.

# CHAPTER SIX

## SEBASTIAN

"Bas, really, you could've stayed home. She would've understood." Pia eyed me from behind her giant Jackie-O sunglasses, patting my hand like she was excusing me from a root canal.

"Wild horses couldn't keep me away from one of Vela's games. You know that. Besides, I feel fine." The words were one thing. The tone I said them in told a different story.

Spending sixteen hours in the emergency department at West Hills Hospital and Medical Center hadn't been my idea of an ideal Friday night. Or any night. While the care I'd received was excellent, the episode of food poisoning left me feeling like I'd been to battle—and lost.

The final prognosis—I'd live to see another day. So even though they'd poked and prodded at me and had done what seemed like every test known to modern medicine, the best explanation anyone with a fancy title before or after their name could come up with was I must have eaten something in the previous twenty-four hours that was bad.

And now, here I was, sweltering under the noontime Southern California sun. Thankfully, I'd opted for a pair of loose athletic shorts, in favor of comfort instead of style.

My niece gave me a big wave from the sideline bench,

along with a smile as big as her entire face to go with it. A matching one broke out on my mug, and we did our secret sign to one another above the heads of everyone who sat between us. One hand curled into a letter C that formed one half of a heart. When we finally saw each other later, we would push them together to make a whole heart, as we always did, and then I'd scoop her up into my arms for a big Uncle Bas bear hug.

*How will I survive when she's too old for all our special things?*

Eventually, it'd happen. She'd become a little shit like all kids do. Her friends would be way cooler than her uncle, and her makeup and her clothes would be much more interesting than the stories I had to share with her about when her mom and I were her age. And so help me God, the first time I saw a boy look in her direction. Even thinking about breathing in the same zip code she lived in . . . I shuddered at the thought.

"You okay?" Pia bumped my shoulder with hers.

"Hmmm? Yeah, fine. Why?" Her question shook me from my murderous daydream. Probably a good thing. We were at a bunch of eight-year-olds' soccer game, after all.

"You're growling," Pia said through gritted teeth, trying not to be overheard. "Honest to God, Bas. Growling."

"Oh, sorry. It's nothing," I said, scowling.

"Thinking about her growing up again, weren't you?" My sister smiled then, knowing damn well she'd busted me.

I turned on the bleachers to face her. "Are you sure there isn't a way to stop it? You swear you've looked into it? I have money, Pia. So much money."

"Sebastian. Albert. Shark. Stop."

I faced the field. "It's a standing offer. We'll just leave it at that."

"Stop. We are not stunting my child's matriculation because it makes you uncomfortable."

"Standing offer," I repeated while holding my hands up in surrender, signaling I was dropping it.

A quick change of subject then. "Is she in goal today?"

"Bas, they're eight, and this is a rec league. They care more about what they're having for a snack than they do about the position they're playing."

"You're kind of a downer today, Dub. What's up?"

"I am not." She swung her head to look at me, and I knew I'd hit a nerve. Shit. I'd seen that look before. I was still exhausted from the hospital bullshit, and the last thing I wanted was a scene with Pia.

"Sorry." It wasn't a word I used carelessly, and very few people deserved to hear it from my lips. Pia would forever be one of those people. She and I went through the shittiest childhood together, and we'd always had each other's backs.

When our mother died giving birth to our baby brother and our father became best friends with Señor Patron, all we had was one another. Pia had been just three years old. I'd become a little man at the tender age of seven, but I took my role very seriously. My father's resentment had grown a little more each day. We'd stolen the one thing in his life he truly loved. The one person who had ever loved him in return.

The morning he never woke up from his nightly bender, I didn't even cry. He was just one less person I had to worry about. One less person to take care of.

Vela's coach called the girls to a little huddle, and they all put their arms toward the center. She gave them a few more tips on ball handling and then shouted, "On three, Blue Jays!"

The girls all deepened their sweet little voices and

chanted with their coach "One! Two! Three! Blue Jays!" Then the swarm of royal-blue jerseys took off running onto the field. Ponytails were popped high on tiny heads with oversize white ribbons that matched the numbers on the backs of their togs.

I focused on our mini number four running as fast her tiny legs could carry her down the field to take her spot in goal. Vela loved playing keeper. If she stuck with the sport and honed the skills of the position, she could really shine. Most players shied away from playing goalie, but a handful were born for the job. If you weren't naturally fast but could kick hard and you weren't afraid to dive and put your body in front of the ball, you could be as much of a star on the team as a midfielder.

We watched the game, cheering the Blue Jays when they had possession and managed to work the ball down toward the opposition's goal. A father of one of Vela's teammates paced along the sidelines, yelling at his daughter as if she were playing in a Chivas game. I wanted to stretch my leg out and trip the guy.

*Accidentally, of course.*

The little girl was so confused, and between her father screaming instructions to her, the coach trying to do her job and coach from her spot on the sideline, and the three officials on the field, she burst into tears and crumpled to a heap in the middle of a play.

"What's going on?" Pia had been looking down at her phone when the commotion erupted.

"Jesus Christ." I shook my head in disbelief.. "This asshole." I motioned to the dad with my chin.

Pia followed my gesture, glaring at the parent. "Oh, him again." She shook her head. "Every single game he does this to her. Even at practice he berates her. I don't know why the coach doesn't say something to him. I think she's afraid of him too. Poor Naya is in tears more than not."

"This will be the last time it happens," I growled. Seemed like I was growling a lot today.

"No, Bas. Don't get involved. Let Coach handle it," Pia said, gripping my arm again.

"Like she has been?" I retorted through gritted teeth.

"True." Pia let go of my arm.

"I'm just going to have a conversation with the asshole after the game. Man to man. No fists. Just words." My voice was eerily calm, and Pia knew not to argue further.

"Bas."

*Well, I thought she did.*

"Dub," I answered back in the same flat tone.

"I'm serious." She tried to sound threatening. In any other situation, it would be adorable.

"Oh, I know you are, sister. So am I. He's a fucking bully. And that's his own kid." I pointed my finger furiously at Naya, who was still wiping her cheeks with the backs of her hands. "What if he pulled that shit on Vela one day while one of us wasn't here?" I raised my eyebrows, letting the question paint a horrible picture in my sister's imagination.

Pia's face changed as thoughts of her daughter being accosted by the man took over.

"That's what I thought," I muttered half under my breath, but I knew Pia heard me.

We watched the game in silence for a while, and then Pia tugged on my arm again.

"Isn't that the woman who does the catering at your office?" she asked, pointing midway across the park.

Sure enough, Abbigail Gibson and her business partner,

Rio, were hanging a banner on the concessions building advertising something called the Intrepid Entrepreneurs.

The sports park buzzed like a beehive on the weekends with families. Middle- and upper-class folks from nearby neighborhoods attended birthday parties and youth sporting events or were just out enjoying the beautiful Southern California weather.

It was a smart fundraising opportunity for a nonprofit group, and it looked like that was precisely what my sassy little caterer was up to. She and I needed to have a serious heart-to-heart about the food-poisoning incident. Hopefully I could get to her before the police did.

"This couldn't have worked out better. I need to have a talk with that woman, and seeing her here saves Elijah from having to track down her address. That is what the man gets paid for, but it saves me from having to go to her home... Christ"—I closed my eyes in mock horror—"probably in the valley or somewhere equally unpleasant."

Equally horrifying was the salary a private investigator made in this city. Especially if his talents weren't being put to good use. The least he could do was track down Abbigail's home address if I needed him to.

"Oh, stop being such a snob, Bas. There are plenty of lovely people who live in the valley. But maybe you should wait until after the game so you don't miss anything."

"Yeah, you're right. Maybe I'll just go get a bottle of water or something and tell her to hang around afterward so we can talk." There was no way I wanted her leaving the park without talking to me, but I'd feel terrible if Vela made an epic save and I missed it. "I'll even wait until halftime to do that."

"You're the best uncle on the planet, Bas."

"Yes. Yes, I am." Just as I said those words, my little niece dived across the net and caught a low-flying ball before it made it into the goal. She seemed to surprise even herself when she rolled onto her back, still clutching the black-and-white ball to her stomach. Her other little Blue Jay mates rushed the goal to congratulate her on an excellent save.

"Great work, Keeper!" I hollered through cupped hands. "Yeah, Vela! Nice!"

She grinned widely up to Pia and me in the stands, and we both waved to her frantically. So proud of that little girl. Proud as if she were my own.

Stars danced in my periphery from all the yelling and the afternoon heat. I quickly sank back down and planted my butt on the bleachers.

"Shit." I wiped my forehead with the hem of my T-shirt.

"What's up, brother? You look like paste. And it's not a good look on you, if I'm being honest."

"Still not one hundred percent, that's all. The heat is getting to me a little bit."

Pia dug into her mini cooler and handed me a juice box. I eyed her wearily but knew it would make me feel better.

Because my sister was diagnosed with type 1 diabetes when she was three years old, we both knew all the nutritional tricks to raise and lower blood sugar and the quickest way to accomplish the goal.

Vela's team came in off the field for halftime, and Pia went down to the sideline to help pass out snacks and drinks. I took advantage of the break from the game to head over to the concessions stand to have a chat with Little Red Riding Hood. Seeing her outside of my office did even stranger things to my libido than seeing her at work. Couldn't exactly explain why that was, but this woman was making me feel like a teenager trying to work up the courage to ask his crush out on a date.

Jangled nerves. Sweaty palms. Dry mouth.

*Seriously?*

I shifted from side to side in my running shoes, fidgeting with my shirt and checking my watch. Christ, if Grant saw me right now, I'd never hear the end of it.

Rio caught sight of me first. She made some snide comment, and Abbigail's head shot up, abruptly stopping her conversation with another parent midsentence. The woman she was speaking to turned around to see what, or who, had captured Abbi's attention so completely.

"Aren't you—" The woman snapped her fingers twice in a steady beat, as if that would conjure my name.

I offered my hand to her. "Sebastian Shark. A pleasure to meet you." I gave her a practiced I'll-have-your-knickers-in-my-pocket-later grin while I shook her hand, and just like that, she turned into a bumbling schoolgirl.

The woman reached up to surreptitiously fix her hair that was carelessly tucked under a Disneyland ball cap.

"Are you an easy-going Jungle Cruise kind of girl or more of a Space Mountain speed demon?" I asked, nodding up to her cap, still grinning. The first lesson in lady killing—women loved talking about themselves. Actually, to be fair, that rule spanned both sexes.

"Probably depends on the day." She paused, and a sly smile moved across her glossy pink lips. "Or the company." She gave me a flirtatious bat of her eyelashes.

Abbigail coughed loudly, and the woman turned boiled-lobster red.

"You okay there, Little Red? Need the Heimlich Maneuver?"

"No," she answered. "You just stay on that side of the counter, thank you very much." She gestured dramatically up and over the service counter to the ground where I stood.

Once the other woman walked away and Abbi's partner was busy with another customer, I stepped closer to the counter.

"We need to talk."

"Isn't that what we're doing right now?" She shifted her eyes back and forth.

"I'm serious. There's been a situation with the food you brought to my office on Friday. I got very sick and had to go to the emergency room that night. It was most unpleasant."

"So I've heard." The tone was frosty and remote.

"Shit," I muttered.

"So I've heard." A little chuckle followed the comment.

I cradled my face in my palms. How embarrassing. "I'm glad you find it humorous. I can assure you it was anything but." I glared at her, but she wouldn't make eye contact.

"Neither was the visit from the police officers I received yesterday morning. I can't believe you told them I poisoned you. Do you have any idea what something like this could do to my business?"

"I didn't tell them you poisoned me, Abbigail."

"So are you saying the authorities just randomly guessed you had a tummy ache Friday night? And then just came by my house to see if I fed you that day? What a series of lucky coincidences. I mean, I've heard the police around here are a bunch of bumbling fools, so imagine the amount of luck they had to have guessed all that."

"Are you finished?"

"Oh, you can bet on it."

I stared at her for several long beats, waiting just long enough to make her uncomfortable with the silence.

Across the field, the official blew the whistle to commence the second half of the Blue Jays' game.

*Goddammit.*

"I need to get back to my niece's soccer game." I thumbed over my shoulder toward the field. "But this conversation isn't over."

"It appears to be just that, Mr. Shark. And if you need me to formally withdraw my bid for the contract at the Edge, I'll understand. Do you need that in writing? I can email something over when I get home today."

"I said this conversation isn't over, Ms. Gibson. That means *it isn't over.*" The last few words of the comment were delivered through gritted teeth. She was pissing me off, and my fuse was already short because I wasn't feeling well. "I'll talk to you after the game." I quickly turned and walked away before she could sass back with another remark.

I sent a text to Elijah on my way back to the bleachers, asking him to find her home address anyway. In the event she decided to leave before we had a chance to finish our conversation, I wasn't above showing up at her door to say what I needed to say. Abbigail needed to hear that I didn't initiate getting the authorities involved with the food-poisoning situation.

There was no logical explanation why I cared that she knew the truth. But the longer I sat and watched the soccer game, the more amped up I became. I kept sneaking glances over to the snack bar where she worked, and as often as I did, I'd find her staring back. She'd quickly avert her eyes but always a few seconds too late.

When I finally held her gaze, imprinting my dark and lustful thoughts onto her body from across an acre of sports park greenbelt, my cock throbbed to life in my thin shorts. I narrowed my eyes, willing her to feel my breath on her skin, imagine my fingers on her flesh like they had been the other day in my office. I wanted her to sense my dirty intentions, even though there was physical distance between us.

She fluttered a hand to her throat but remained locked in my stare. I could see the rise and fall of her chest beneath the filmy tank top she wore. Her pale skin was already pink from the sun and heat, but a darker flush spread like a storm making landfall.

She broke eye contact and dropped down to busy herself with some task below the counter. I instantly dreamed up several things she could do at that level if I were standing there beside her. If she were on her knees in front of me, looking up at me with those wild green eyes, begging to suck me off, maybe?

*All right, Little Red. Just this once. And only because you've been taunting me with this perfect, sinful mouth. These plush, pillowy lips.*

Of course she'd argue. She always argued. But I'd stop her by shoving my cock past her tongue until she gagged. *Now you better make it worth it. And you better take all of me.* I'd make her gag again until tears sprung from her eyes and ran down her cheeks.

God, the tears. *Why am I so turned on by her tears?*

Pia shot to her feet, cheering enthusiastically. "That's my girl! Nice save, honey!"

Without thinking, I did the same thing—and then just as quickly sat down, frantically looking for something to cover my lap.

*Jesus Christ. Shit. Shit!*

I looked around wildly, hoping like hell no one saw the ridiculous woody I was sporting when I stood up. The shorts I wore left nothing to the imagination, and for Christ's sake, I was at a little girls' soccer game. I'd be arrested if I didn't get myself under control.

"Wow, that was an amazing save," my sister said as she sat down beside me. "Not that you've seen anything for the past ten minutes."

"What are you talking about?" I acted offended, but she was totally right. I didn't even know what the score was.

"I haven't seen you so preoccupied with a female since you were a teenager." Pia kept her eyes on the field while she spoke, probably because she knew if she gave me the full hot seat treatment I'd turn feral.

"I'm not preoccupied."

"Cut the shit, Bas. It's me. Don't insult me, or our history, by lying to me."

I couldn't even meet her expectant stare. She was right, and I had nothing to add in the way of defense. I couldn't explain the draw I had to that girl in the snack shack. I couldn't explain why even though I'd already told the police that I personally didn't suspect her of a crime, I hadn't ordered them to stand down completely on the case. And why the thought of being the one who made her squirm while fearing the fate of her guilt or innocence made my body light up with unadulterated excitement. And I certainly couldn't explain why I wanted nothing more than to have her moaning my name while she shattered with the wildest orgasm of her life while speared on my dick.

"You're right, I'm an asshole, Pia. I'm sorry. And that's

the second time I've had to apologize to you today. Maybe I should've stayed home."

She put her arm around my shoulder and squeezed me closer to her. "Your secret's safe with me, brother. Everyone will still think you're the big bad wolf in town. No worries. But now, that's the final whistle, and here comes our Blue Jay."

As she said it, the referee blew three long toots on her whistle, ending the game. The kids came off the field, high-fiving each other and the coach after a big win over their opponent. I kept my eye on Naya's dad to see how he handled his child after the game.

"Daddy, we won!" She looked up to him, smiling along with her teammates.

"Well, you really need to work on your passing more at home. It's sloppy. You made some crucial mistakes in the first half." He didn't even look at her while he issued the criticism.

My hands curled into fists. She was eight years old, for Christ's sake. I could feel her pain inside my own heart.

"And your team needs a better coach. I have no idea where they get these screw-ups."

"Hey, buddy, why don't you ease up, man? It's a kids' league. They're out here for fun."

"Maybe your kid is, but mine is looking for a scholarship after high school."

"She's eight." My brows hiked up toward my hairline in disbelief. "That's ten years away." I chuckled at his ridiculous answer.

"Show's what you know. Scouts start looking as early as ten." His authoritative tone made him seem even more ludicrous. *Did people really think this way?*

"How many adults make a career out of professional

sports, do you think? And is that really the lifestyle you want for your kid?" Maybe a different approach would get through to him.

Now he was the one to laugh. "What? Should my kid idolize jackasses like you? Dipshits who have women killing themselves because they fell in love with them? It's funny that you're handing out career advice." He shook his head and began to walk away.

"You have no idea what you're talking about. Asshole."

He turned on his heel at the insult. "What did you just call me?" He stalked back to where I stood.

"You heard me." I squared my shoulders, preparing for a physical blow.

Pia grabbed at my arm, but I moved from her reach.

"Bas, come on. Just let him be."

"You're a bully and a terrible example for your daughter." I pointed my finger in his face. "If I hear you berate her or any of the girls on the team ever again, I'll contact Child Protective Services. Mark my words. It's a game. It's supposed to be fun. Fun doesn't end in tears, idiot. There are enough screwed-up adults running around this world. You don't need to do your best to make another one." I gave him one last head-to-toe scan, only moving my eyes. "Piece of shit."

At that point, I was the one to turn and walk away, leaving him standing there with his mouth hanging open. I suspect he wanted to say something but couldn't organize his thoughts quickly enough to muster a comeback.

"And a mental giant to boot," I said to Pia as I took Vela's outstretched hand.

Most of the team's parents had stopped to watch the altercation. As I walked away, a few started clapping in appreciation for what I'd said to the man. Apparently a lot of people felt the same way but no one ever had the balls to put the guy in his place. By the time I cleared the throng of people, everyone was applauding.

Vela was jumping up and down beside me, having no clue what was actually going on but loving the commotion.

"Why's everyone clapping, Mama? Because we won?" she asked as she bounced along.

"Yes, that, and because Naya's daddy is going to try to be kinder to her. Won't that be great?" My sister ran her fingers through Vela's sweaty hair, brushing it back off her forehead.

"That would be the best thing ever!" She released my hand to clasp both of hers in front of her chest. "It's really sad when Naya cries. Her dad is so mean. I just stay far away from him." She shook her head and transitioned right into the next subject seamlessly, as only children can do. "Can I get a snow cone? They have them at the snack bar."

I chimed in. "Snow cones for everyone. My treat!" Snow cones and a quick conversation with a certain redhead—how convenient.

Pia eyed me over Vela's head, knowing the game I had in mind.

I shrugged unapologetically. "We have unfinished business."

"You've got it bad, brother."

"I have no such thing, thank you very much."

"We'll see." She walked with Vela to the line that formed at the snack bar's window while I went off to the side of the building where the service door stood propped open.

"Abbigail. Can I speak to you for a minute, please?" I asked, peering into the block building.

"No, you can't. I'm swamped," she said without looking up.

"You have a horde of volunteers standing around with nothing to do. It'll just take a minute. Come." I strode away from the door and around to the back of the building. There was glorious shade from a mature oak tree, and I took a minute to let the breeze waft over me and cool my skin.

Another minute passed. She still hadn't come around the building. I was thinking of at least three ways to extract her from the concession stand when she appeared with a cold bottle of water in each hand.

"You looked like you could use this," she said, offering me one of the bottles.

"Thanks. I think you're right." I cracked the top open and drank half the bottle in one long pull. "I feel like my stomach turned inside out Friday night."

"Listen, Mr. Shark. I told the police all I knew. I really don't think it could've been from my kitchen."

I closed the space between us because I couldn't stand to be so far away from her when it was just the two of us there. A wooded area lined the park on the back side of the building, so no one had a reason to come back here. The parking lot and all the sports fields were in the opposite direction. It was doubtful we'd be interrupted.

"Why are you here today? At this sports park, I mean? I've never seen you working in the snack bar before."

"Oh." She thumbed over her shoulder toward the building. "I mentor a girls' club. Middle and high school girls—young entrepreneurs."

She was fumbling for words, and for some reason it turned me on. Normally the insecure type did nothing for me, but I'd seen the fire in this woman's spirit. I knew it was solely a reaction to being near me.

My dick twitched as I put the pieces together.

*Yep. That's what was doing it.*

I nodded in approval. I appreciated business owners who gave back to the community and especially to youth groups. Having had the rough upbringing I had, I knew the value of outreach programs like hers. "That's a great idea. You'll have to introduce me to your group."

"What makes you think they'd want to meet you?"

I cocked my head to the side. *Be serious.* I was on the *Fortune 500* list for the past ten years in a row. And that was just for starters. I was a self-made success story, and I had a ton of valuable information and advice to teach young business people. She knew it, I knew it—hell, even those high school girls knew it.

"Abbigail." Her name left my mouth on a sigh, and it felt so right on my tongue. Just like I knew she'd taste so right there too. Her lips. Her skin. Her pussy. Yes. All of it would be perfection. I took another step toward her, invading her personal space exactly like I had in my office earlier in the week. She was so easily dominated. She *wanted* me to take control of her pleasure. She all but begged me to with her vast green stare as she watched me move incrementally closer.

"Hmmm?" She tilted her head back. That particular way women do. She looked up at me, screaming *kiss me* but not saying a word. My cock knew what she was asking. The bugger was jerking in my shorts with every bat of her eyelashes.

*We'll get there, big guy. This one's going to be worth the chase.*

"Why is it?" I ran my thumb just above her eyebrow,

smoothing out the line of tension that formed there. "Why is it I can't keep my hands off you when you're near me?"

"I— I don't know. Is that an actual question?"

"Mmmmm." I hummed low in my throat and traced my thumb around her eye to the apple of her cheek, where the sun had kissed her pale skin. She glowed a rosy pink from the afternoon heat. I cradled her face with my other hand, reaching my strong fingers around the back of her head while I caressed her lips with my thumbs.

"I'm going to kiss you, Abbigail," I growled roughly.

"Yes," she breathed out in response.

"I wasn't asking. I know you'll let me. It's written all over your face." I moved my mouth closer to hers. "Your glassy eyes."

Closer.

"Your sharp little breaths."

Closer.

"Your parted lips."

Closer still. Until my lips were just a hair's breadth away from hers.

"I can smell how much you want me. I can smell it on your skin." I touched my lips to hers but not a true kiss.

"From between your thighs."

Then I crashed my mouth together with hers. Mastering her lips apart with my tongue. Calling hers forward, only to retreat when she responded. Again. And again. When a frustrated mewl worked its way up her throat, I gave her what she wanted, twining my tongue with hers, stabbing and thrusting in deeply until she panted through her nose for air.

"That's good." I pulled back, grinning. "I can definitely work with that."

# CHAPTER SEVEN

## ABBI

For a second, I wondered why I was still breathing. Or standing upright. Or conscious, for that matter.

I urgently worked air in and out of my lungs. A mix of fire and ice that claimed my legs—as well as the throbbing currents at their crux. My head felt like a marble tossed in a steel bowl. My ears clanged. My eyesight was foggy. My equilibrium swam.

And I instantly wanted more.

How could I not have known? How could I have roamed this planet for twenty-two years and not realized this was what lips were meant to feel like? That a heart was supposed to feel like it was about to explode from my chest? That colors were supposed to be this vivid, scents were supposed to be this mouthwatering, and one man alone was supposed to be the center of my need just seconds after he'd moved away from me?

Away being relative. Thank God.

He hadn't gone far. I hoped it was because he was lost in the same how-am-I-still-breathing mire as I was.

I gave in to the craving to confirm it. I raised a hand to where his chest was surging like a violent sea. But there was nothing liquid about the texture beneath my touch.

"Oh," I croaked, touching the defined muscles beneath his T-shirt. I let my hands drift across his pecs, appreciating the firmness as his torso heaved with each breath. Air sawing in and out like waves on the shore . . . a steady, strong cadence . . . a pulse reflected back through the ocean-blue eyes that bored into me while I explored.

"Oh," I repeated again, sounding more like a moan of appreciation the second time, though.

"Fuck." Sebastian's husk jolted through my whole body. "*Fuck*," he said again, lowering his forehead to mine and then rolling side to side where we touched, intensifying our heated connection.

As if his action was my unspoken permission, I slid my free hand around his nape. Holy crap, he even had muscles back there. I prodded and squeezed, hoping to elicit another addicting F-word from his firm lips.

"Abbigail." Not quite what I was going for but equally perfect. The man's dark baritone was instant fire at my core. "Abbi," he whispered.

Oh, yes. Perfect.

Especially if he planned on finishing it by kissing me again.

Oh, how I needed him to kiss me again.

*Damn it. Please kiss me again . . .*

"Hmm?" All right, so signals got lost between the seductress in my head and the naïf on my lips. Not that Sebastian noticed, based on the hard length pushing through his nylon shorts *and* my flimsy skirt. How I savored the feel his need. Of his . . . his *erection*.

As I forced myself to consciously think it, I gulped hard.

So did Sebastian.

Right before he trailed his lips along my hairline, rasping as he did, "Oh . . . Abbigail. What the hell are you doing to me?"

"Well, nothing involving poison." Though I tried to laugh it out, the effect was more of a pathetic croak. "Which was why you all but dragged me back here by my hair, right?"

His determined growl vibrated through both of us. "If I drag you anywhere by your hair, girl, you'll beg me for it first."

And just like that, I was even more bewildered. Thank God he somehow had me pinned to the back wall of the snack shack, nearly holding me off the ground with the weight of his body. "Well, that sounds . . . splendid."

Not that this wasn't. Holy crap, our flirting was a lot more fun than I remembered it being with others in the past—especially as Sebastian reacted by grinding in until my thighs were fully parted for him. And then laved my neck and earlobe with heated licks and bites.

"Ms. Gibson," he finally asserted in a sexy murmur, "I don't do splendid."

"Hmmm." My heartbeat galloped as I did my best to sound coy. "What *do* you do?"

He pushed a low growl into the curve between my neck and shoulder. "Well, I can promise a few more S-words will likely be involved."

"Like sensual?" I smiled, letting those three carnal syllables swirl down through me. "And slide . . . and satiny . . . and screw?"

Holy wow. I'd never said all that before. The words, yes. But all in one sentence? With one specific motivation? For one beautiful, dominating man? Never.

But I was nailing it.

I was a freaking femme fatale—and I was pretty sure I'd

just drawn blood.

For all of two seconds.

Before Sebastian Shark twisted his head with the focus of a lion about to dig into his prey.

He growled into my neck, sending liquid lust through every membrane of my being. And then anchored my head with a commanding hand so he could bite into the meat of my earlobe.

Hard.

"*Uuhhh!*" I repeated the soft but high yelp as he slid to the tender spot below my ear, nipping brutally again. He used the flat of his tongue to soothe the abrasion, though I told myself not to be lulled back to any sense of safety.

It was wise counsel.

I was stunned all over again as he leaned back and impaled me with the blue steel of his gaze. Dear God. This man and his hypnotic eyes.

He only magnified the torment—the magic—when contrasting their sapphire splendor with an onyx-dark scowl. "All right, Ms. Gibson," he said, his tone a sudden clip of all-business purpose. "It's time we got clear about some things."

I sensed him wanting to hold up his fingers, just like he'd done the first time he had me trapped and horny like this. But this time, I refused to lose my focus to furious tears. I was a temptress, after all. "I'm listening."

A long-suffering look clouded his handsome face, matched by his heavy sigh. "I don't do sensual. I do sex. And I don't slide with satiny intent. I pound with one clear goal. And I sure as hell don't screw, either." By the time he finished the litany, he almost looked amused, and I went from sexual seductress to silly schoolgirl in the flash of five sentences.

I shifted my weight—as far as was possible, anyway, with my body still locked by his—and forced myself back into the temptress's head space, trying to salvage the moment along with my dignity. "Fine. You don't screw." I nudged up my chin, proud of how the words flowed as if I'd said them a hundred times. "You fuck."

He compressed his lips tighter. "No."

Oddly—and thrillingly—the air hitched in my throat. "No?"

"I take." He moved back by a step, seeming to sense I needed the space.

He wasn't wrong.

"Not forcibly, but not tenderly." He squared his shoulders. "I take what's consensually offered to me. My partners enjoy themselves and are fairly compensated for the experience. In the end, everyone goes away happy."

Thank God, even more, for that extra space. I was positive I sucked down every bit of air between us as I dropped my hands and then dug my fingertips into my thighs. "But there's an end." I abhorred every note of dejection that weaseled its way into my voice. I shouldn't give a flying crap about his "ends," happy, consensual, or otherwise. Nothing about today had changed a thing between us. It sure hadn't changed anything about him, no matter how hard he rocked the hot, doting uncle bit.

Come tomorrow morning, Sebastian Shark would still be Sebastian Shark. High above the city in his cushy tower, snarling at those below. Even his bromance sparring sessions with Grant Twombley would remain. And of course, complaining about my salad dressing—or the color of his napkin.

Or maybe none of it—if he still intended to push legal action about my food messing with his sensitive stomach.

A concept that should have knocked my pulse back to normal but didn't. It was simply impossible to imagine this looming panther as a weak kitten on a hospital bed. My mind's eye just wasn't capable of seeing it.

Which meant only one thing.

It was time to get back to my girls.

"So…" I went ahead and spoke up, since our silence had stretched to the point of uncomfortable. "Now that we have that cleared up, thanks for stopping by today. Don't call us; we'll call you."

I almost added a small snicker—until Sebastian made it clear he wasn't laughing. Not by a glowering long shot. I ended up gulping instead, when he hitched back into place in front of me. Every drop of moisture in my throat evaporated as Shark extended one arm to the wall beside my head. In so many ways, this position was more unnerving than his intrusion for the kiss.

"Hmmm." He dipped in his head, studying me even deeper. "Tears to deal with the fury…but a headlong sprint into sass when someone decides to open up a little." He closed in tighter, lighting the shadows between our faces with the brilliance of his gaze. "Is this how you keep all the boys away, Abbigail? Or is it just me?"

I was back to reining in a salty laugh. *All the boys? Ohhh, silly man. If you only knew.*

Except that there was nothing to know.

Leading me back to the behavior that, damn it all, proved his point to a freaking T.

"And is this how you keep all the girls close and bunched in the panties, Sebastian? By claiming you've actually 'opened up' to them?"

*What the hell is wrong with me? Why am I purposely provoking the bastard who holds all my cards right now?*

He turned the tables on me again as he scrutinized me from down his noble, carved features, just before rocking his head back a fraction—and bursting with one of the fullest, loudest, most unexpected laughs I'd ever heard in my life.

I half expected a camera crew to pop out of the bushes and yell some catchphrase from a television show that hadn't aired yet. Maybe they were shooting the pilot and Sebastian Shark was an executive producer who agreed to star in the season opener to lure viewers...

My confusion had to be broadcast across my features as I waited for him to summon some composure and swing his sights back down on me, seizing me all over again with his intense blues. And immediately intensify the effect with his riveting physical grace and predatory energy.

"Ohhh, Ms. Gibson."

And that bestial grumble...that did equally primal things to every nerve ending in my body.

I shifted my eyes left, then right, and then back to him. "Yes?"

He curled in toward me. Over me. Drove that blue crystal gaze into me while that devil's smile kept playing across his lips. "You talk to me like nobody else does," he husked. "Like nobody else dares."

"Maybe more people should."

"Maybe we should just keep this between us."

His mouth returned to its granite line, but his eyes kept up the smile. I was so entranced by their intensity, I forgot to breathe. When I finally did, my senses were filled with his spicy, masculine musk. My sights were consumed by the defined planes of his chest. My sex was achingly aware of its nearness to his.

"What does that mean?" I finally countered. "That you trust me now?" I cocked both my brows. "Or are you holding on to the delusion that I poisoned you?"

"I didn't say that."

"But you didn't say I'm exonerated, either." I aligned my hands at the center of his chest. "Do I have to stab in here and jerk it out of you?"

His gaze narrowed by a telling fraction. "Not the spot I'd envisioned you jerking, Red."

I plowed past his filthy inference. I had to stay focused on the important subject here. "If I'm facing a court action tomorrow, I need to know."

Aha. Progress. At least that was what I hoped as he drew in significant air. "I haven't instructed the sheriff's office to keep pursuing things. But I haven't told them to close the file, either."

"Which means what?"

As his assessing scowl became an insolent sneer, I wondered if it was the look he gave business rivals before telling them they'd been bested. "It simply means that I may need to be further...persuaded...about your innocence."

"Persuaded? How?"

He stretched out his other arm, thoroughly fencing me in with his rippled guns. He waited one more second, as if really-but-not-really weighing options, before murmuring, "Have dinner with me."

"Ex...excuse me?" A laugh spurted out before I could stop it. "You want to have dinner...with *me*? At night? Sitting down and actually talking to servers like they're human?"

He tilted his head to the other side. "Yes, yes, and no."

"Sorry?"

"Yes, I want to have dinner with you. Yes, at night. But absolutely no on the civility with servers." He straightened his head before qualifying, "Actually, no on the servers, period."

I shook my head. "I . . . don't follow."

"It's simple. You'll come to my place."

So this was what frozen dread felt like. "I will?"

"Not tonight, of course."

"Of course," I repeated lightly. However, I did so mockingly. "Let's just—"

"I'll have Craig reach out to set something up. You have any allergies or culinary hard limits?"

"Hard . . . limits?"

Dear freaking God. It sounded like I'd never heard the words before. I had—just never in the same discussion as dinner.

With hypnotic finesse, Sebastian handled my query with a steady stroke along the side of my neck. "Things you can't or won't eat, Little Red."

"Uhhhh . . ." I opened my mouth. Closed it. Forced my lips to connect with words again. "No. I . . . ummm . . . enjoy all kinds of cuisine. But—"

"Outstanding."

His smile widened, opening a chasm of bliss in my chest. The man's smile was more devastating than his eyes.

"I'll instruct Craig to get his ass to Belcampo Meats and grab us a pair of steaks. We can talk while they're on the grill. You like California or French reds better?"

"I—" Was still having issues with basic language, apparently. "Wh-Who's Craig?"

"My personal assistant. He'll make sure you get the address and all the proper NDA forms."

"Your personal assistant? That's not Terryn? NDA forms?"

"Terryn is my executive assistant. The NDA is standard protocol, Abbigail. Practically the same agreements you signed when Shark Enterprises signed you on as our caterer."

With massive effort to focus, I finally stepped away from his potent hold. "I'm still your exclusive caterer?"

He pivoted, looking as regal as a king while handing my phone back. "For now, yes."

I matched his imperious regard while taking the device. "Depending on how much you enjoy yourself when I fix you dinner?"

"When *I* fix *you* dinner."

It didn't surprise me, but it didn't put me at ease, either. "With reimbursement for everything . . . after dinner?"

That shot the man's smile way past devastating. For several seconds, I struggled for a decent descriptor beyond that but had to give up. Words were impossible when I thought about paying the man back for a juicy steak. Basic thoughts were impossible. Where the hell was my inner temptress when I needed her?

"Why don't we start with you bringing dessert, Little Red?" He amped the agony of the moment by maintaining the few feet of distance between us—despite the illicit ideas sparkling so clearly in his sapphire gaze. "And then we'll see what develops after some chocolate and wine."

A protest surged up my throat. I was ready to give it full rein, along with a dozen more reasons why this "date" was a bad idea. Topping the list was my own cardinal rule put in place by my sound business sense—which had borne a huge black eye the second I let Sebastian lay his lips on me.

But if I didn't do this...

"You know this is bordering on extortion, right?"

It needed to be voiced. Without snark or lip or anything except what it was. The truth.

Trouble was...it also gave Shark a damn good excuse to reclose the steps between us.

Then to tunnel his hand back beneath my ponytail.

Then to move in even tighter, invading my space and my energy every way he possibly could.

Then to flood my senses with all his heat and size and power and determination...

*Oh, this is so nice...*

"Extortion might work." His voice was like a gathering storm, vibrating my senses with wild anticipation. "But I choose...exploration."

I dragged my gaze up to meet his. Sure enough, he was already starting the expedition. His mesmerizing blues raked every plane of my face. "Like a modern Daniel Boone?"

He dropped his voice lower. "Like a modern Bluebeard."

And again, he sucked the air from my lungs and the stability from my legs. "This really isn't fair, Shark."

"Life isn't fair, Ms. Gibson."

He stepped back once more. I was swaying. He was swaggering.

"That's one lesson you can skip," I said. "Learned it already."

"Then at least you'll get a great steak out of all this."

"And you'll get my triple chocolate orgasm cake."

His eyes flared. I'd handed him that one on a silver platter, but it was worth it. No matter what quip he cued up now, I knew he'd have as much trouble waiting for our dinner as I would.

"Uncle Bas?"

A little girl popped into view. I hadn't met Vela Shark in person yet, but thanks to the photo shrine of her on the credenza behind Sebastian's desk, it felt like I already knew her. She was even more endearing now, standing in all her I-came-and-conquered glory. Her socks were slouched, her legs were grass-stained, but her face lit up when she saw her uncle.

"Hey there, Vel." The affection in Sebastian's voice exposed him at once. "What's up?"

Vela approached and burrowed against his side, and he affectionately tugged at her ponytail.

The girl bounced back a huge grin. "Guess what?"

Sebastian curled up an answering grin. I watched, enraptured, as the girl's pinky finger and that man's soul got tight with each other. "What?"

"The Intrepids don't just make snow cones." *Wrap, wrap, wrap.* Yeah, *very* tight. "They also have ... brownies!"

"Whaaat?" The man's deadpan was, hands down, one of the sexiest sounds I'd ever heard. "You don't say."

"I do say. And they. Are. The. Best. Ever."

As I succumbed to an even bigger smile, Sebastian replied, "Did you know that the Intrepid Entrepreneurs only sell those treats? The person who actually makes the brownies is this lovely lady right here. Ms. Abbigail Gibson."

Vela broke into a wide grin. "You're really good at your job, Ms. Gibson."

"Well, thank you, Vela." I gave her a little bow while arching an eyebrow at her uncle. "Some people don't exactly agree all the time."

"Well, they're losers," Vela snipped. "Seriously, your brownies are even better than the ones at Chocolate Bash. And I love those brownies more than my own breath."

"Wow." I used my stunned expression to force back my laughter.

"Okay, missy," Sebastian said. "In my world, this is called trying too hard."

She pouted. "But you always tell me to try as hard as I can at everything."

A darker scowl from her uncle. "What do I also tell you?"

She thought for a few seconds. "That asking is half of the getting?"

He pulled her in close and bussed the top of her head. "Do you have something to ask me, Little Star?"

Though Vela kept her smile, she swept back from her uncle with practiced confidence. "Mr. Shark, I'm enjoying these brownies quite a lot—and in light of the fact that I helped the Blue Jays win today, I feel you should buy me another one." She notched her head higher. "Perhaps two."

"Well done, Miss Shark." He shook her hand and left behind a folded cash bill when he released his grip. As I recognized the picture on the note—Benjamin Franklin—he was already speaking again. "Go tell the Intrepids that's to be used for buying out *all* their chocolate brownie stock."

"Yes, sir!"

But as she got ready to scamper off, I parked my hands on my hips and a new glower on my face.

"What?" Sebastian spread his own hands with a return challenge.

"My girls are here to learn usable business skills and

entrepreneurship, Mr. Shark. Not 'smile pretty and wait for a sugar daddy to buy out your inventory.'"

"What's a 'sugar daddy,' Uncle Bas? It sounds yummy."

Sebastian nodded toward the front of the shack. "Just go hop in that line and buy those brownies, Vela."

"Is . . . Is it okay with Ms. Gibson?"

"It will be."

The second Vela cleared the shack's corner, I bit out, "It won't be." I meant it even more as the man swept in on my personal space once more. "Damn it, Sebastian. For the record, this part's not fair, either."

His inky brows crunched in on each other. "Explain."

"Because I'm supposed to be teaching these girls—"

"And you have been," he said with the serenity of a yoga master. "All goddamn day, in this infernal heat. Now, it's time for them and you to be compensated for the hard work so they can go enjoy being kids. Set them free, Abbigail. Let them get out of here and go to the mall, or the nail salon, or the boba joint, or the coffee shop—which honest to shit makes no sense to me on a day like today, but—what?"

At first, all I gave as an answer was my perplexed sigh. "I just have no idea how to use this as a teaching moment," I finally admitted.

"*Pffft.* Of course you do."

I reared my head back. "I do?"

"You do." He reached in and squeezed my hand with the same insolent confidence he'd lavished on Vela. "We'll schedule an afternoon for you to bring them over to the offices. I can show them around and tell them about how much work there really is—"

"Whoa." I stepped around, jerking on his poor arm like

we were choreographing a crazy dance routine. "The...
offices? Are you offering—do you mean—*your* offices? Shark
Enterprises?"

Up went the man's signature smirk. The arrogant, radiant
resilience that had sunk a thousand competitors—but in this
moment was the wind beneath my wings.

"What you're doing with these girls is great, Abbigail. A
field trip like this would make sense, right?"

For a long second, I could only gape. At last I stammered,
"I . . . I have no idea what to say."

"Hmmm." His smirk didn't falter while pressing even
closer, molding our bodies with the same intent his stare
offered to my lips. "I'd say 'thank you' would suffice, but that'd
be passing up a prime opportunity."

My breath shallowed. "An... An opportunity...for
what?"

"Adding it to your remuneration. For the steaks and wine."

"Oh," I rasped. "Of... of course. St-Steaks and—"

Who needed to say the word when the crush of his lips
already had me joyously buzzed? As his body rocked with
mine, communicating how intoxicated he was too? As our
sexual inebriation got better with every mesh of our mouths
and tangle of our tongues?

This was crazy. So damn desperate. Maybe even pathetic.

There was still an open investigation on me with the LA
Sheriff's Department because he had been poisoned. He had
the final say on what company would be landing the catering
contract for his new tower. Sleeping with him was probably the
worst idea on both fronts.

But God help me, it was all I craved.

All my mind could conjure and my body lusted for.

I needed close, carnal knowledge of Sebastian Shark.

The agonizing admission matched the painful wait I was about to face over the next days.

I seriously never thought I'd crave steak and wine this much in my life.

# CHAPTER EIGHT

## SEBASTIAN

"What does that mean in English, Brookside?" I looked at my watch while pulling the cork from the wine. The decanter Pia had given me for Christmas would finally get some use, as I planned to let the young Bordeaux sit for the two hours remaining before Abbigail was due to arrive.

"It means we're ready to break ground, Shark. Exactly on schedule. I thought you'd be ecstatic." Annoyance laced his voice, but I held my tongue.

"I am. I wanted to be sure I understood you correctly. So many roadblocks have been put in our path, I think I was just expecting you to be calling with another one." If he expected an apology, he'd be waiting a while.

*As in, forever.*

The soils engineer's report had been in my email inbox that morning, and trying to make heads or tails of most of it was like trying to decipher the human genome map. I had talked to Grant about it for fifteen minutes before we both agreed to wait for Brookside's call and hear his personal take on the information.

It wasn't helping matters that most of my mind was preoccupied with making dinner for the feisty young redhead who was due—I looked at my watch again—in an hour and fifty-two minutes. Time was ticking away, and I still had a hundred things to do in order to have all the components of the meal come together at the same time. I'd tried to keep the menu simple so I wouldn't make an ass out of myself with overcooked meat and undercooked potatoes. It was a bit unnerving preparing food for a professional caterer, but I wouldn't let the stress get to me. For all she would know, I had this mastered, like everything else I took on.

"Shark? You still there?" Brookside asked.

Shit. Totally forgot I was still on the phone.

"Yeah." I cleared my throat. "Yes, I was reading an email that just came in. Listen, I need to take care of this. Where do we go from here? We have the ceremony for the press in a few weeks, but what's the next step on-site?"

"Well, the survey team should be there to mark off the auger cast piles. That's according to the last copy of your GC's schedule—that I have, at least. I'm sure you have a copy of that too?"

It was more of a dig than a confirmation. Almost a *you should be asking your job supervisor these things, not me, you idiot* type of remark.

"That's scheduled for Monday and Tuesday," he continued. "If all goes well and they did their homework, you could be digging by the end of the week. All depends on your sub's schedule."

"Thanks for all you've done, Jonathan. I'll reach out to Ricardo to see if he has everything lined up. I'm sure he does, but you're right. It wouldn't hurt to check in with him." I tapped out a note on the nearby iPad I was using to look up dinner recipes.

"And if he's worth what you're paying him, he won't

mind you babysitting him a little bit. I've seen that man's fee schedule. You've got one of the highest-paid generals in the country on your job site. He should be serenading you every day like Elvis."

I chuckled. "Right, okay. Just send your bill to the project's accounting department. I'm sure Terryn gave you that information when you were at the office?" I asked by way of ending the conversation.

"Yep, we're good to go. Good luck, Shark. I look forward to seeing your building in the LA skyline."

"You and me both." I stabbed the End button and tossed my phone onto the kitchen counter.

First order of business was peeling and dicing the potatoes so I could get them cooked. That way all I had to do after Abbi arrived was mash them and add the roasted garlic.

I had coated the bulb of garlic with olive oil and wrapped it securely in foil. It was roasting in the oven on a nice, low temperature, and it filled the kitchen with the heavenly smell of earthy, pungent garlic. My mouth watered just thinking of how delicious the meal would be. And, if things went like I planned, how delectable Abbigail would be afterward.

I was anxious to get her on my turf and in the complete privacy of my home. She had sent back all the necessary documents. Most of them were signed, but a few items were lined out and others were highlighted. Even that made me chuckle and throb in my boxers.

She had the strangest way of getting to me, and working her out of my system was becoming an urgent need. The biggest project of my life was finally taking shape, and I really didn't have time to be skirt chasing. I needed to be one hundred percent focused on my building.

The appetizers were easy to make but delicious. Grape tomato, baby arugula, prosciutto, and fresh shrimp Craig picked up at the farmers' market that morning. The perfect combo of flavors nestled on a mini skewer. The shrimp were marinated in a zesty citrus blend beforehand so the flavors would pop in your mouth when you bit into the snack. It was the impeccable starter for the beef-heavy meal.

I had an hour before show time. Off to the shower to freshen up while the water came to a boil for the potatoes and the roasted garlic cooled enough to spoon from the skin. I'd fire the steaks on the grill just before we ate, and the asparagus would be roasted on the grill too. Everything was completely under control. I'd had Craig set the table out on the patio before he left earlier this afternoon, so I was right on schedule.

Forty minutes later, I paced back and forth in the foyer. How could I be so nervous? And why did I live in such a big house? It was impossible to be near the kitchen to keep an eye on the food and close to the front door after the guards at the gate let me know Abbigail was on the property. Me and my big ideas to send the staff home early so she wouldn't feel awkward with other people milling around. These were the exact reasons I had people paid to work in my home, for Christ's sake.

When the doorbell chimed, I nearly jumped out of my skin. I'd gotten so wound up in my browbeating, I'd all but forgotten why I was wearing a path in the large flower pattern of the entryway. I took a calming breath and pulled open the soaring twenty-foot-high leaded glass door. The dark walnut wood and inlaid glass made the thing weigh a ton, something I had never really appreciated before. It might have been the first time I actually opened the door myself.

"Hello. You found the place, I see."

"Jesus. Christ. Sebastian." Abbi walked through the doorway and continued right past me, turning in a full circle in the foyer. Her mouth hung open as she took in her surroundings.

Seeing the house through her eyes was a whole new experience. It was a large home. Everything about it was over-the-top. The sweeping staircases, one off to each side of the entryway, that seemed to float up to the second floor with no support system beneath, were the first thing to capture a visitor's attention. An ornate wrought-iron banister lined each flight, topped by gleaming walnut that echoed the front doors. The stairs' risers and treads were polished rust-colored marble, the same stone found in the pattern of the flower on the foyer floor. Malachite and Carrara came together to make the other parts of the floor's design.

She finally met my eyes, and her cheeks flushed with embarrassment. "God, I'm sorry."

"What are you sorry for?"

"I'm looking around like I've never been inside a house before. But seriously. This is incredible. How long have you lived here?" Her gaze darted from one place to the next, trying to decide where to settle.

I thought for a moment, trying to remember how old Vela was when I moved in. I could remember being terrified of the pool out back, and with the home being over fourteen thousand square feet, how could we keep track of her all the time and be sure she wouldn't wander out to the pool?

"Five years. Give or take." I couldn't take my eyes off her. She looked radiant with her hair hanging freely around her shoulders and down to the middle of her back.

"It's enormous. Do your sister and niece live here too?"

I smiled. "No, but not for lack of trying to convince her. Trust me. Vela is all for the idea. She loves the pool. Can't keep her out of it when she's over. But surprise"—I rolled my eyes dramatically—"my sister wants her own life."

Abbi laughed.

"Let's go out back, if you don't mind? I have the food going in the outdoor kitchen, and I can't keep my eye on it standing here in the foyer."

"Lead the way. Where can I put this?" She held up a Tupperware type of container, which I assumed had the dessert inside.

"Does it need to be refrigerated?" I called over my shoulder as we strolled straight through the living space to the sliding glass doors that made up the far wall. I had all four wide open to catch the evening breeze. We stepped out into the backyard.

"Oh, wow. This just gets better and better. Sebastian, this is unreal."

A rush of pride filled my chest as I watched her take in the pool, guesthouse, gym, outdoor kitchen, spa, and patio.

"This is probably my favorite part of the property. I spend as much time as possible out here. Especially since I spend so much of my day cooped up in the office. When I'm not there, I'm usually out here."

I walked over to where she stood, rooted to a spot in the middle of the patio. "Let me take that." I held my hands out for the dessert. "Can I get you a drink? Wine? Something else?"

"There were promises of wine and steaks, were there not?" Her green eyes always glowed a certain way when she was mischievous. I could picture her as a child in those moments.

"Indeed there were," I said, letting her mood infect me.

"Well, then? I'll have the wine."

"Good choice. It's decanted and chilled to the perfect temperature."

"Of course it is."

"What's that supposed to mean?" I walked over to the wine cooler and pulled out the decanter.

Abbi followed me and took a seat at the terra-cotta bar of the outdoor kitchen. She accepted the glass of Bordeaux I handed her but waited to sip until I had my own glass poured.

"Just that I'd venture to guess you do everything perfectly." Her eyes darkened to a different shade of jade, and she shifted restlessly in her seat. Maybe I wasn't the only one feeling the spike of sexual tension.

"Well, I endeavor to. But I don't always get it right." I held my glass aloft, offering mine toward hers in a toast. "To new endeavors."

"I like that." She smiled softly, and a warmth swept through my body—and I hadn't even let the wine touch my lips yet.

"I like *you*," I said quietly, my glass obstructing my mouth.

"You're very smooth, you know that? And this wine is outstanding. Mmmm." She took another eager sip.

"Wait till you taste it with the steak. Even better together. What temperature do you like yours cooked?"

"Medium, please."

"Medium rare, then. Good choice." I gave her a quick wink.

"That's not what I said."

I smiled while taking a drink from my glass. I could sense her getting ramped up.

"Why bother asking me a question if you aren't going to

listen to the answer?" Her little temper was so easy to fire up.

"Just because I asked you for directions, Abbigail, doesn't mean I'm going to change the route I planned on taking." I leaned across the bar and toyed with the ends of one of her curls. "I like your hair like this. You should wear it this way more often. It suits you."

"Just not always practical around food, you know? People don't appreciate long strands of red hair in their meal. And way to change the subject."

"Whatever it takes. And it's the truth. You look stunning this evening."

I went to the refrigerator and pulled out the appetizer. I grabbed a small bowl for the skewers from under the counter and placed the plate and trash bowl in front of Abbi.

"I hope you like shellfish. You said you were up for anything."

She already had one of the skewers in her fingers and popped the whole thing in her mouth and chewed, eyes going wide as the flavors exploded on her tongue. When she finished chewing, she took the small cocktail napkin I handed her.

"Jesus Christ. Where did you learn how to cook? I can't believe you do this well too." She shook her head in dismay. "I'm so screwed."

"That's the plan, yes. Several times, if I have my way." I leveled my stare to hers, and she immediately looked away. Where was the brass balls girl from the park on Sunday? I wanted to call her out on it, but I lifted my wineglass to my lips instead, never taking my eyes off her.

She swallowed a few times more than necessary to clear her throat of the bite she'd eaten before finally speaking. "I meant because of your enormous ego."

She was pitching them right over the plate, and it was all I could do to hold back from swinging. There were at least five comments on the tip of my tongue that involved the word *enormous*, but she was already a deep shade of pink from the last remark I'd made.

So, instead, I made an obvious adjustment to my thickening cock. I watched her eyes follow my hand the entire time and then turned to put the steaks on the grill.

"Can I help with anything?" she asked from right beside me. I was so lost in my lusty thoughts, I hadn't noticed her approach the grill.

"Will you refill our wineglasses and bring them to the table? Also, there's a pitcher of ice water in the refrigerator behind the island." I motioned with the tongs in my hand. "Would you mind filling the glasses on the table?"

"I'm on it!" she said enthusiastically. Abbi looked happy to have something to do besides sit and watch me mill about.

When I had the steaks seared, I moved to mash the potatoes and put the asparagus on the grill. They would roast quickly, so I had to keep my eye on them. Last, I folded the roasted garlic into the whipped potatoes by hand. A quick turn on the meat and asparagus, and everything was ready to be plated.

"All right, my lady, take a seat. Looks like everything is just about ready." I hustled all the food off the grill and onto the serving dishes I had set out earlier. When I brought the meal to the table, Abbigail looked amazed. I took the seat beside her rather than across from her. I reached across to grab the place setting, silverware, and wine, and set up shop where I sat. She watched me with interest but didn't say a word.

"It would appear I have the need to touch you when you're

near me. I can't do that from all the way over there," I said unapologetically.

"Oh" was all she said, but a smile started at a corner of her mouth and then spread to a full grin.

"Can I serve you?" I asked, taking her plate. I would do it regardless, but I was attempting to prove I possessed manners. I just didn't always choose to display them.

I put reasonable portions of food on her plate and placed it back in front of her. If she wanted more, she would be welcomed to it. There was more than enough for seconds. I loaded my own plate and waited for her to cut into her steak. Guessing she'd object to the temperature of her meat, she surprised me when she put her fork right into her mouth and immediately moaned.

I had to give Craig huge props on his selection at the market. He'd really picked two fantastic cuts, and it was simple to make them shine with just salt and pepper and the right amount of heat.

Abbigail pointed at her beef with her fork, mouth still too full to speak. "Mmmm"—*point, point*—"mmmm."

"Good, right? Try the wine right after. You won't believe how different it tastes," I said before taking a bite.

She swallowed after chewing the last bit and dutifully picked up her glass and had a big sip, eyes bulging out in appreciation.

"How can that be? That's incredible. Oh my God. Freaking heaven. Right there on my plate and in my glass."

"I told you, didn't I?"

"You did. You did," she said and then tucked right back in for more. "I don't think I will ever get enough of this."

After her next bite and swallow of wine, I had to stop her.

I had to taste the wine on her lips. I couldn't stand the torture any longer. I put my hand on her wrist to stop her from lifting the glass back to her lips.

"What's wrong?" she asked, almost alarmed.

I took the glass from her hands and sat forward to the edge of my chair. "I need to taste your lips."

Her green eyes widened, looking like jade in the dwindling light of the evening. I watched her features change until our lips met. Much softer than the day we kissed in the park. I licked along her top lip first, tasting the salt and beef stock from the steak. Groaning, I swept in deeper, tasting the heady tannin of the wine mingling with the copper tang from the rare portion of the meat.

I pulled back to look at her, her eyes still closed. She looked like a doll, with her milky skin nearly glowing in the new moon of the evening.

"You are so beautiful, Abbigail." My voice was husky with need.

Her eyes fluttered open, and she seemed surprised by my compliment.

"Thank you. And thank you for this amazing meal. I'm completely blown away."

"The pleasure was mine. And will be mine." I grinned. "But first, we eat, so this doesn't get cold."

We ate in companionable silence for a few minutes, just enjoying the food and sounds of nature from the backyard.

"Have you always lived in SoCal?" I asked her while cutting a piece of steak.

"No, I grew up on the East Coast. Rhode Island, specifically. And before you ask, no, I don't miss it. I miss my family that still live back there, but"—she looked around the backyard—"nothing compares to this paradise. Granted, I don't live like this—not even close—but my place is nice by my standards. And I'm doing it on my own, and that's the most important thing."

"Why is that the most important thing?"

"What do you mean, why? Isn't it obvious?"

"Not really." I put my hand atop hers. "I'm not trying to make you feel defensive, Abbigail. I'm just trying to get to know you."

"You're right. Sorry. I think I've always felt like I've had to prove something to someone. No matter what stage of my life I was in."

"Explain."

She narrowed her eyes at me over the rim of her glass while she sipped. I wasn't sure why, exactly. Was she deciding how much to open up to me? Did talking about her childhood make her uncomfortable?

*Shit, I knew that one all too well.*

"Again, not trying to make you uncomfortable. We can change subjects if—"

Abbi shook her head. "No, it's not that. Not at all. I was letting my cynical side run away with me. I've been trying to be better about that, but honestly, being around Rio all the time doesn't really help in that department."

"I've noticed she's a bit of a bitter pill. Kind of glad to hear it isn't just for my benefit."

She laughed. "You definitely ramp her up, not going to lie. But no, it's not just you. She has some history. But most people do, right?"

"Definitely. It makes us who we are," I said, nodding. "No one should ever feel bad about their history. It's what defines us. At least that's how I see it."

"I like that approach. It's fair. And honest." She looked at me thoughtfully.

"What is this look?" I asked, trying to interpret it but coming up short. I had a lot of experience with reading people's body language in business situations, but with personal exchanges, not so much. I'd always limited myself to certain types of personal interactions, and feelings and conversations weren't part of the mix.

"There's a lot more to you than I think I expected. I feel"—she paused, considering her word choice—"honored? Yes, I feel honored to share this time with you." She nodded in agreement with her statement, seeming pleased with the delivery.

"Well, so far, I'm enjoying spending time with you too, Ms. Gibson. Tell me more about your family." I made a mental note to circle back at some point in the conversation to why she felt like she had to prove herself to people. For now, I would stick to lighter topics. "If Rio is your sister-in-law, you must have a brother? Older or younger?"

The twinkle in her eye could've lit the entire backyard. "I'm the youngest of five. My parents married young and wasted no time starting a family. Irish Catholic. Need I say more?"

"Was it good or bad having that many siblings?" Having just one sister, I often wondered what a large family would've been like.

"I love it. For the most part, I mean. I have four very protective brothers. I've seen the way you watch Vela. Imagine that feeling times four. Bram, Flynn, Sean, and Zander are all probably what would be called alpha males, I guess?" Her smile stayed in place even after she finished talking.

"Which one was brave enough to lasso Rio?" I grinned, thinking of partnering with that strong woman.

"That would be Sean. They moved to California first, and I followed the week after I graduated from high school. Came out to visit them spring break of my senior year and fell in love with the palm trees and sunshine. My heart came back to life after being dead for so long after..." Her face fell into complete sadness.

I couldn't resist taking her hand. She needed to be comforted. Whatever she was remembering caused great pain and grief. I brought the back of her fingers to my lips, placing a gentle kiss there. "I'm sorry. Whatever it is, I'm so sorry."

"You don't even know what you're saying that for." She met my gaze, looking like she was near tears.

"Doesn't matter. I can see the sorrow on your face. I can almost feel it from where I'm sitting. It was not my intention to drag up a bad memory."

"Oh, it's okay. It's always right there." She touched her chest, right over her heart and looked away. "Right under the surface, you know? Well, of course you don't know. What am I saying?" She took a steadying breath and then continued. "Our mother passed away when I was in high school. Massive heart attack on our kitchen floor. It will be burned in my memory forever."

"I *do* know." My words were steady even though I spoke about the most significant pain I'd ever known.

"Hmm?" She shook her head slightly, trying to make sense of my remark.

"I know what you mean about the pain being right here." I thumped on my own sternum. "All the damn time. Pia and I lost our mother when I was just seven."

She snatched her hand back from mine to cover her mouth in horror. "Oh my goodness, you were just a baby. And that means Pia was just what?"

"Three."

"So your father—"

"Became a sad-sack alcoholic." I had to cut her off before she made him into some sort of hero he had never been. "I get the fact that he was brokenhearted. Not only did he lose the woman he loved but their newborn son as well. But he had two living children who needed him." Brewing in my gut was the familiar anger that was always present when I thought about my father.

"He was neglectful on his best days, and then Cassiopeia was diagnosed with type 1 diabetes the same year. So instead of my father getting his shit together and being the parent he should've been, I had to learn how to monitor her sugar and inject her insulin. Because she would've died if she had to depend on him."

By then, we had both finished our meals and were just sitting at the table, talking. I suggested we move to the more comfortable furniture near the fire pit. There was a sofa and love seat around the lava rock–filled ring, along with two high-backed chairs that swiveled on attached bases. All the furniture was arranged atop a coordinating earth-toned outdoor rug that tied the look together. Pia outdid herself with every project she took on around my house.

We sat side by side on the love seat after I lit the fire pit with the gas assistance and a few dry logs that were already arranged inside.

"Where is your father now? Do you have a relationship

with him?" Somehow, she still held hope in her voice.

"Six feet under."

Blank eyes stared back at me.

"He drank himself to death by the time I was sixteen. I raised Pia myself, begged the neighbors not to turn us in to the authorities so we wouldn't be separated in foster care."

"How did you manage that? You were just a boy. How did you earn money? Provide food and pay rent and all of that?"

I shrugged. "Where there's a will, there's a way. I'd been taking care of us for most of our lives already. My dad was worthless, even while he was alive. I learned to hustle on the streets of East LA when I was really young. That's when I met Grant. He was a hustler too."

A grin played on my lips as I remembered what a cocky asshole he had been. We'd thought we could take on the world. "I worked legit jobs too. It wasn't only...ummm... questionable endeavors."

I slid my arm behind her along the top of the sofa cushions so I could toy with her hair while we talked. I'd never felt such a strong need to touch a woman like I did with Abbigail.

"That's unreal. You're an amazing man, Sebastian. Really, just...wow."

I looked away. "I did what I had to do. Some of it? Not so proud. Other parts? Damn proud. No matter what, though, like I said earlier, it made me who I am today."

The mood surrounding us had gotten way too heavy and needed to change. I'd already lived through my shit life once, and I did everything in my power to keep it in the past. Once again, Abbigail Gibson had an uncanny ability to make me do things out of character.

I refilled our wineglasses, emptying the bottle from dinner.

"Enough talk of the past. Let's talk about the present. The right now."

"Oookkaaayy." She drew out the word, looking like a skittish kitten.

"Are you always this nervous around men? Or is it just me?" I chuckled, running my index finger under the neckline of her open collar. She had an odd style for a young woman. Different from other girls her age.

Although, when I thought about it, I typically kept the company of dancers and escorts. Women who intentionally dressed to be provocative. In comparison, Abbigail dressed like women twice her age and possibly one who worked in an abbey or correctional institution.

"I'm not nervous," she said, swallowing so forcibly I could see her throat work from top to bottom. And it was so damn sexy. Calling to me to kiss her there. Suck her. Bite her.

I took her wineglass from her trembling hands, set it on the wide tiled ledge of the fire pit, and placed mine beside it. When I turned to face her, I slid off the low cushion of the love seat and onto my knees on the padded outdoor rug.

"Open your legs," I directed quietly.

"What?" She gulped.

"Spread your knees apart so I can get closer to you." I tapped the insides of her knees with my fingertips.

She complied while her breath sawed in and out, making her chest rise and fall steadily.

"Are you comfortable there? On your knees?" Her skeptical look vanished with my ensuing comment.

"It's not my body I'm concerned with, Abbigail," I answered with a wink, reaching forward to unbutton the top button of her shirt.

One by one the buttons came loose, and more of her creamy flesh was revealed. Light brown freckles spattered across delicate skin, even over the swells of her breasts that peeked out from the lacy white cups of her bra.

By the luck of the lingerie gods, her bra had a front clasp, and I zeroed in on it with skilled fingers. I watched her eyes, looking for any objection.

"We have complete privacy out here. And no one lives in that house on the left." I bent my head forward and kissed her, just above the bra, teasing along the lace with the tip of my tongue before spreading the halves away to expose her breasts to my view.

I inhaled sharply.

*Perfection.*

"Jesus, Abbigail. You're so damn gorgeous. Look at you. Just look at you." I stared at her breasts like they were the first pair I'd ever seen. As if I were a twelve-year-old boy copping my first feel. I thumbed the baby-pink nipples and watched the way they sprang to attention from the stimulation—my cock responding in kind.

"Need these in my mouth." I kissed her lips first, though. Roughly. My need had spiked from touching her. Seeing her. She was unraveling my control, and I went from casual explorer to lusty conqueror in a few short beats.

My tongue spread her lips, gaining entrance without asking permission and sweeping deeper with each pass. Little mewls vibrated up from Abbigail's throat and into mine, spurring me on. She liked it. She liked me. I could feel her need.

I wanted to devour her chin, jaw, ear, and then her neck. I would consume her by the time I was through. Something had possessed me after seeing her tits. I'd become a beast.

Even worse than usual.

Women always amazed me. They had pretty parts and soft places to nestle and touch. But Abbigail? Oh, shit. Abbigail was a species all her own. Definitely not like the others. No. Not even close.

Her skin tasted like elements of the Bordeaux we shared. Black cherry... plums, maybe? Some sort of flower danced in my nose when I pulled away. I already knew the smell would tease me for hours after she left my bed.

"Sebastian," she moaned as I sucked the underside of her breast into my mouth. Women always loved that spot caressed and nipped. I swore it was more sensitive than the nipple for some. I reached up with my hands to knead the mounds roughly, and she arched beneath me, lifting her back off the cushions, her face pointing to the nighttime sky.

"More? Is that good?" I asked, looking up over the sexy arch of her throat. The urge to sink my teeth into her was so strong, I had to fight it off with everything I had. I pinched her nipple between the side of my thumb and index finger when she didn't respond.

"Shit! Yes. God, yes! It's good. So good." She narrowed her eyes at me but didn't pull away.

"Don't be sassy, girl. Just an answer. That's all I wanted." I nibbled the place I'd sucked, and she closed her eyes. Abbi threaded her fingers in my hair at my nape, scraping her nails through to my scalp.

"Mmmm. I like that." I closed my eyes too. Felt so good. I knelt up tall again to capture her mouth, grinding my cock into the side of the love seat's cushion.

"Fuck. Fuck, yes." I rutted harder while we kissed, simulating thrusting into her heat.

I worked the button of her jeans with my fingers. I needed to feel her dampness on my fingers and lips. I needed to taste her.

And then a cell phone rang. Her damn cell phone rang from where it sat on the island by the grill.

"No. No way," I gritted against her lips.

She chuckled in response and then let out a heavy sigh.

"No. Seriously?" I grated.

"Let me just get rid of whoever it is. My father is getting up there in age—"

I backed away immediately. I'd never forgive myself if I were the reason she didn't respond to an emergency.

She answered the call while walking back toward where we'd been going at it. "Abstract Catering. This is Abbigail."

*Who the hell would be calling her business number at this hour?*

"Oh, yes! Hello, Mr. Blake."

*Blake? As in Viktor Blake?*

But how many Blakes must live in Los Angeles? I was acting ridiculous and testy because I had a goddamn hard-on I could break wood boards with like at a martial arts demonstration.

Thoughts banged in my skull, and I wanted to rip the phone from her hand and chuck it into the fire pit.

"Oh, no, it's fine. Don't worry about it. How can I help you?" Abbi said to the caller.

*No, he should totally worry about it.*

"Hmmm, yes, that is quite a pickle. You're right. No, we can totally help you out. How many are you expecting? Fifty? No problem. What time do you need service set up by? Eleven. All right, no worries. Will the usual assortment work? And what about drinks? Yes, mm-hmm. Okay, yes. No, no worries at all. Oh, you're welcome, Mr. Blake." Then she giggled.

Fucking giggled.

"Fine, I'll call you Viktor. Okay, see you tomorrow, then. And thank you for the opportunity. Bye."

*Red.*

A blood red haze settled over my backyard, and I physically blinked my eyes two or three times to clear the strange film that toyed with my vision. I wanted to tear something or someone apart with my bare hands.

Not that it was Abbigail's fault. She didn't have a clue that I hated that man. Viktor Blake. Bastard. How dare he call her while she was at my house? I was seconds from having my mouth on her pussy.

Goddamn asshole.

Talk about a mood killer.

"I'm so sorry about that. Now, where were we?" She reached her hands forward to stroke my chest. I grabbed them, stopping any chance of us picking up where we left off.

"Maybe it's time to call it a night. If you need a ride because of the wine, I'd be happy to have my driver take you. One of my security team can follow in your car."

She winced.

My tone sounded curt even to my ears. It couldn't be helped. That phone call was the equivalent of a bucket of ice water down my pants.

Again, not that she knew any of the history between Viktor Blake and me. Nor was I about to share it with her. She'd already heard enough of my history for one night.

*For one lifetime.*

"I'll walk you out," I said without emotion.

"I think I can manage. Since I'm being dismissed so coldly, why don't we just go for broke?"

She was pissed. Honestly, she had every right to be. But, in typical Shark fashion, I wouldn't do anything to change it.

"I'm not dismissing you. I had a lovely evening."

She tilted her head to the side, calling me on my bullshit.

"Abbigail," I said in a frustrated huff.

"Sebastian," she said in the same delivery.

"Clearly, you have a busy day tomorrow. And now it's busier than you expected. I'm trying to be considerate."

"Look at you, then. Mr. Considerate. Right."

We walked toward the front door.

"Let's not end a wonderful evening on a sour note."

*Am I pleading?*

It sounded an awful lot like pleading.

Sebastian Shark did not plead. With anyone.

"Good night, Sebastian," she said, resting her hand on the door handle.

"Until next time, Little Red." I leaned forward to kiss her, and she thrust her cheek out as the only available option.

*Get your head out of your ass, man. Or out of your cock, wherever it may be lodged. This girl is playing you. Another man just called her.*

I kissed her softly on the cheek and chuckled.

"What's so funny?" she asked over her shoulder as she stepped out the front door, still looking for an argument.

"I am," I answered without emotion. "I think *I'm* the joke at the moment. Good night, Ms. Gibson. Drive safely." And then I closed the door to my very big and very lonely house.

# CHAPTER NINE

## ABBI

"Indigestion, irritation, celebration, or recuperation?"

Rio's soft but knowing query had me looking up from the fresh sourdough slices I was drizzling with secret sauce. The kitchen's air was still laced with the bread's tangy scent, though my sister-in-law's nose crinkled as if one of the loaves was burned.

"Umm...excuse me?" I knew where she was going with the query but wasn't sure about exposing my emotional flank to her incisors. "You tackling the *Times* crossword again? Didn't I order you to stick to sudoku?"

Rio's gaze darkened from the warmth of whiskey to the umber of melted chocolate. And of course I had to conjure an image of the dessert I made yesterday—leading my brain back to the man responsible for redefining the triple chocolate cake for the rest of my life.

No. Not for the rest of my life, damn it.

Sebastian Shark didn't get to redefine anything for me again. Not after the fiasco of last night.

*Fiasco.*

The word fit perfectly into the mental parking space I had reserved for him. I could come up with a handful of other words for Sebastian personally. Jerk, jackass, dick—all justified quite thoroughly after the way he threw me out of his home not even nine hours before.

Correction. His church-sized palace.

His sprawling, lonely castle.

And why was that still such a surprise? Especially now?

"Abbi."

"Whaaa?"

Holy crap. I'd been deep into the recall this time—but wasn't amazed or sorry about it. I had just returned to the moments after Viktor Blake's call. At least I hadn't been basking in every sizzling, tingling memory of what had happened before that...

"Okay." Rio chuckled. "That really did just fly in one ear and out the other, didn't it?"

"Just lots on my mind," I mumbled. "We've got all the last-minute details for Blake's order to double-check, and—Crap." I smacked my forehead with one hand and snapped my fingers with the other. "I just remembered. He asked for the cold buckwheat noodle salad instead of the rainbow macaroni. That means we'll have to boil the noodles and then—"

"You mean boil them...like this?" With the grace of a game show hostess, she swooped an upturned palm over the pair of pots on the stove's back burners. Then with her other hand, she dumped a pile of chopped tomatoes into a bowl of diced feta, asparagus, and scallions.

"I bow in worship." I dipped my head low. "You are officially crowned the Queen of Multitasking."

"Yeah, yeah. You can kiss my ring later." She grabbed a slotted spoon and stirred everything in the bowl. "Especially because it frees you up now to finally giving me some answers, woman. Oh wait." She flicked the spoon up as if brandishing a sword. "I just figured it out!"

"Should I be scared?" I teased, hoping like hell she hadn't really.

She notched her chin higher, holding me hostage with her perceptive gaze. "Oh, yeah." She added a solid nod. "And now I know I'm right too."

I avoided squirming under her scrutiny. Barely. "You willing to put money on that?"

"Are you?"

She wasn't wavering. And my clamoring stomach knew it. Still, I kept up the outward appearance of confidence with my brazen invitation. "Go for it, Sherlock. Let's hear your theory."

"Sebastian. Shark."

Her deduction didn't exactly blindside me. I was just less prepared than I'd expected to be—which made me mad. But if I could keep the resulting sting contained behind my eyes . . .

"That's a name, not a theory." Why did it sound like I was conducting my side of this conversation through clenched teeth?

"You saw him. Not in his office or as part of the lunch route. You saw him last night, didn't you?"

I plunged my stare back down, focusing on the stack of avocadoes that needed to be sliced, crisped, and placed on the bread along with Rio's salsa. "H-How . . . did you know?"

"Because if you'd been out with anyone else, you wouldn't be hiding it from me." Her shoulders dropped as she voiced her theory. The sadness in her tone boomeranged off the walls in the otherwise quiet kitchen.

I worked harder at finding a place to fix my stare. "So this is guilt by omission, then?" And now why the hell did I sound so defensive?

"You're not guilty of anything, Abs. Except maybe believing that wolf could change into a decent housedog."

I felt my face twist in aggravation. "What makes you think I want a dog?"

She rolled her eyes. "Fine. Okay. Whatever you thought you'd be getting from the man, then. The changes you thought you'd be seeing in him, just bec—"

"What makes you think I expect him to change? Or want him to?"

"I've been around the block a few times, Abbi. It's a common pipe dream we all share. We, as women, I mean. We meet a guy, maybe he's a little rough around the edges, he's good but maybe not great, you know? But we think, 'I can change him.' Or the better one or worse one"—she huffed a derisive laugh—"depending how far gone you are, 'For me, he'll change.'"

"You're way off base on this, Rio. It's not like that. Not at all like that." But before I could continue, she went on as if I hadn't uttered a word.

"And I know what I witnessed at the park on Sunday. An hour of you and Sebastian Shark trying to hit vital organs with your glares until he dragged you behind the concessions stand. Then when you both returned wearing Revlon's Fatal Apple across your lips . . ."

I inspected the ground again. "Well, hell."

"Looked more like you'd been to heaven and back by all the stars that had collected in your eyes." She bumped up a coy shrug. "But whatever you say. If you're not ready to talk about it, that's cool. I want you to know though, Abs"—she waited until I met her brandy-colored gaze—"I'm here when you decide you are, okay?"

"Why?" I leveled, still battling the guilt of not sharing. "Why, if you noticed all of that, did you not say a word?"

Rio shrugged. "I think I was hoping that if I shoved the guy's behavioral blip aside, you would too. I also know you, little sister. Discussions involving affairs of the heart happen on your terms. And not a moment before."

At my nod, she added with a small lift of her mouth, "Actually, I think that's a Gibson genetic predisposition."

"So then what? You thought—or hoped, rather—that I'd come to my senses and forget about Sebastian and go out with Viktor Blake instead?"

"Let the record show that I wasn't the one to bring up the hot Russian this time. But now that we're here—"

"No."

"Oh, come on, Abs. You know it's not a complete conversation with me if the Russian hunk angle isn't exploited."

"Well, I've had enough exploitation lately, all right?"

The trash can wobbled after I viciously tossed in some avocado pits, and Rio let a heavy pause go by. Then another.

"All right," she finally uttered. "You know Sherlock Gibson isn't going to erase that one from the notepad."

*Crap, crap, crap.*

New heat crawled up my neck and spread across my cheeks. I dug my fingernails into my palms to extinguish the emotion. "Okay, listen. I'm not a victim here, Rio. Shark may have been holding a figurative gun to my head, but all the bullets were in *my* hand." I opened my fingers from a fist to reveal my empty palm, as if there were bullet casings lying in my flat hand between us. "I agreed to his ultimatum with barely a fight. I did it willingly."

"His... ultimatum?" A confused look replaced her half

smirk. "Okay, slow up. What the hell are you talking about, 'ultimatum'?"

I returned both hands to the avocado task. "Exactly what it sounds like."

"Can you indulge me? Pretend I don't know what it sounds like. Because I don't like the way my brain wants to fill in those blanks."

"Fine." I started chopping avocadoes like a ninja shredding balsa wood. "When Shark and I were... talking... out behind the snack hut, he told me he'd consider asking the police to close up the food-poisoning allegations—*after* I had dinner with him."

"After you had—" She squeezed her eyes shut while mouthing a countdown in order to cool down. I tracked the silent four, three, two...

"Shit, Abbi," she finally muttered. "Why didn't you tell me?"

"Because I wanted to go. There. I said it. I wanted to go, Rio." I watched her shift her gaze heavenward before looking to me to continue. "I know that's not what you want to hear. But it's the truth. I'm attracted to him. Very attracted to him, as a matter of fact." I felt heat creep up my chest and neck again, just at the admission.

"So what happened? He made you literally put the proof in your pudding? And likely expecting some juicy 'side dishes' too." After she air quoted the innuendo, she propped her hands to her hips and waited. "And Mr. Uptown actually drove to Torrance for this?"

"Oh, dear hell." While I loved my bohemian corner of the world, the idea of Sebastian stepping foot in my condo was as ludicrous as it was disturbing.

Really disturbing.

Yes, even after everything we'd shared last night.

Because when all was said and done, even after all the romantic razzle-dazzle, none of it was supposed to be more than a casual fuck. A way to get what we both wanted. I'd have a check mark on the bucket list, closure on the food-poisoning claim, and an orgasm I hadn't rubbed out for myself. He'd have a nice notch on the bedpost, the best chocolate cake of his life, and an orgasm he didn't have to rub out for himself. Everybody was supposed to take home a W.

But a funny thing happened on the way to the winner's circle.

"Dear hell indeed." Rio's high gasp sliced into my thoughts. "Does . . . that mean . . . ohhh, shit, Abs! Did you go to his place? His *mansion*?" She laid heavy emphasis on the last word.

She finished it by pushing the bowl of salsa toward me with enough force that the stainless-steel bowl slid across the worktop and almost sailed right off the edge. I caught it with a scowl.

"Easy, killer." That would've set us back at least thirty minutes we couldn't spare.

"It *was* a mansion," she charged. "Wasn't it? You need to spill, Abbigail. Better yet, did you get any pictures?"

"Pictures?" My mouth fell open to react, but all I came up with was: "You think I had time for pictures?"

"And you waited a full hour into the workday to start telling me about this?"

I chuckled softly. "To be honest, I wasn't planning on telling you at all."

"Excuse me?" Her dark brows hiked farther into her hairline than I thought possible. "And that reasoning is why?"

I made her wait as I slid the avocado slices under the broiler. "Oh, where to start, sis? The judgment? The fact that Sebastian Shark isn't exactly your favorite C-Suite hottie."

She canted her head. "He's starting to grow on me a little. *A little*," she qualified, jabbing a carrot my direction. She started shucking the vegetable's skin, and I breathed in relief that she was only wielding a peeler. With what I had to relay next, I worried about the woman being anywhere near a knife.

"Well." One more deep breath before I went for it. "At the moment, I can say he's not my favorite, either." I clamped my mouth shut before sharing more.

Clearly, that wasn't what Rio expected me to say. Still, she was calm about rebutting, "Guess it's a damn good thing we still have Blake's order to fill, then." In her old *Finding Nemo* tee and cuffed jeans, the woman planted her hands on her hips and tapped a flour-covered Doc Marten on the floor. "Time for explanations, sister."

"Nothing much to explain." I gave a small shrug.

Rio's emotion-filled *tsk* spliced the air. "Why don't you let me be the judge of that?"

"Because judges are supposed to be impartial?"

"And that's really what you want from me?"

"What I want is to not be judged at all. And maybe a longer pair of these." I held up the steel tongs I was using to flip the avocado slices and narrowed my gaze with pretend sinister intent.

"Juicy." She rubbed her hands together. "I'm in. Where do we start? At the top of the mushroom or the fun bouncy balls?"

As usual, I couldn't decide whether to hug the woman or break down and soak her in my confused sobs. The good *and* bad thing was I knew she'd be okay with either choice.

"Abs." She grabbed my free hand with tender meaning. "It's me, honey."

"I . . . I know."

"Tell me what happened."

But now that we were at this place in things, I pulled back my hand, adding an apologetic glance. I already knew it wasn't necessary; Rio was well-accustomed to the Gibson shutdown, courtesy of her experiences with my difficult brother.

*Difficult.*

Wasn't that the fitting word of the week, courtesy of the maddening Y-chromosome beast in my life? But how did I summarize it all for Rio without violating Sebastian's NDA provisions?

And there was the new rub too, as stupid and pointless as the agreement itself. Because seriously, I was just fine about keeping his street address secret, as well as agreeing not to set a drone free in his house, and even maintaining radio silence about the expensive wine he'd poured with our meal. None of that meant as much as the connection we'd shared. Well, that I thought we'd shared—until it all went up in smoke after thirty seconds of a basic business phone call. And while Viktor Blake had no way of knowing how he'd daggered up our night, it was hard not to let my irritation ooze onto him too.

But Rio didn't deserve my bitter backlash about all that. I took a deep breath and went straight for the point. "What did he do, sister?" I drawled. "Well, let's ask the more relevant question here. What didn't he do?" As I spoke, Rio's concentration didn't waver—which justified the speed of the comprehension that ignited her features like a sunburst through storm clouds.

"Holy. Shit." She punched both words with astonished

gasps. "Are you telling me what I think you're telling me?"

I bunched my eyebrows, completely confused. "Umm... what am I telling you?"

"That Sebastian Shark, man about town, couldn't perform when the curtain finally rose? Was the curtain the only thing that rose?" She grinned at her own joke.

"No." I brought my hand down over hers. "Oh, holy hell. *No*," I groaned.

"What? Are you not allowed to tell me or something? Did he make you sign an NDA, like we had to do before delivering to his offices?" At once, her features bugged wide. "Oh, he did. That's why everyone still thinks he's a fast player. They all think he's got an erection for the ages, and—"

"It *is* an erection for the ages!"

Unbelievably, her stare got bigger. "And the Trojans came marching in," she exclaimed. "At last. Yes! You cashed in your V card?"

"Oh no, sweetie. No Trojans marching—though they might have stormed the barricades. Maybe a little."

Rio's first response was a litany of F-bombs and something about a sawed-off cactus stump that I couldn't quite make out because I was laughing so hard. As she walked the pots of noodles over to the strainer in the sink, she finally said, "All right, NDA or not, you're going to spill everything. I've got freaking whiplash. Which Shark are we dealing with here? The Jaws who rocked your world or the guy from here"—she jabbed a thumb toward her T-shirt—"who wanted to just be friends?"

I dug my teeth into my bottom lip. "Oh, I don't think he wants to be friends."

Rio studied me like I was a Jenga tower and her next move had the potential to topple the entire stack. And I loved my sister-in-law a little more for her cautious treatment of the subject. "But he never moved things into the other category?"

"It was...amazing," I finally whispered. "Oh damn, Rio, he was amazing. We were on his patio, and the wind was blowing in from the canyon..."

"And he brought out a throne and then slid your feet into a pair of glass slippers?"

Her undercurrents were sarcastic, but her tone was all dreamy fantasy. And this was still Rio I was dealing with. I could work with that. "Better than that," I sighed out. "So much better. All the right words. All the right ways to touch me..."

"But..." She pitched it up into a question at the end. The rest was up to me, but I didn't want it to be. Why couldn't I live in the fantasy forever?

"But my phone rang."

"Okaaay." Rio narrowed her eyes while drawing out her bafflement. "I don't get— *Oh shit.*" But then obviously, she did get it. "Your phone rang...right when you were getting to the good stuff?"

Feeble nod. "Exactly."

"And you answered it? Oh, God. Don't tell me. No; you have to tell me."

"It was the forwarding ring from the business line."

"And you've got this modern gizmo called voicemail," she said. "It's the coolest thing. Just go with me here. If somebody calls you and it's after hours, you can let the phone ring a few times. And then—here's the really magical part—"

I stopped her by raising a hand, extending one select finger. As Rio leaned over as if to bite off the digit, I tapped its tip to her forehead. "If I'd left it for voice mail, we wouldn't be flush by thousands more of Viktor Blake's dollars."

"Whoa." She reared back and slammed her hands on the rims of the noodle pots. "The call was from him? Hottie Russki Viktor?"

"I believe I just said that?"

"But needed to about five minutes ago," she snapped.

"Huh?" I didn't hide my genuine confusion.

She explained while walking the pots into the cooler. "You know they're notorious rivals, yes?"

"Professionally. Which stands to make sense because they're in the same business. But we're in an ambitious field too. If we got pissy every time some healthy competition came along and—"

Her high chirp of a laugh cut me short. "Dearest, there's nothing healthy about the way those two go after each other. If Shark and Blake could actually make 'cutthroat' a thing, you'd see blade sharpeners next to their desks. Probably the huge stone ones, like from the Middle Ages."

I shook my head and groaned. "Can we talk about things that don't involve them wanting to behead each other?"

"Won't eliminate the fact that they *do*."

"But why?" I held up a hand, conciliatory despite the big yellow oven mitt I'd just donned. "Go with me here, okay? From where I'm standing, Viktor and Sebastian have achieved damn near the same level of corporate god status. True, Shark Enterprises has more employees here in LA, but that's because Blake split his HQ teams between here, Singapore, and St. Petersburg. While Sebastian is commended for keeping the majority of his core workforce in America, Viktor has been praised for strengthening foreign relations through commerce. They both feature fine art and high-end brands in their offices. They both wear bespoke suits—"

"Someone's been doing her homework," she said, rolling her eyes. "And you could be rattling down this list for the next hour. Point made, girl. The crowd gets it."

"No." I launched into an adamant head shake. "I don't think we do get it." I turned and pulled the finished avocadoes out of the oven. "What's really going on between those two?"

"It's a mystery to most of us, Abs." Rio returned to shucking her stack of carrots. "But it's real, as you saw with your own eyes—and paid for with a crying clit—last night."

I'd picked the wrong moment to slug down some water. After choking on the stuff for the better part of a minute, I finally croaked, "Want to warn a sister before doing that again?"

"What?"

She blinked big Bambi eyes. My giggles replaced the chokes.

"Crying clits usually aren't the best side dish for a plate of unanswered questions."

"A plate? Girl, you're working on a whole damn platter by now."

"Agreed." My laughter faded. "Especially after getting tossed out of the manor like I'd crossed some sacred line of the emperor's."

"He tossed you out? Seriously?"

"Not literally. And it wasn't like I was little Olivia Twist and he threw me into the snow with a starving belly."

"Fine." She stuck out a rebellious pout. "But I'll bet he brought the ice all the same."

"Damn it." This time, she'd struck the nail so perfectly on the head, all I could do was hand over the point. "I hate it when you're right." I smacked my flat hand on the stainless worktop.

Rio rushed over, yanking me into a fierce hug. "Ohhh, Abs. Sometimes I hate it too."

"No you don't." I hugged back, and we snickered together.

"I'd gloat, but unlike your favorite customer of the day, I'm not about kicking people when they're most vulnerable."

"I'm not vulnerable. I'm pissed."

"There's a difference?"

"Right now there is."

"Which would normally earn you my full vote of support. But since ripping up the contract with his company is off the table—"

"Wait."

Her whiskey golds nearly became fireworks. "You mean you *will* rip up the contract?"

"I mean that there's another way. At least I hope so."

"Well, you've already used the ice-out option."

"More than aware of that." I folded my arms with determination. "No ice this time."

She perked her head back up. Her gaze was twice as brilliant. "Blowtorches instead?"

"Right idea." I half laughed it. "But wrong execution."

"My inner pyromaniac is open to options."

"Tell me you're kidding."

"Why don't I tell you 'no comment'?" She averted my stare by inspecting her cuticles.

For the sake of my sanity, I decided she was just going thick on the sarcasm. "Maybe turning up the heat *is* the ideal answer here."

She amped the mischief in her grin. "Go on."

I rocked my head back on my shoulders before doing the same with my weight distribution, appearing like a satisfied designer watching my creation head down the runway. "It's really quite simple. I'm going to kill him with kindness."

★ ★ ★

The extreme kindness Olympic trials would be calling any second. I just knew it.

If only my plan hadn't hit one semi-crucial glitch.

When I arrived at the Shark Enterprises penthouse, the man's office was dark.

I stood in the middle of the luxurious space, all but scratching my head about the dilemma. But that would've meant moving, and somehow, I thought I might alter this reality by simply holding still long enough.

Someone softly cleared their throat near the door.

I spun around, plastering on a smile. "Oh, hi there. It's Terryn, right?"

The young woman with the mouse-colored hair and the darting gaze wasn't much of a talker—which had probably played in her favor in keeping her position with Sebastian. Still, she stated in a concise voice, "May I help you, miss?"

"Is, uhhh, Mr. Shark in today? I mean, we received the order for his lunch last night, but—"

"Of course he's in today." Her reply was a whip of sound. *Sheez*. The little mouse that could—and did. "He's just not in right now."

Screw the whip. The woman's emphasis was a whole flogger, flailing across my brain. I backed up by a few steps.

*He's not in right now.*

But that wasn't what she'd said. Not really.

*He's not in for* you, *Abbigail Gibson.*

"Uh. Okay." I didn't understand how I maintained my polite smile. Whatever the source of my strength, I was grateful for it. The last thing I needed was to expose my disappointment to Terryn, who'd clearly appointed herself as Sebastian's secret spy. "I guess . . . I'll just drop his food here?"

"That's fine," she responded, continuing to tap at her smart pad. Recording the four breaths I'd just taken, probably.

I loaded his tray up with a sandwich, drink, and dessert, but instead of setting it down, I handed it to the woman who looked ready to cut up the man's food and then serve it to him while on her knees. If he insisted on going the adolescent route today, I could roll with that. I'd just be back tomorrow— probably after a long hard talk with myself tonight regarding this plan of mine.

*Time is my ammunition, Mr. Shark.*

★ ★ ★

I showed up the next day with a new lunch ready to roll—

To find out he still was still expertly playing his hand.

Oh, yes. "Project Avoid Abbigail" was still in full swing that afternoon.

And the next.

And the *next*.

And even after the weekend, which had brought a botched supplies order, a broken coil in the walk-in cooler, and a panicked what-do-I-wear-to-an-internship-interview call from one of the Intrepids—all leading to my Monday morning attitude of truly not caring if the bastard decided to avoid me for the rest of freaking time.

Or so I told myself.

Had even almost convinced myself, through most of Tuesday.

But when Wednesday came, I had to confront the disgusting inevitable.

I *did* care.

Which was beyond ludicrous and well past stupid—a perfect description for the behavior he'd descended to, not me. Behavior for which there'd never be an apology.

On top of all that, I gave up hope that the man—if I ever saw him again—would confess he'd actually liked the evening we'd been enjoying before my phone call. There'd be no real resolution of what had really killed his mood that night. I'd never know if it was truly Viktor's interruption or if the call had saved him from having to be polite about my awkwardness and clumsiness.

But I was over playing the guessing game about it.

Just like I was over trying to wear him down with kindness.

Right now, I just wanted to be over him, period.

But to make that happen, I had to face a new truth. Closure with him meant involving him—if only for one last time. And this time, I meant it. No more duck-and-hide between us. It was time to hit the reset button . . .

During a surprise ambush.

*Snap.*

I'd just arrive at his office thirty minutes before my normal time. It was so easy, it was scary. The fact was confirmed by Rio's fast support of the plan. She came into work early so we'd have everything ready and loaded to go. And yes, she did it without a single line of snark. In every molecule of the kitchen's air where that droll sarcasm would have gone, she'd instead inserted humming.

*Humming.*

And not her typical alt-rock favorites either.

The category of the day: peppy eighties tracks.

I almost started recording the occasion for posterity but figured nothing would beat the woman's rendition of "Eye of the Tiger" as we loaded the final batch of sandwiches into the van. Accompanied by her warbled cheer for me to rise up and stalk my prey, I headed out onto the delivery route...

Hoping that was just as easily done as sung.

★ ★ ★

Traffic was astoundingly light as I approached downtown, which meant I'd be super early to my first stop on the route: the Blake Logistics building. As I rode the elevator to the penthouse, an eerie anticipation accompanied me. The tweaked schedule meant I'd be walking in on Viktor unawares. I was both scared and intrigued by that.

Okay, so I didn't expect to catch the guy cruising YouTube in his underwear and munching on pork rinds, but what was Viktor Blake like in his natural habitat? What did he do and how did he act when he didn't know I was already in the building?

As I parked the cart in the penthouse lobby, next to the ornate gold door that led to Blake's office, a woman emerged from inside. She was dressed stylishly, as everyone in the company usually was, but her posture was hunched, with one hand cupped over a lot of her face.

A face that was streaked with makeup.

I saw enough to figure that part out—or maybe it was just my instincts kicking in. Tears were my psychological specialty.

While I wished that wasn't the case, all those intuitions surged into high gear now, telling me the woman hadn't just been letting off some mild emotional steam.

As soon as she dropped her hand, my hunch was emphatically validated. In the vivid colors of the mark consuming her left cheek.

The reds, fuchsias, and purples of a fresh, hard slap.

It was impossible to restrain my gasp. And my concerned reach, landing at the ball of her shoulder. "Hey. Are you—"

But it was all I got out before she sob-hissed at me. Then wrenched, spun, and fled, bolting for the stairs instead of waiting for the elevator.

"What the..."

"Abbigail?" Viktor's hail, which sounded like he'd just been relaxing in the park with a mimosa and a puppy, heaped more confusion on my psyche. "Well, look at this. It *is* you. What a day-brightening surprise."

"Uh...Mr. Blake..."

"How many more times do I have to remind you? It's Viktor, remember?"

"Fine. Viktor." I jabbed my voice with the same rough edges as his. None of this was feeling right, and I wished more than ever for his typical formal facade. "Th-That woman... she was..."

"Lost," he said, motioning me to come into his office as if he had a spare mimosa for me. "She tripped in her office and hit the corner of a filing cabinet on her way down. She got mixed up in the elevator about what floor the First Aid station is on. She'll be *fine*."

I rolled my shoulders, focusing on settling my nerves. The explanation made sense—or so I tried telling myself. Instead, my memory flashed to the dickhead dad from the West Hills soccer game—and yes, I'd know that even from across the grass. The same way I'd watched in awe as Sebastian put the pig back into place—and how easily I could imagine those same words growling out of Viktor after his wife or kid *accidentally* hurt themselves running into a door.

*She'll be fine.*

But what was he going to do about the bile my stomach had begun to churn?

All the mental hand-wringing wasn't helping a damn thing. It was time to hike up my big-girl panties, plaster a smile on my face, and grab the lunch that had been ordered for Viktor today. I wasn't surprised to see a veggie loaf and a green salad through the clear plastic lid.

"All right, well . . . lunch is served."

The man's warm smile was a reassuring sight. There was no way for a guy to be that sincere and friendly if he'd just physically injured someone, right? That crap took strain and adrenaline. But as Viktor stepped back so I could walk in, it appeared like he'd really had a few swigs of his imaginary cocktail. But he looked that way every day. Nearly as tall as Sebastian, he was more graceful about handling his massive muscles. He was relaxed in his skin and surroundings, whereas Sebastian always jolted and sprinted as if all of it was too small for him.

At the moment, I was feeling more of the latter, as well.

Viktor's office was expansive and airy, composed of a lot of glass, steel, and white surfaces. Didn't stop the space from feeling weirdly confining.

Especially as Viktor shut the door behind him with a loud *clack*.

"Umm." I worked my lips together after muttering it. "Where do you want me to set everything down? The desk or the table?"

"Anywhere is fine."

Viktor's murmur was as polished as the curved front of his designer desk. While delivering to the desk trapped me behind the massive furniture for a few seconds, it also gave me a viable exit route. Fortunately, the penthouse office had a side door too.

"Rio added extra sauce to the veggie loaves today, so they should be really good."

"They're wonderful every day." His voice was still all brushed steel and shiny glass, an ideal match for how he practically glided back into the middle of the room. But while his movements were full of dancer grace, everything north of his shoulders was locked in weight-lifter intensity. Even the smile I'd first considered charming when I met him now favored dry plaster. "But the best thing about them is the service that accompanies them."

I scooted out from behind the desk, nervously fingering the apron ties at my nape. "Well, we're happy that you're happy."

"Very happy." He moved into the space between the desk and his chair, and I inwardly high-fived myself for escaping when I had the chance. "Except for one thing."

"Oh?" I shoved aside the weird paranoia about my safety, returning to gut-deep paranoia about my business. "Is there a problem with something?"

Viktor leaned down and opened a drawer. My heart throbbed to the point of pain. I barely subdued the lump that rose in my throat as panic slammed my senses.

Was this it? The other shoe that would drop, validating Sebastian's food-poisoning claim? Did Sebastian know about this already? Was that the motivation behind his avoiding me, instead of the bratty act I'd been assuming?

And how I knew every danger about assumptions.

"Well...yes," Viktor finally said. "There is a problem, Abbigail." He hitched up one side of his mouth while I visibly squirmed—which piled on more layers of weirdness to this exchange. Were Blake's urbane exterior and golden-god looks just a front for a vile masochistic streak?

"You know I'm always open to feedback." I stunned myself by sounding like I'd rehearsed that a thousand times, when this script was as cold as an ice block to me. A faint clicking sound vibrated the air, and I wondered if it was passing high heels in the hall or my knocking knees.

"I'm glad to hear that. Because I'm supremely uncomfortable about something."

*Deep breath in.*

*Deep breath out.*

"I'm all ears."

"It's occurred to me that you filled a full lunch order for fifty last week with less than twenty-four-hours' notice."

"It was our pleasure to do so." An attempt at a smile. Major fail at execution.

"And my comrades thoroughly enjoyed the meal." He leaned over toward the open drawer. "But there was something missing."

"Oh. I'm so sorry." Screw the smiles. I was furious. Why had he waited a full week to bring this up?

"The chance to properly thank you."

"Well, I'm sure if you just tell me what the—wait, *what*?"

Viktor's grin was full of pleasure as he extended both arms. In his hands was an intricately painted oval. I dropped my sights to the beautiful object, absorbing all its details. The face with the big eyes, wrapped in a painted red head scarf. The painstaking detail in the pink and purple roses and the cheerful yellow daisies along the base.

"Oh . . . wow," I finally stammered and then shot my gawk back up to his face. "Nesting dolls. Right?"

"In Russia, they're called *Matryoshka*," Viktor explained. "This set was handmade in the Khotkovo region, where my family is originally from."

"But not you?" I asked, tentatively running my index finger over the delicate brushwork on the doll, still resting in his outstretched palms.

"No." He laughed softly. "I was born and raised in Ohio. The Buckeye State."

I joined him in the chuckle, though mine died out as he slipped the doll into my grasp. "Viktor. I— I can't accept something so—"

"You can and you will," he insisted. "It's special. Like you, Abbigail." He closed the drawer and then hitched his thigh up on the desk, sitting lower to bring our faces level. "The big green eyes remind me of yours. But they symbolize much more."

I would've dropped the thing back onto the desk but was more agitated than before about getting even closer to him. "I know that they represent family, home, and connection. That's why you should maybe think of giving them to—"

"I see the dolls as a metaphor for other things."

As he issued the interruption, he stood again. Then— *damn it*—edged closer to me, to where he could lift the top off the biggest doll as I held it in my unsteady hands.

"Layers," he murmured, securing my gaze as he did. Viktor's eyes were the color of myrtle cacti, complete with the turquoise streaks and the ruthless needles. "Layers," he repeated, pulling off the next shell. "And how we all hide our most precious selves beneath them."

"Inside rose-colored dolls?" I prayed he'd catch my sardonic hint and back away from the intensity.

"Or behind rose-colored glasses, maybe." So subtle hints were not the guy's forte. "Or under layers of humor. Or even buried in meaningless numbers that stand for meaningless things, splashed across meaningless screens on our desks."

He waved to the monitor gracing the other corner of his workspace, but even that and his modest smile didn't convince me he'd issued the statement in self-deprecation.

Somehow, in some way, he was saying he knew.

*He knew.*

About how powerfully I was drawn to Sebastian Shark. About the man's attraction to me in return.

But it wasn't just that he knew the truth.

He was hell-bent on thwarting it. Changing it.

"Thank you, Viktor. It's a lovely gift." I'd take the damn dolls. Not because I wanted to. But at this point, that was the best option for getting out of there the fastest. "It was unnecessary but sweet."

"Abbigail." He quietly commanded it while wrapping his grip around the back of my elbow.

Flinching involuntarily, I tried to cover my response with a forced smile. "I really have to be going now."

"Why? You're here early. Far ahead of schedule."

"On purpose," I clarified, subtly moving out of his hold.

"Because of pressure from Shark?" His prickly blues

narrowed to accusing slits. "Has he threatened you?"

Miraculously, I held back a laugh. *This* from the guy who'd shrugged off a weeping woman fifteen minutes earlier.

I narrowed my eyes at the comment but quickly offered, "One of my brothers is in town, visiting from back east. We have plans." A large part of me wished I'd told him my schedule wasn't his business. Instead, I jerked up my chin and said, "Mr. Shark has nothing to do with it."

Damn good thing we weren't playing *Three Truths and a Lie*.

"That's good." Viktor studied my face. "Because, for the record . . . I'd like the chance to know what's under your layers, Abbigail." He stepped back but continued watching me in earnest. "And to let you see a few of mine, too."

I was saved by my watch's buzz. It was just a last-minute order change from Rio, but he didn't have to know that. "Umm, I really need to go."

"Will you . . . at least think about it?" His steely blue eyes studied me.

I was out the door before he finished the question.

And wishing I could be like the last woman who'd left and opted for the stairs.

Fortunately, the elevator was already open. While riding it down to the next floor, I hurriedly tucked the dolls into an empty cup holder on the top of my cart—fighting not to think about all the expectations that had been offered along with them.

*What a day-brightening surprise . . .*

*They're special, like you . . .*

*I'd like the chance to know what's under your layers, Abbigail . . .*

Thank God a lot of the Blake employees were out getting ready for the company's summer beach party today. I finished delivering to the building in under an hour and was never happier to hear the melodic ding that signaled my return to street level. I shoved my empty cart up into the van, fired up the engine, and pushed the speed limit to get away from the place as fast as I possibly could.

My record delivery time at Blake Logistics was a welcome dovetail into the day's bigger plan. I was fifteen minutes ahead of my planned schedule—meaning a good forty minutes earlier than my normal delivery time—when I pulled the van up to the usual cutout in the curb on Hope Street.

"Sandwich goddess." Maddon strolled up as I loaded the preorder bins into the delivery cart. He wore his normal grin along with a curious stare. "This is a surprise."

"Hey there, Mads." My reply was breathless but friendly. "Not really a surprise, buddy. Just the usual, though a few minutes early."

"Uh, yeah. *Early*." For the first time since I'd known the kid, he appeared jittery. He averted his gaze while shifting his weight, conveying nervous energy that hadn't even been there during the media circus after the Tawny Mansfield incident. "Did, uhhh, Mr. Shark ask you to switch up the schedule?"

"Nah. Just running ahead today and thought I'd—"

"So his office doesn't know you're here? Like, right *now*? You didn't call his assistant to tell her—"

"Maddon." I hopped down to the pavement and then punched the button for the lift to lower the packed cart. "You seriously think Terryn wants to be bothered with this?"

"Yeah," he cut in, showing authority for the first time. Ever. "I do."

Regrettably, I believed his paranoia—mostly because he mentioned Terryn. The woman probably had nightmares in which she'd neglected to tell the cleaners that Shark wanted heavy starch in his shirts, not medium. But I also knew that if Terryn was put on alert that I'd arrived, she'd find some way to alert Sebastian.

Not. Happening.

"Come on, Mads." I laughed it out this time. "I'm delivering lunch, not state secrets."

And if I just happened to have a chunk of indignation to get off my chest, along with two dozen questions for which I was really entitled to some answers . . .

Terryn had to stay out of this picture.

Time to break out the heavy artillery.

"But rather than calling upstairs, do you have time to sample a new menu item and tell me what you think? I could really use an outside opinion." It was all I could do not to singsong the temptation, especially when the young guy jogged up a brow. "Nutella and caramel cheesecake . . . with vanilla wafer crust."

The guy groaned at once. "Damn. I love Nutella."

"Perfect, then! I had no idea." *Too easy.*

Okay, fine. Maybe scrolling the guy's Instagram feed counted as having an idea. But I wanted to cover every possible roadblock. I'd attempted the same to learn Terryn's sweet tooth weak spot, but aside from a bland LinkedIn account, the woman had zero social media presence. Which, in a modern world for a twenty-something young woman, was creepier than Viktor Blake and his nesting dolls.

It was go time. Time to get in front of Sebastian and settle this . . . this . . . what? Situation? Problem? I didn't even know what to call it.

The one thing I did know was this time when that particular Shark smelled blood in the water . . . it would be his own.

# CHAPTER TEN

## SEBASTIAN

Secrets were hiding in the intricate crosshatch pattern of streets that wove between downtown buildings in Los Angeles. Old and new tales waiting to be told, if you just stopped long enough and listened.

Dawn broke just after five thirty that morning, and the sun rose fully twenty minutes later. By then, the whispers stopped, and anyone interested in hearing the riddles would have to wait until tomorrow for another chance to get in on the magic.

It was my favorite part of the day, and it was well worth getting up early to experience it. My driver had learned years ago to fuel up the car the night before, and he did the same for himself, stocking his cup holder with a venti Americano for the journey.

I watched the streets below my building yawn and stretch and come to life with the first commuters arriving to work.

What did my day have in store for me?

I'd finally gotten a good night's sleep—the first since the shit-show dinner with Abbigail Gibson. I'd vowed not to waste another minute analyzing the subject of her. In any form at all.

My initial consideration that she was too young for me to be involved with was validated that evening after she left my home. I was better off putting the whole Ms. Gibson experience in a tidy storage box marked Goodwill.

I'd set it out by the curb next to the other unused charitable efforts.

It was time to refocus my valuable time and energy on what mattered most. The Edge. It was everything to me. Everything. And as I looked down at the streets below, watching humans move about, the familiar excitement returned.

In less than two years, thousands of people would flock to my building, my dream—my legacy—to spend their day working, shopping, and playing. Sebastian Shark and the Edge would become household names. Synonymous with Gucci and Rolls Royce.

The best part would be the secret behind the success. The story the streets of Los Angeles knew but others didn't. Because they never stopped long enough to listen or cared enough to ask.

When I watched the city below, in the quiet hours, I knew there were others like me. I knew the streets whispered hardship and pain. And I knew those who overcame the adversity life had dealt them would rise above the storm and find success.

The Edge would be more than just another icon in the city's skyline. When my story was finally heard, it would resonate with underdogs everywhere. Boys in the projects would relate to my childhood, and young entrepreneurs would connect to my business acumen. My persona would speak to everyone on their own personal journeys for success, and the Edge would be the physical symbol that represented it all.

It gave me a hard-on just thinking about it, and if I had a willing body to fuck, I would. I needed to blow off the excess energy surging through my system. I was on a career and life high, and I needed an outlet for it all.

"Siri, compose an email to LuLu Chancellor."

Siri's voice filled my office. "What would you like to say?"

"Good morning—comma—my friend—comma, new line—Would you happen to have a redheaded pony in the stable currently—question mark—I really could use a lap or two around the track today—period—Please let me know as soon as possible—period, new line—Kind regards—comma, new line—Sebastian."

Siri then asked, "Would you like me to read your message back to you?"

"No, that won't be necessary. Just send the message to Ms. Chancellor, please."

"Your wish is my command, Mr. Shark."

That was why I preferred Siri to my living, breathing office assistant. She was much more agreeable, for one thing. And setting up appointments with LuLu via Terryn gave Terryn more information than she needed to have. There were certain parts of my private life I preferred to keep . . . private.

As the office came to life with people, I shrank into my usual solitude.

I never interacted with others.

Even less so since the experience with Abbigail.

I'd found an excuse every day to be out of the office before she arrived with the lunch deliveries and returned after she was sure to be gone. Even if that meant circling the block three or seven times until her delivery van had cleared from the curb out front. But no one would know that beyond my driver. And, like everyone else on my payroll, he'd signed an ironclad NDA, so one word about my comings and goings to anyone and he'd lose his very well-paying job.

Grant stopped in for the morning report, as he liked to call it. I got the reference from watching *The Lion King* with Vela a few hundred times when she went through her Disney phase. Thankfully, that didn't last long. The girl was on to the next thing before the old thing ever had a chance to grow roots.

Pia assured me it was typical childhood behavior when I worried that nothing held her interest. Frankly, I worried about everything where Vela was concerned. I was like an overbearing second-string helicopter parent my sister didn't ask for or need. But despite my best efforts to rein it in, I couldn't help myself. I merely wanted the absolute best for my niece. It wasn't like her father was around to make the same claim.

"What do we have on the agenda today, boss man?" my COO asked, strolling through my office.

"I seriously despise that nickname," I grumbled from behind the monitors on my desk.

"I know you do, man. I know you do," he said with a smirk. "Do you want some coffee?" He stopped in front of the Keurig, picking through the pods for the one he liked best.

"No, I'm amped up enough. I finally slept well last night, but I know it won't last. I need to burn off some steam." I held up my hand to stop him before he even suggested what I knew would come next. "I emailed LuLu this morning. Do you want to come?"

"Yeah, see if Shawna's available, if you don't mind." A wide smile split his face. "I had an exceptional time with her last visit."

"Actually, I think I'll have them come out to the house. Are you good with that? I'm not a fan of going to LuLu's place anymore. She's going to get raided soon. I can feel it in my bones. Too many people know about her now."

Grant stood silently while his coffee brewed and then replied, "Good call, Bas. I bet you're right. You usually have a good sixth sense on this sort of thing." He stirred cream into his coffee and sat down on the leather sofa closest to my desk. "So, what happened to the sandwich girl? She turn you down?"

"Other way around." I forced a laugh. "When's the last time you saw me get rejected? By anyone?" I shook my head at the ridiculousness of the notion.

He nodded thoughtfully. "You've got a point. Still, I thought you were into her. The way you looked at her." Then he shrugged. "I don't know, something seemed different."

"Well, you thought wrong. Plus, she's involved with Blake somehow. I don't know the extent of it, but he called her the other night when we were having dinner, and she all but came in her panties while talking to him. Total deal killer." Fury burned in my gut just thinking about it, but I kept my face expressionless.

"Oh, so there's the real story."

"What are you talking about?"

"Why you're rejecting her. Or whatever." Grant waved his hand dismissively.

"Well, yeah. I don't play seconds to anyone. Especially not Viktor fucking Blake."

Grant knew the history between Viktor and me. Every sordid detail of it, from childhood on. Of all people, I would expect he would understand why I wouldn't want to associate with Abbigail after discovering she was with Blake. Regardless of the extent of their relationship.

"Dude." He waited for me to meet his stare before he continued. "Don't you think you might be overreacting? For all you know, she could be his lunch lady just like she is yours."

"So what?" Finally, my veneer was beginning to crack, and a bit of ire seeped out.

"So that's enough to cast her out?"

"Yes."

"Bas."

"Grant. There. We both know each other's name."

"Be serious. You like that girl. Why are you acting like this?"

"Like what?" I finally gave up on what I had been working on and stood up behind my desk. Grant wasn't going to let this go, apparently.

"Like an eight-year-old! No, wait, Vela acts more mature than you. Like a five-year-old. Pull your head out of your ass."

"I'm not acting like a child." I came around my desk and leaned against the edge, stretching my legs out in front of me. I remembered taking a similar pose when Ms. Gibson was in my office the week before.

"Are you sure?" Grant challenged.

"Did you come in here to talk about the day's schedule or my social life?"

"At this rate, you're never going to have a social life. And paying call girls doesn't count as a social life. How nice would it be to fuck a woman and not have to pay her beforehand?" He raised his brow in question while sipping his coffee. I had a dark fantasy of him burning his lips and tongue on the brew.

*At least then he'd shut up.*

I just stared at him. What was I supposed to say to that? I mean, really? I didn't relish the fact that this was what my social life consisted of right now. I didn't expect this was where it would stay forever, though, either. It was a moment in time.

A necessary phase—like Vela and the Disney movies—a place I was but wouldn't grow roots before I moved on to the next phase.

There would come a time when I would find a woman to settle down with. Share my life with.

*Maybe.*

I just hadn't been there yet.

*So fine, it wasn't a phase, it was a rut.*

*Or a lifestyle.*

I scrubbed my hands down my face and then back up again. I hated when he called me on my shit—especially when he was right.

"You just had about nine points of self-discovery, didn't you?" He laughed his trademarked throaty snicker.

"Shut the fuck up, Twombley. I don't know why I let you in that door half the time. I don't need this right now. You know that as well as I do. Seriously, man. You're supposed to be my friend. I mean, you are, aren't you?" I looked at him in utter bewilderment. He was the only person outside of Pia I showed weakness in front of. Definitely the only man.

"You're my best friend, Bas. That's why I don't want to see you screw this up." Sincerity filled his voice, his words reaching straight into my chest and putting my heart into a full nelson.

We were both quiet for close to a minute. Grant finally spoke first—he always did. He was more uncomfortable with silence than Vela, for Christ's sake.

When he finally spoke, his voice was rough with emotion. "It was the way you were looking at her. Watching her. I don't think I've ever seen that look on your face before, and I've known you your whole life, man. At least the part that matters, anyway. There's something different about that girl."

Full nelson to a single leg takedown. The emotions referee smacked the mat. One. Two. Three. It was an easy pin, and Grant may as well have raised his arm in victory.

"She's so young, dude," I finally offered in defeat. "I've got a dozen years on her." I tried to come up with any sort of reason I should stay away from Abbigail Gibson.

He grinned widely, knowing he'd just taken a cool W. I'd made it too simple. "So what? I mean, she's legal, right?" At least he spared my dignity and played along like we were still trying to argue about it.

"Yeah." I hung my head, feigning shame. If I were honest with myself, it stoked the fire hotter. "But barely," I said, exhausted but slightly lightened by the thought of pursuing her again.

"That might even be fun."

"You're such a dog." I knocked him in the side of the head, messing up his perfect hair before it flopped right back into its perfect place.

"I'm just saying what you've already thought." He shrugged, still grinning like the scoundrel I knew he was.

"With my luck, she'll tell me she's a virgin or some shit. Jesus Christ."

"Oh my God. Don't even joke about that shit," Grant said, sobering.

"I know, right?" With a deep, cleansing breath to banish the horrifying thought, I went back to sit at my desk. "Let's get to work. Freight doesn't move itself."

"True story. Do you ever just take a minute to appreciate how far we've come?" My best friend was still in the mood for the touchy-feely stuff, apparently.

"Every single day, Grant. There will never be a day I take it for granted. I know what everyone thinks of me. I know people think I'm a giant asshole, that I sit up here in the penthouse suite, acting like the king of all things. But I will never—not for one single day—forget how much blood, sweat, and tears it took to get here. Whether it was mine or someone else's is beside the point. Fluids were spilled. And someone paid in pain. Sometimes it was me, sometimes it was another. But every day, I remind myself of that."

"That's why no one will ever get the upper hand on you, man. As long as you want to stay on top of the logistics game, you will," Grant added thoughtfully.

"*We* will. You've been right beside me from the time we hustled to get jobs in the neighborhood in East LA, doing courier jobs on our bikes. Now we're moving full shiploads across oceans, Grant. We did this together. That's another thing I never lose sight of. You are my brother. My family. In all the ways that matter. You will always be taken care of like my family." I waited for him to meet my gaze; the touchy-feely sort of talk wasn't something we usually dealt with. "I hope you realize that," I finally added when our eyes locked.

"I do. Why are we getting all creepy this morning?"

I laughed. "I have no idea. This has gotten a bit heavy though, hasn't it? Don't think I'm going to hug you or any of that shit, though. So, what do you have today? Aren't you meeting with the city?"

"Yes, finally. After two canceled appointments, I'm finally meeting our appointed Development Services Case Manager from the city's Department of Building and Safety."

"Damn. Are you kidding? I really thought that happened weeks ago."

"Nope. I guess the guy had kidney stones or something,

but he swears he's the picture of health now and we have his undivided attention. The beauty of being accepted into this program is that they hold your hand and walk you through the phases that can get really tricky with the city, like permitting, entitlements, public improvements—especially the parking situation, which we still haven't seen a viable solution from the architect, I might add—other public improvements the city will probably require, and utility design."

I held up my hand up in a full stop motion. "You're giving me a headache, man."

"I know, it's stressful. That's why getting in with this management program with the city is golden. They liaise with all the different bureaus on our behalf. They know who to go to with what questions and problems. They cut through the red tape for us."

I twisted my face. "What's in it for them?"

"The city wants you to build your building here, Bas. Not in Houston—or Boise, for that matter. People are leaving LA faster than they can pack their two point five kids in the minivan and get the hell out of Dodge. They want to keep your business and all the future business you will bring with you right here in the City of Angels. Makes perfect sense." He shrugged and rightfully so. It wasn't rocket science.

"Well, keep me in the loop. What time is your meeting?" I asked, looking at the octagonal bezel of the Audemars Piguet on my wrist. Expensive timepieces had always been one of my personal indulgences. The one I wore today was a favorite of mine, even if on the casual side of my collection.

"My meeting is at ten, so I need to get over to the conference room. Do you want to have lunch today? Oh wait, I forgot about LuLu's. Message me the time on that, will you? I'll keep my phone on silent, but I'll sneak a look when it vibrates. It'll give me something to look forward to so I can get through the snore-fest of a meeting."

"Will do, but you need to focus. Everything that goes on from this point forward is vital."

"Bas." He put his hand up to stop me from launching into a full lecture. "I know. I got this."

As the tall man opened the door to leave, I jogged my memory for the name of the girl he wanted me to ask for at the stable. "Who did you want me to ask for? Silvia? Shanna?" I scowled, knowing I was coming up short. It was frustrating that I couldn't remember something so simple as a name from twenty minutes before.

"Shawna," he called over his shoulder, grinning the way he had the first time he mentioned her name. Maybe I needed to ask for her instead. She certainly had left an impression on my buddy. While I was preoccupied with Grant, Terryn had walked up behind me and patiently waited for me to finish the conversation.

"Good morning, Mr. Shark. Have you had a chance to review your schedule for today?"

"Of course I have. Did you need something?" I answered without emotion in my tone or expression on my face.

"No, sir. I was just checking if I could help with anything before the day gets going," she said sprightly, as if she were trying to be upbeat enough for the both of us.

I just stared at her. What was she playing here? I shifted my eyes from one side of her oval face to the other. "Have you finished the container supplier spreadsheet I asked you to create three days ago?"

"Yes. It should be in your email. I sent it when I got in this morning. I also put a copy in the company's Dropbox files." She looked very pleased with herself as she gave her report.

I narrowed my eyes, trying to remember what else I had tasked her with yesterday afternoon.

"I need you to look at my schedule for the next two weeks and see where I can fit in a tour and thirty-minute meet-and-greet with a youth outreach group. Sometime after key business hours and school hours. You'll have to investigate the LAUSD middle and high school release times and estimate commute time to the office. I don't mind if I have to stay late to give the tour and presentation myself." I paused briefly, giving that point a bit more thought. "In fact, I want to do the tour myself."

Terryn wrote feverishly on a notepad she always had with her and then asked a follow-up, "Do you have a contact person for the group you'd like me to call to set this up?"

"No, I'll handle that. Just give me two date options I can present. You can send that information to me in an email as well. I don't want to be disturbed until I leave for lunch." I finished the decree as I went through my office doorway and closed the door swiftly behind me.

Of course, the moment I sat down at my desk, my plans changed. An email arrived from the legal department insisting documents needed my signature before they could be submitted to the planning commission. Two more messages back and forth, and I threw my pen across the suite so hard, it ricocheted off a chair at the conference table and into the floor-to-ceiling window on the opposite wall.

"Jesus Christ." I stood abruptly, my chair slinging into the low bookcase behind my desk, rattling the pictures and potted plant on the shelves. When I stormed past Terryn, I said, "I'm going down to legal."

My office door stood wide open, but my computer would go into sleep mode in thirty seconds without activity, and everything else that was sensitive inside those walls was under lock and key. The lights were motion activated as well to save on energy, so they would shut off on their own after about five minutes.

Thirty minutes later, I returned to my office, madder than a nest full of hornets. The papers that needed my signature weren't ready when I arrived, so I stood around wasting valuable time while the intern who initially emailed me fumbled around the office, trying to load a new toner cartridge in his printer so the documents could be printed. I finally took matters into my own hands and not only fixed the printer but sent the file to the printer from his work station, signed the documents, scanned them, and emailed them back to myself from his email account.

Talk about just doing things yourself if you wanted them done right the first time.

As I rounded the corner from the elevator, I noticed the light was on in my office. Maybe Grant was finished with his meeting and had returned to fill me in. Terryn knew better than to let anyone else in there without me present.

As she came rushing toward me looking like she knew her job hung by a fragile thread, I knew it wouldn't be Grant inside my personal sanctum.

I glared at her, and she clamped her mouth shut, taking a few steps back from the doorway.

When I cleared the arch, I saw Abbigail Gibson standing at the windows, looking out over the city like she had every right to be doing so. I quietly closed the door behind me, not alerting her to my presence until the knob clicked into the slot that kept it closed.

"What an unexpected surprise," I said nonchalantly, strolling over to my desk. I didn't couple the word *pleasant* with *surprise* in my comment because I could feel the offensive waves pulsing off her. Not defensive this time.

No, not this visit.

She was here to attack. Full artillery in place. And it would appear her sights were set directly on me.

Perfect.

Because this day wasn't enough of a shit show already.

"We need to talk, Mr. Shark," she said, not turning away from the window. Her voice was cool and calm, missing its usual oozing caramel seduction or emotion-filled rasp.

"Funny. I was thinking the same thing. Just this morning, in fact," I said low in my throat, volume barely in the range of normal conversation. A shift from my usual commanding mien.

She finally turned to look at me. "Really?" she asked with a hopeful look before catching herself and schooling her features.

"Yes. Because I believe I owe you an apology."

"Just one?" She folded her arms across her chest. Classic closed-off body language on display. "Or is it a blanket sort of thing? A cover-all for myriad transgressions?"

"I hadn't thought that far, I guess. How many transgressions are we talking here?" One side of my mouth kicked up in amusement. She was sexy as hell when she was trying to stay mad.

"Is this amusing? Or are you genuinely offering contrition right now?" She tilted her head to the side in a challenge as I came around the front of my desk and approached where she stood.

"I can't help smiling when you're near me, Ms. Gibson." I stepped closer to her. "Much in the same way I can't help touching you when you're near me." I reached for the hands she wrung together in front of her apron like I'd seen her do several times before.

"No." She dropped her hands to her sides so I couldn't take them in mine. "You don't get to do that right now. You really sent some crazy signals the other night at your palace. I can't repeat a spin cycle like that again. If that's your normal routine, I'm going to say no thank you. To all of it." She took a step back so I couldn't touch her.

"Nothing about this"—I motioned between the two of us—"has been my normal anything, so I'm flying blind here, Abbigail. Maybe admitting that to you will earn me some slack in the forgiveness zone?" I raised my eyebrows with the question.

I waited for her to say something, but she didn't. She just watched me, maybe trying to reorganize the attack strategy I'd upended. I could only guess since she wasn't giving me a clue.

"Say something," I finally bit out harsher than I intended, and she recoiled slightly at the tone.

"Listen, I appreciate the apology. I do. It's much more than I expected, actually. Thank you for that. But I would also appreciate some sort of explanation. One minute, your mouth was doing fantastic things to my body; the next minute, your front door was nearly spanking my ass. That was whiplash-worthy behavior if I'd ever seen it, Sebastian." She looked at me expectantly. The ball was back in my court.

I dropped my chin to my chest, kicking my own mental

ass for making her feel the way I had. It was shitty the way I acted, and now...hell. How would I explain what drove my ridiculous behavior without getting into the history behind it? Because I sure as hell wasn't about to do that.

"Let's sit down for a minute." I motioned toward the sofa grouping where she usually set up my lunch. "Can you spare the time?"

"Yes, that's why I came early today. I wanted to talk this out with you, and it hasn't escaped my notice you've been avoiding me for seven days. Nine if you include the weekend. But who's counting?"

I chuckled at that, hoping she'd join in as we both sat down. No such luck. We lowered to separate couches but faced each other.

"Contrary to whatever you've let yourself believe, I have a hectic schedule, none of which had anything to do with seeing or not seeing you." That was a lie. I had most certainly adjusted my schedule to avoid her. But I had to do what I had to do. Starry-eyed girls who hoped to find their Prince Charming didn't fit into my life. If she were going to stay a part of my world—still just a strictly hypothetical concept—she'd have to adjust her mind-set and fast.

"Okay." She swallowed hard, and the familiar surge of need pulsed in my dick.

*Jesus, girl. What is it about you?*

I watched her, fascinated. Entranced by the physical pull of her nearness. Until she broke the spell, short as it was, by continuing the inquisition.

"Why did a business phone call make you so upset? *You.* Of all people. I have to assume you do business at all hours of the day to have grown your business to this magnitude." She looked around the office as a visual reference to go along with her remark. "I mean, I'm not wrong, am I? It was the phone call?"

"It wasn't the call as much as it was the caller."

"Viktor Blake?" She looked confused at my tone.

"I hate that man."

"Yep. Picking up that vibe." She nodded swiftly. "Loud and clear."

"I hate that he called you. I hate that he called you at my home." My voice grew darker with the memory, so I tried to ease up. I really did, I swear. "I understand you are a business owner, and I understand he may very well be a client of yours."

"That's exactly right, Sebastian. He's a client. And that's all he is at the moment."

My face—and gut, for that matter—twisted at the last part of that comment, but I soldiered through it, not giving up my position in the conversation. I had an actual point to make, goddammit. We could circle back to the "at the moment" wording in a minute.

"I hate that he called you when I was three seconds from pushing my tongue inside your cunt."

"Seeh…baas…tiiaann." My name came out of her mouth in three lusty syllables. All with rushes of needy breath in between. Her hand fluttered up to the base of her throat as she said them.

My cock was a steel rod. It was begging for a way out of my suit pants, pulsing against the inside of my zipper. I had to adjust myself to find a more comfortable position to sit without causing some sort of blood-supply emergency.

"There. You wanted an explanation. There's your explanation. Happy? I'm a jealous son of a bitch on top of controlling, tyrannical, egotistical, dictatorial, and let's see, what else? I'm sure there's something else."

"Asshole?" she squeaked.

I gawked at her from where I sat.

"You think I'm an asshole?" I nearly whispered, actually feeling wounded.

"Not really. But a lot of people do," she quickly corrected.

"They can go fuck themselves." I shook my head dismissively. "I only care what you think. Whether I'm crazy for admitting that out loud is yet to be determined." I had to look away. I couldn't maintain eye contact while I waited to be gutted by her possible rejection.

"No. I like you. That's the problem. As foolish as it may be, I can't deny it. I like you, Sebastian."

I moved faster than she could track. One second, I was sitting where I had been the entire conversation, and the next I was crowding her against the back cushions of the sofa where she was sitting. My thigh pressed along hers, the heat of my body melting into the heat of hers. We could burn this damn building to the ground.

I toyed with the apron tie under her thick ponytail. I wanted nothing more than to undo the knot and tug the front down, pull her T-shirt up, and lick my way from her navel to her lips, imprinting myself there so she'd feel sinful even considering speaking Viktor Blake's name again.

"Whoa," she whispered, eyes enormous and watchful, so full of arousal.

"What? What is it, Little Red?"

"I'm . . . I'm not sure. The look on your face. You look like you could eat me alive right now."

I laughed deep in my throat. "Oh, baby"—I shook my

head—"if you only knew the things I want to do to you with my mouth." I leaned forward and kissed the tip of her nose and then pulled back.

She kept her eyes closed for a few seconds, and when she finally opened them again, she looked even more aroused than before.

"Sinful things, Little Red . . ." Like lightning, an idea struck me. "Hey, let's go away for the weekend. Get out of this town and away from the distractions."

"Whaaa?" she squawked.

"Away. Weekend. Follow along, Ms. Gibson. It's not that complicated," I teased, hopping up from the sofa. She followed, and we both stood in front of my desk.

"Okay, maybe you *are* an asshole." She was the one grinning then, so I knew the teasing tables had turned. This girl would give as good as she got.

"I'll take care of all the plans. You just clear your schedule. I'll have Terryn email you the details." It was as good as done. When I made up my mind, things happened.

"But I—" she protested, but I held up my hand, basically ending our talk.

"It's settled, then." I bulldozed right past any objections she was thinking up by taking her roughly in my arms and kissing her. When I released her, her cheeks were flushed, lips a bit swollen, and eyes dazed.

"But I—" she said again before I cut her off.

"Ms. Gibson, I have a ton of work ahead of me today. So, unless you want to have a preview of how we're going to spend the better part of the weekend, right here on the top of my desk? I suggest you hurry on your way."

I gave her a very wolfish grin while ushering her to the door.

"Check your email." I winked and all but pushed her out the door for the second time in our very short time of knowing each other. But this time, the promise of much better things danced in my imagination.

# CHAPTER ELEVEN

**ABBI**

It was officially the day that couldn't get any more bizarre—until it had.

Sebastian Shark had devastated me.

Had melted me with his contrition. Gutted me with his naughtiness. Rocked me with his growling protectiveness—before turning me to mush with his dominant passion.

He'd teased me about having his way with me on his desk, right then and there.

I'd almost called him on it. Okay, probably more than almost. I'd damn near begged him for it. How I'd wanted him, in every dirty, decadent way he was inferring.

Yet I'd let him usher me out his door, complete with my dazed senses and my needy sex. Somehow, I'd finished my deliveries through the rest of the building, but I barely remembered doing so. No wonder, since every inch of my bloodstream felt like neon rope lights and every breath in my lungs became an open temptation to scream.

Instead, I concentrated on the contacts list in my phone—more specifically, on one name.

Sebastian.

Just standing there, imagining my fingers typing a text to him, made my chest throb with twice the agony as before.

What the hell was I supposed to say, anyway? Sure, the truth was a good place to start—but actually doing it? Actually tapping out the words?

*Hey there. Before you start packing, I thought you might want to know that I snore sometimes. And oh yeah, I'm a virgin.*

Oh, dear God.

"Anyone in the mood for a train wreck?" I mumbled. Because today hadn't brought enough of those already. But as my thumb hovered over the Send key, my screen switched to signal an incoming text from *him*. And a smile broke out across my lips.

> *Hi there. Pesky neighborhood*
> *asshole here.*

My giggle was instant, bouncing off the walls of the mercifully empty elevator. I gulped it down, ignoring the hot blush and tremoring fingers that followed. For Christ's sake— all this from a text message. Somehow, I managed to tap out a reply.

> *Hello again. Neighborhood*
> *sandwich goddess, at your service.*

> *I've always dreamed of being*
> *serviced by a goddess.*

> *Flattery will get you everywhere.*

My new giggle was fed by substantial nerves. "Oh, my

God." This was such strange territory for me. Even in my early teens, long before my mom died, I rarely ventured out of the friend zone with boys. Having four brothers gave me a distinct advantage to understanding the male mind-set, but that didn't always bode well in the dating department.

Those same brothers had impossibly high standards for potential suitors, which meant my affections often went unrequited. Silver lining on that? I was never in a position like this. A slave to my phone screen—and the merciless charge of my damn libido.

I'd never been this scared to death, either.

Or so freaking exhilarated.

So full of wild, giddy life.

This was like that first ride on Space Mountain, when you pull back in to the platform and you don't know whether to laugh or throw up, but you know for damn sure you want to go around again.

My breath hitched as the little dots from Sebastian's side of the conversation started dancing again. And then stopped.

*Are you still in the building?*

I bit my bottom lip, once more debating my answer. And then . . . not.

> *I just finished lunch rounds.*
> *On the elevator down to the lobby.*

My delay in his office had only lasted fifteen minutes, but I'd taken advantage of the extra time to stroll through my deliveries as if floating through the clouds his kiss had taken me to.

*Well, send the thing back up.*

And the heaven he now beckoned me back to.

*I'm already ten minutes behind.*

*But you're still in my building.*

*Only the top thirty floors
are yours. So technically...*

No dancing dots this time.

I was pierced by disappointment and victory at once. Guess I was the winner of this round.

It was time to focus on the next downtown delivery. King Holdings was a smaller office with easier drops, and I looked forward to getting in and out of a building without navigating overbearing assistants, sobbing strangers, or men with agendas other than what they'd hired me for.

After the elevator doors closed, I pulled out my smart pad and started focusing—well, attempting to—on the orders I'd need to load up for the King building.

I got as far as scanning the first batch before looking back up, perplexed about why the elevator wasn't moving. I'd pressed the damn button, but the car hadn't moved an inch.

"What...the..."

"Ms. Gibson?"

I jumped a little and then whirled around. "Wh-Who is—"

"Apologies, ma'am." The voice was a professional baritone. For a second I wondered if God was using the elevator speakers to rebuke me for every filthy thing I'd imagined about Sebastian Shark over the last hour. But God didn't usually apologize and probably would have used my full name.

"Wh-What's going on?"

"Are you Abbigail Eileen Gibson?"

*Shit.*

"I swear, only a couple of the visions got really carnal. And I promise I'll go to confession on Sunday—oh, damn it—I mean darn it—I'm going to be out of town on Sunday. Can Monday be okay? Confession is open then too, right?"

"Please just answer the question," the voice cut in.

"R-Right..." I hauled in a deep breath. "Yes. I'm Abbigail Gibson. Is there a prob—"

A loud buzz erupted from the speakers, indicating my holy intervention had ended. Probably a good thing, since a new string of *shit-shit-shits* spilled out of me as the elevator moved at last.

Shooting straight up instead of down.

Holy crap.

What was going on?

My careening mind supplied a few ideas. Option A: Someone had keeled over after eating lunch, and the Abstract Catering box was already being blamed. And B: Sebastian Shark had a higher operations clearance in this building than God himself and had ordered that my elevator destination be overridden.

As the elevator doors opened again, I was definitely rooting for Option B.

Light flooded into the car, and as I shielded my eyes from the glare, a perfunctory voice yipped out at me.

"Ms. Gibson."

I jumped inwardly but plastered on a friendly smile. "Hi there, Terryn. Long time no see."

My sarcasm didn't amuse her. As she turned and began clacking her heels along the marble, she twirled a finger in the air. "Come along," she instructed. "Bring the cart if you need to. He wants you again."

"Oh . . . all right."

Better than all right.

I followed Terryn into Sebastian's innermost haven, and he shoved back from his position near the window, stealing my breath as he moved with alpha-wolf stealth. On his way over, he tossed aside a report he'd been reading. Though his stare never left me, the report swooped to a perfect stop in the middle of the conference table.

"Thank you, Terryn," he murmured. "That'll be all for now."

"Of course, Mr. Shark." Only now did I realize Terryn had been holding her breath too. "Oh! Your water pitcher is empty. Let me fetch you some more—"

"Later." The man still barely blinked, continuing to bathe me in the dark-blue tide pools of his gaze.

"But I'll only be a moment. It's no trouble at—"

"Later!"

Holy shit. The wolf was ready to bare his fangs any second. I warmed to the thought at once, despite how he flashed me a roguish wink. His action lowered the intimate bubble around us, even as he raised his voice to a boom that could have filled the Staples Center arena.

"And Terryn? Shut the door thoroughly. Hold all my calls. I'm not to be disturbed for the next half hour."

"Y-Yes, Mr. Shark."

My nerves were ready to concede an alliance with the woman's wobbly voice, but as soon as Terryn was gone, they were drenched by a wave of curious calm. I expected it to recede as soon as I stepped out from behind the cart, especially as Sebastian stalked over as if leading the wolf pack to take sample bites out of me. But as he dipped and did just that to my neck, I wrapped my hands around his head and bent back, exposing even more flesh for his questing lips and tongue.

Yes.

What this ferocious, demanding, force of nature did to me...

"My God, woman."

Especially when he growled things like that into my skin.

"What's this about, calling me back here?" I managed to ask, despite my shallow breaths and deepening desire. The crevice between my legs turned into pure heat, a torment from which he gave me no mercy, digging his teeth into the sensitive valley beneath my ear.

In answer, he turned the flat of his tongue into a searing sweep along the front of my neck. My long moan was his vibrating reward, but he didn't halt the sweet assault. Down he trailed, to the ridge of my collarbone. "So delicious," he murmured along that oh-so-sensitive ridge. "So perfect."

And clearly, the man was just getting started. Sebastian worked my lips apart with a spearing invasion and then circled his tongue with mine in hot, thorough domination while he claimed every moan I could spare, every mewl I could manage, every tremble I could muster. As he did so with the twisting, meshing, searing proof of his passion—a hunger I never knew any man was capable of possessing, much less expressing with this fire and fury and lust.

It was so good.

So *damn* good.

No. It was beyond that. I was dizzy. Floating. Then falling. Completely limp in his arms, confirmed by the brazen smile defining his beautiful mouth as soon as he pulled away and stared at me through half-lidded eyes.

"You are a feast fit for a king, Abbigail."

A new smile quirked my lips. "Whatever you say, Your Majesty."

"Hmmm…" He stood taller, finally loosening his hold—though not before making me yelp from his possessive smack to my backside. "Glad we're in agreement."

I freed a laugh as he slid one of his hands into mine. "Dear God, you're a piece of work."

"So I've been told." He tugged me across the room, toward his desk. "A piece of artwork, actually. I think the exact words were 'a masterpiece carved by the angels.'"

"Now that sounds like one I need to research more. For verification purposes, of course."

"Of course." He glanced over his shoulder, the arrogant smile still in place. "And while we're on the subject of fulfilling that goal…" He sank into the big executive chair, scooting it away from the dinged-up bookcase with practiced grace. In the same motion, he hauled me all the way down into his lap. "There are a few things you need to see here."

"And a few things I need to feel, as well?" The line popped out before I could help it, courtesy of something else that was popping up from between his thighs. It was a little unnerving, how perfectly his erection notched against my core.

"Oh, yeah…" While his comeback was smooth, his breathing wasn't. He expelled that ragged air against my lips before clutching my face and compelling me into another tongue-filled tangle. Holy shit, the man did this stuff really well. And the steamy *après*-kiss stare thing too.

At last, he broke our silence again. "Thank you," he murmured, cupping his hand to the back of my neck. His fingertips toyed with the ends of my apron ties.

"For what?" I was genuinely curious. Shouldn't that have been the other way around?

"For..." He stopped, seeming to catch himself. His eyebrows crunched inward. "Well, for letting me haul you all the way back up here."

I was damn near sure it wasn't his original pick of confessions, but the acknowledgment was nice. *Really* nice. "My pleasure. Though I didn't quite have a choice about it."

"Truth." His smirk was a perfect cocktail of sexy and smug. "But at least I got the chance to practice my manners a bit more."

"Ah, yes." I beamed a wider smile, enjoying how it made his crotch swell against my ass cheeks. "Well, you're doing beautifully, I might add."

"And you are a quick study in acquiescence."

My heart hammered harder. "That...uhhh...reminds me." I straightened as much as was possible, given our positions. "There's something we should prob—"

"Hold that thought." His firmness made it an order, but his enthusiasm made it a seduction. He turned his head, jiggling the mouse to wake up all three of his monitors. "For the record, I don't usually go paging the security office to recall elevators. There was a real method to my madness."

"Besides needing to kiss me until the room turned upside down?"

"Well...besides that," he volleyed, as if I'd just told him his suit looked nice.

With an equally confident nod, he directed my attention toward the screen in front of us.

For the three seconds before my astounded outcry.

"*Sebastian.*"

Each of the monitors was consumed by a different image of high-end luxury. One was a tropical canyon centered on a small palace, similar in architecture to the one he owned. The next looked like a mountain chalet, complete with a courtyard waterfall. The last was a seaside villa with a negative-edge pool overlooking a deserted beach.

"Was that a gasp of pleasure or horror?"

I flipped my gawk from the monitors back to his face—where the subtle worry in his eyes kept my attention glued. "You're kidding, right?"

His cocky smirk returned in its heart-halting resplendence. "Which one do you like best?" he asked softly. "They're all available this weekend, so I want you to have the final vote. If you want to see more pictures, I can pull those up too."

"I—I'm not sure..." I looked closer, noting the URL at the top of each search referred to something called *privateluxury. net* with a substring that said *sharkbite3000*. From there, I snapped the pieces together. He didn't want to sweep me away for the weekend. He wanted to sweep me *away* for the weekend.

"Hey." He rubbed my back reassuringly. "Don't stress about this, okay? These places have screened their staff for decorum and discretion."

"With three-page NDA forms?"

I made the joke evident in my tone, but Sebastian's nod was all business. "Likely. As well as additional training on top of that for things like security awareness and service standards."

"Of course. I mean, that's a given, right?"

A low chuckle from him now, appreciating my jest, before he started nibbling at my neck again. "I guarantee you, Abbigail, there will be a lot of things given on this trip."

Shockingly, I was able to form some actual words into a response. "That sounds like a really good agenda."

"Hmmm, yes." He hummed it into my ear. "So let me enlighten you about the options." He clicked first onto the mansion that looked like his place. "This one's the closest. Palm Springs. It's hotter than Satan's balls out there right now though, so clothes aren't a concern."

"At—at all?" I squeaked.

"At. All." He nipped at the curve of my jaw. "And hey, look at this. The master bed is on a rotating dais. We can get... creative... with positions."

Hard swallow. "P-Positions?"

"Oh, definitely. What's your favorite, baby?"

"I... uh... hadn't really thought about it." Not a lie. Not by a long shot.

"Well, there's your homework before we go. I want top three by the time we leave on Friday."

"Wh-What's the next one?" I used the question as an excuse to calm my throbbing sex. The wicked fantasies he'd started spinning—especially the totally naked part—had turned me into a glob of helpless arousal. I liked it. I hated it. Oh, God, I was a mess.

Even more so as he moved on to the Alpine Chalet.

"Ahhhh. The Tahoe place. Just an hour or so by jet," he

explained. "But once we're there"—he advanced through photos of a modern-themed place bordered by thick evergreens—"also completely private. Probably a good thing, because I'd want to bury myself inside you on that table ... and on that stairway ... and in front of that fireplace ... and—"

"And what's the last one?" A real rush now, since the thought of him screwing me on the deep rug in front of that fireplace was equivalent to jamming a hand down my pants and stroking myself.

"Playa del Carmen, in Cancun. A longer plane ride but worth it. Right along the water, with some very ... interesting ... architecture."

My breathing halted as he clicked through the images. Many contained pieces of heavy wooden furniture that were definitely not designed for simple relaxation. One big apparatus even had a curved leather swing device hanging from it, with cuffs strategically placed at the sides.

"Uhhh ... yes," I finally grated as my imagination took that kinky ball and sprinted with it. Right away, my mind's eye was consumed with the idea of being suspended in that thing, with Sebastian's naked form fitted between my legs. His fine, muscled buttocks would flex and release with every new thrust into me. He'd go harder and harder as his desire spiraled ... and mine along with it ... "Inter ... esting," I blurted. "Ah ... yes."

His satisfied chuckle was a dim sound against the roaring blood in my ears "That settles it. Playa del Carmen, here we come." He placed a quick but sensual kiss on my mouth. "Hopefully, in a bunch of different ways."

I dared to take the lead on initiating our new kiss. One, because I couldn't resist the allure of the man's smiling lips. Two, because I knew he didn't indulge in smiles very often.

Well, not this kind. An expression that was authentic and true instead of a show he put on for others.

It was that openness that I spoke to with the tender touch of my lips. It was what he returned to me in his silken caress along my nape and his velvety groan into my throat.

It was magical—nearly surreal.

I was moved.

And inspired.

Enough to take a deep breath and finally murmur, "Mexico sounds . . . really awesome."

His grin kicked higher. "Awesome is only the start, baby." And his growl dipped lower, vibrating through my chest as he loosened the knot behind my neck, dropped my apron, and delved his face into the V of my T-shirt. "And I'm going to start the trip by freeing these beautiful mounds as soon as we get on the plane." He nosed his way inside, just beneath the edge of my left bra cup. "Abbigail, you're a constant, vibrant revelation."

"R-Revelation?" I stammered. "I—I'm not sure I under—"

"Don't worry." The adoration in his voice was like a physical caress. "In all the best ways, I promise." He stretched his tongue, flicking my nipple . . . igniting every cell of my blood. "Christ. Look at you. Look at these tits, so erect and stunning. You make me feel like a virgin again. No, even better. Back to third grade again. These definitely put Miss Dandelion to shame."

"I'm . . . I'm glad they please you."

"I'm positive *all* of you is going to please me, Little Red."

"I can't wait to please you in a lot of ways, Mr. Shark."

"And I can't wait to fuck you in just as many ways, Ms. Gibson."

I gasped as he unclasped my bra with his teeth. But it was

an exclamation of mixed sensations—especially as I swallowed hard while tangling my hands into his thick hair. "Then you'll get to be *my* revelation."

He growled out a chuckle into my bare cleavage. "That so? Tell me about it, baby."

"Well..." I let go of his hair as he dragged his stare up. His bold features and thick stubble were mind-meltingly beautiful, even in the garish fluorescent lighting. *My prince.* The thought was reassuring. He was my prince, worthy of entrusting with my deepest secrets. "The... virgin part."

Between one breath and the next, all his warmth vanished.

Between the next two seconds, so did mine.

I broke out in an all-over shiver. Sebastian did nothing. Said nothing.

"Is that going to be... a problem?" I attempted to insert some humor by diving into my best BBC anchor accent and quipping, "You know, a few hundred years ago, a gentleman of your ilk would pay a hefty purse for my—"

Sebastian lurched to his feet, toppling me down from his lap to the corner of his desk before spinning away. "Well, I'm not a fucking gentleman," he spewed, balling his hands into fists against his nape while coming to a violent stop next to the coffee table. "Of any goddamned ilk."

"Fine." I pushed at his chair with a foot, adding a fresh set of nicks to the unit behind it. "Just to be clear, I'm not asking you to pay for it."

"To be equally clear, that's not exactly a deal-breaker for me."

"Wow," I spat past viciously stinging eyes. "Let's alert the press about that one. Oh, wait. Someone already did."

He jerked back around. Our glares directly clashed again.

"Well, that was swinging low."

I lurched off the desk, letting my arms spread wide. "It's not like you're unfamiliar with the equipment involved. Maybe if you just practice some patience while warming it up—"

With a burst of a roar, he shut down my rant.

With a couple of wide stomps, he was back in front of the desk.

And with a swoop of strength, he had me splayed on my back across the top of it.

Two of the three monitors crashed to the floor. His keyboard and pen cup followed.

"Oh!" I cried, but not in distress. In welcome. Yes, of all of it. His unbridled anger. His ruthless power. His fierce retaliation. His blatant frustration.

He pressed his full weight atop me, and the folds at my core ached to the point of torture.

Yesss.

"Obviously, you need me to be clearer about this, Little Red." He clutched my wrists in tighter increments. "I am a very patient man, Abbigail—especially when it comes to warming up the … 'equipment.'"

He used the heels of his hands to maintain the pressure of his hold while shifting his thumbs up until he was driving them into the center of my palms.

"But let's be clear. Once I get a woman warm, I don't stop until she's hot. Until she's wailing. And begging. And screaming for me to use her body." He lowered until our breaths tangled and our noses nearly touched. "Do you understand, Abbi? I tear women up. I break them apart."

"I … I understand. I … I w-want that."

A ferocious rumble broke from his chest. A visible change

in his gaze, the cobalt shadows hardening into a thousand shards of glass. The swollen rod fitted between my legs thickening into a hot hammer of lust.

And my answering breaths, doubling in their tempo of need as his lips parted. His stare sharpened.

Oh, God. I got it now. I really understood.

My helplessness turned him on. Worse, it turned *me* on.

"You don't want this, Abbigail. Not from me, you don't."

"Why?" I spewed. "Because you're that convinced you'll break me? Is that it? Or is that now a convenient way to skew this?"

He clenched his jaw and ripped his glare through more of my defenses. "You think it's my easy out?" He slowly shook his head. "*Christ.*"

I wanted to echo the word—with joyous thanks. It was the moment I'd prayed for but didn't think would come. His own vulnerability. And yes, it was only a tiny chink in his armor, but I'd take it. Would work the angle whatever way I could.

With gentle focus, I lifted my fingertips to his jaw. In a purposeful rasp, I pleaded, "*Sebastian.*"

But I barely got the whole word out before he whipped his head back and out of my reach. His whole body followed.

"Do you think I'm enjoying a second of this, Abbigail?" He crunched through the electronic wreckage, turning his computer keys into plastic shrapnel. "Do you think I haven't tried to be the guy worthy of your pretty whispers? To be a normal bastard who can screw in time to slow jazz and ocean waves instead of a deviant who can't get off until I've pounded the whites from a woman's eyes?"

I sat up, my fresh circulation bringing a new throb to my wrists and palms. I couldn't ignore the matching rhythm in my sex. "Eye whites are overrated." My bloodstream was pure fire now. Raw hunger. Consuming need. Even now, with raging tears coursing down my overheated cheeks, every drop of my blood was ablaze for him. My whole body clamored and cried for his.

"You don't know what you're saying."

"Because now you're the expert on me?" I spat back.

He chuffed. "Well, that's clearly not the case."

"Meaning what?" I demanded.

Sebastian turned back around with rough steps. He kneaded his neck and looked me in the eyes. "You're really still a virgin?"

I was glad for a chance to laugh, even if it was drier than gluten-free bread. "I think I'd know if I'd checked off that box."

"Checked off the box." Bafflement twisted his beautiful face. "So, that's what it is to you, then? Just a little square to be stamped?"

"Isn't it?" His immediate glower had me visibly prickling. "Oh, come on. Don't tell me you burned your V card with any more ceremony."

He jutted his chin. Dear God, he had one of the most perfect jawlines on the planet. "That was different," he answered, looking away.

"How?"

"I was a teenager!"

"And things would've been different if you were my age?"

A new huff. "Well, that never would've happened."

"Then go with me for a second. Use that imagination I'd bet is very capable. Would things have been different?"

He rubbed his furrowed forehead with his thumb and forefinger. "No," he finally growled. "I doubt it would have been any different."

"But for me it should be? Why? Because I'm a woman?"

"You're damning me no matter what answer I give here, Red." His frustration morphed into resignation.

But I couldn't drop the subject. He needed to hear my point. "I'm a woman who has been focused on learning my craft and building my career instead of taking time for a full-on relationship."

Sebastian yanked in a sharp hiss, pointing at me with gusto. "And there it is."

"There *what* is?"

"The word," he bit back.

"What word?"

"Relationship."

"What the hell does that have to do with anything?"

"Do you think that's what this is right now, Little Red?" He spoke it like an accusation, and I was pretty sure he meant it like one too. "Between us?"

I slid off the desk with enough force to send his blotter over the opposite edge. "The word's not going to give you hives or any of my clingy girlie cooties. You can say it out loud."

"All right. *Enough.* Obviously this is a broken merry-go-round. We're getting nowhere—and you know what? I don't have the right tools to fix it."

I cocked a brow. "What are you saying?"

He answered that with scary silence. The still air thickened, adding layers upon itself until it hung over the room like a funeral pall.

At last, I slumped my shoulders. So did he. The sight impacted even the darkest corners of my gut. Watching the man reveal that small sign of defeat... It was like the cosmos had reversed the planet's orbit. It wasn't natural. Clearly Sebastian agreed—and fought it with a new march across the floor. The air was riddled with metallic and plastic crunches as he decimated more of his fallen electronics.

As soon as he stopped, our stares locked and held.

He'd picked a damn good metaphor for the occasion. We were on a merry-go-round, but the ride was broken. And the longer we tried to talk this out, more things were getting broken.

"Damn it." The serration in his voice scraped at my heart. "Abbi…damn it. I wish the situation were different." He dropped his arms and curled his hands into fists. "But they aren't. They just aren't. Period."

I rocked backward, unsure of what to say. I went with the only words that made logical sense. "So maybe it's just time to stop this ride. I want to get off."

"This isn't a ride you can just stop, Abbigail."

I ticked my head to the side. "Do you have a better idea of what to call it?" I turned it into a question for the sake of the conversation, though I was in complete agreement about his assessment. I'd oversimplified—and God only knew, there was nothing simple about this mire.

"It's…a pause button."

Oversimplification for the win.

"Explain." I folded my arms and hoisted my eyebrows. While I purposefully threw his trademarked phrase back at him with an infinitesimal grin, it was all the support I could lend right now. "Until when?"

"Until you get that"—he waved his hand up and down my frame, as if displaying a prize heifer at auction—"that… situation…handled. As soon as fucking possible."

"That *situation*?" I couldn't unlock my folded arms if I tried. For his safety and mine. He was in very close danger of getting a five-knuckle imprint on that perfect jaw I had admired only minutes before.

Sebastian flung a stare full of daggers. I hurled just as many back—not that it helped one ounce of the chaos he churned through me, even as he grabbed my hand and hauled me across the room, back toward the office's door. Unlike an hour ago, when he'd ushered me out of here with devilish smirks and winks, he now handled me with grim, silent possessiveness. It didn't change as he hooked his other hand around the handle of my cart, pulling the thing toward the lobby with us.

Until he halted in his tracks and caused me to stumble to a stop.

And then added to the tension with a snarl. "What. Is. *That?*"

He sounded like he was staring at human body parts on my food cart rather than lunch service supplies.

But when I followed the line of his glare, I wasn't sure whether to giggle or cower. He was blustering at the compartment where a round wooden head, painted with a red kerchief and pink roses, peeked out.

"Nothing." A defense. "Well, a gift." Then, an idea. "Nesting dolls." I pulled the pretty oval all the way out. "From a grateful friend."

Sebastian's glare grew hotter than the sidewalks outside. "A friend named Viktor Blake?" No. His voice was beyond that now, jabbing intimidation up and down my spine.

He was getting pissy again about Viktor, and I was egging him on.

At least I could control the outcome of the second bit.

And damn well would.

"As a matter of fact," I finally said, matching his bad temperament, "yes. A friend, and a client, named Viktor Blake." The universe had crazy timing. Before this afternoon, I wouldn't have felt right about using my rapport with Viktor like this. But the guy owed me a solid for all the bizarreness during my delivery to him today, and this was definitely the moment to collect. "A client who wanted to thank me for a job I did for him last week. It was a last-minute order, and—"

"I know. I was there, damn it."

I slipped easily out of his hold—a good thing because his rage was like a nuclear blast zone. *Shit.* I didn't remember Sebastian approaching DEFCON status when we'd last talked about Viktor . . .

But right now, that just happened to be a good thing.

"Ohhhh." I swerved my tone up and down, purposely playing up my grand epiphany. But Sebastian didn't have to know that part. "You know . . . I just had a great idea . . ."

"No." He slammed it out before half my smile dawned.

"But Viktor's a nice guy. And beautifully built, at that. I'll bet he'd love a night of diving into all my situational misfortunes."

"No."

"And I think I noticed some free evenings on his calendar as I set up his lunch today. We could probably make this happen real s—"

He pounded a palm onto the cart so hard, the nesting dolls hopped right over the edge. "You set up his lunch for him?" he seethed. "Like you do for me?"

I bent and picked up the dolls—realizing the action was as good as slapping the grizzly across his face. Or so I hoped.

"He's a steady and valuable client, Mr. Shark. Just like you. But unlike you, he doesn't think there are any *situations* with me. Quite the opposite, actually."

To the point that the guy and his urbane facade—make that facades, many of them—had me craving a shower after leaving his office today. But Sebastian didn't have to know that either. He'd turned my virginity into an issue and then an ultimatum. And then, even a war. At the very least, another Shark-style skirmish. I was simply fighting fire with fire.

"Fuck." Sebastian enforced the growl with a new grasp around my wrist. I glared, but he didn't relent. "Fine." He yanked on me hard, and I burst into a wince that dissolved into a moan as he crushed my body back against his. "I'll do it."

And just like that, more pain.

The crappy inside-my-chest kind this time.

My psyche shriveled as shame and indignation stormed in. As humiliation punched between my ribs and fury turned my heart into an ember.

Weirdly, I fixed my stare over to the nesting dolls again. Viktor's metaphor about them was a haunting echo in my head.

*Layers. We all hide beneath them.*

Layers.

Yes.

The ones I thought I'd been seeing beneath Sebastian's shell. The parts of him I'd started to like, despite everything. Despite the beast who roared at everyone, the asshole obsessed with erecting a tower, and the lover who got mentioned in desperate suicide notes. Because I'd also seen the guy who stood up for little girls, the man who liked cooking me dinner, and even the boy who had to learn about diabetes before he even learned algebra.

But what if that was the shell?

"Abbigail? Did you fucking hear me? I said I'll do it, okay?"

What if the big bad wolf was his true self?

Because right now, that made the most sense of all.

"Don't. Bother."

# CHAPTER TWELVE

## SEBASTIAN

Last night ended in a blur. What started out as a nightcap turned into a top off…then fine, just one more…and then well, shit, I might as well finish the bottle. Now it felt like there was sand in my eyes and sawdust in my throat. I knew I was definitely too old to deal with feeling this hungover the morning after a clusterfuck of that magnitude.

A cluster *not*-fuck would be more accurate.

The unwelcome face of my best friend appeared in my line of sight when I looked up from my hands, where I had my head cradled, massaging my throbbing temples.

"I guess this explains why my messages went unanswered last night," Grant said with his usual lighthearted chuckle.

"How's that?" I asked, squinting at the harsh light of the fluorescent bulbs overhead. "Jesus Christ, I think I'm starting to hate Scotch."

"I'll get you some water. A few aspirin probably wouldn't hurt either. I thought you were staying in last night?" Grant asked, walking over to the refrigerator.

"I did," I moaned.

"Shit, man. Drinking alone in that castle of yours?" He shook his head ruefully. "That paints a sorry picture, man. Even for you. What happened?"

As much as I wanted to talk to my best friend about the problem at hand, I knew the moment I put it out into the open, it would only get worse.

*Is that even possible?*

"Out with it, man." He slammed the water down in front of me with a bit more force than necessary. Liquid sloshed over the rim and onto my desk. I met his stare with a reproachful one of my own.

"You're cleaning that up."

"Oh, I'm sure sandwich girl will be along any minute to mop up behind you. She seems to be coming earlier and earlier every day. Soon she'll be waiting here with your breakfast when you walk in."

"I can guarantee that won't be happening today. I'll be lucky to get stale bread crust with moldy cheese by supper."

"Ooooohhhhh. This little fright fest this morning has to do with her. Interesting. Now you definitely need to tell me what happened."

I watched Grant open the door to my office and stick his long neck around the corner to where Terryn sat at her desk. I couldn't hear what he said, exactly, but he closed the door behind him when he came back, mischievous grin firmly in place.

"What did you just do, Twombley?"

"I told your assistant we weren't to be disturbed. I know how she likes to busybody around here when I've been in with you too long."

"That was mighty presumptuous of you, no? What makes you think I want to involve you in any of this?" Damn, I was irritable.

"Because you look like shit, you already admitted you

drank too much last night—which is way out of character for you—and I know how tied up in knots you've been about that girl. The fact that you canceled our plans with LuLu's girls yesterday just adds icing to this mucked-up cake you've baked."

Grant flopped down on the black leather sofa but arched back up just as quickly, reaching behind him. "What the...?" He pulled out one of Vela's Barbie dolls from between the cushions. She must have left it behind the last time she came to visit. "That hurt, you skinny bitch. Eat something, woman," he said to the doll before tossing her onto the table. Then he pointed at the furniture across from him. "Come sit down and talk to me. Stop being a stubborn dick and tell me what happened. It will do you some good to get it off your chest."

I huffed out a frustrated sigh and pushed away from my desk. "You know that bossy shit you pull with the females doesn't work with me, right?"

"It's good that you recognize this behavior in another, at least. Seeing how you taught me everything I know." He watched me with a fixed stare while I came to sit down on the sofa, giving him a knock on the back of the head as I walked past.

"What was that for?" he asked, laughing while he finger-combed his hair back into place.

"This is all your fault." I pointed at him. "The more I think about the conversation you and I had in here yesterday morning, the more I realize that."

"Oh boy. Can't wait to hear this logic. It's off to a magnificent start. The wise and all-knowing Sebastian Shark not admitting fault. No way." Grant rolled his eyes.

"I'm serious, man. I think we were sitting right here, even. I'm having the strangest sense of déjà vu." I took a big swing of the water he'd gotten me.

"Enough with the riddles. Unless we're reenacting the tale of the 'Three Billy Goats Gruff' here. You're the Troll, if you haven't looked in the mirror this morning. Seriously, what are you talking about?" Grant finally lost the friendly tone. It took a while to push him to his limit, but apparently he'd reached it.

"That was such a random literary reference." I just stared at him, rubbing my throbbing forehead.

He simply shrugged in response. "Quit stalling."

"Pia always says, when you speak something into the universe, you make it come true. We did that. You and me. Sitting right here in this office. Yesterday morning."

"Oh. My. Fucking. God. Bas. Say what you mean. I'm going to punch you in the next minute, swear to all things that are holy."

"She's a virgin." Boom. Mic drop.

He stared at me. Just stared. Opened his mouth to say something. Closed it. Then stared.

"What's wrong, Grant? Billy goat got your tongue?" I worked the staring bit then.

"A virgin?" His eyes bugged wide. "Are you sure?"

"Well, no. I didn't get down on my knees and check under her skirt. I mean . . . I pretty much took her word for it."

He started quietly at first, a little chuckle in the back of his throat. I thought he was chuckling at the visual I had just painted of verifying Abbigail's hymen remained intact. But then Grant's eyes darted around the room, as if looking for a hidden camera to catch the practical joke on film, and then back to me, laugh building as he did so.

"I can't imagine why you're laughing," I said with very little emotion.

His laughter bubbled up and over like a pot of scalded milk on a hot stovetop. He laughed and laughed, for several long minutes, complete with knee slapping, tears streaking, back stretching—the whole nine yards.

I, on the other hand, remained completely stoic. There wasn't an iota of amusement to be found in the subject as far as I was concerned. Growing impatient, I got up from the sofa and strode back to my desk. If I could drag Grant from the room by the collar of his shirt, I would.

"Oh my God." He finally sucked in a breath. "Oh shit. Dude." He leaned forward, putting his head down halfway between his knees and gasping for air.

*Drama queen.*

"That's hilarious. I'm sorry. I don't mean to laugh, but you have to see the humor in that. I mean, if you're honest with yourself, you see why that's funny." He finally took a look at my face, no trace of humor to be found on it, and tried to get himself under control. "Ironic at least, right? Of all the men to have to deal with a virgin? You? I mean . . . Bas. Come on . . ."

"Shut up, Twombley." The words were snarled more than spoken. "I'm not amused. At all. Not one little bit. It doesn't matter anyway." I shrugged and mindlessly shuffled papers on my desk. Never mind that I didn't even see the words written on them. I just needed something to do with my hands.

"What does that mean? Doesn't matter? What did you do?" He popped to his full height and strode over to my desk, looking panicked. "Please tell me you didn't send her packing over something like this."

"Why would you care if I did? That's my first question. Why are you so invested? And *you*." I stood quickly and reached across my desk, pointing my finger right into his chest. "You know better than anyone"—*thump, thump*—"that I don't have the psychological tools to deal with a fucking virgin." *Poke.* "I'll cause that girl harm she won't get over. She doesn't need a bastard like me in her life." I sucked in a breath through my nose and flopped back into my chair, rolling back slowly until it bumped into the bookcase. "Certainly not on some moony memory page of firsts in her scrapbook."

A solid minute passed before either of us spoke again. I stood up and went around to the front of my desk where he stood. I felt awful for getting physical with him, but I'd lost my temper. We'd done far worse to each other over the years—and over dumber things, too.

"What now? Are you still going to see her?" Grant finally asked, rubbing the back of his neck.

"Don't know," I answered quietly. "I pretty much left it up to her. I told her to go take care of the problem, and if she wanted to still see where things could go from there, she knew where she could find me."

"Take care? Of the problem? Did you actually use that phrasing?" Grant stared at me as though I had sprouted a second head.

"Yeah, more or less." I shrugged. "That's what it is. A problem. As far as I see it, anyway."

"Jesus, Bas. This is why—"

"Why what?" He was pissing me off again. Well, him and the things he didn't even know yet. Anger percolated in my blood.

"Nothing. It's not important."

*No, not anger.*

*Rage.*

"Say what you were going to say, Grant," I gritted through my teeth.

"Why? It's not going to change anything. You're not going to change." He shook his head.

"Why should I change? I'm not the one with the problem here."

He thought for a minute and then looked at me, a strange smile spreading across his face. It was the same smile he always gave me before he shared an idea I wouldn't like.

"Tell me, best friend," he said, as silky as a mongoose would whisper to a snake moments before it struck. "You wouldn't mind if I have a go with her? Help her with her little 'problem'? She's a superfine piece of ass, after all. Young, untested. I mean, Jesus Christ..." He rolled his eyes back dramatically. "I'm getting a boner just thinking about it." The motherfucker grabbed his cock through his slacks before taking the final strike at my composure. "I'll bet that red hair is everywhere, if you know what I'm—"

I can't accurately recount the sequence of events that came after that. They involved Grant, me, the toppled sofa from the weight of both of our bodies slamming into it, and the items that flew off the coffee table, including a glass lamp and a statue Pia sourced from Sri Lanka—which I never really cared for anyway.

Bodies, furniture, pieces of glass, and pottery made for a loud clatter and a big mess.

*Big mess, indeed.*

Terryn rushed into the office to find Grant and me tangled together on the floor, still grappling with one another. At least one of us shed blood, judging by the red smears on Grant's face.

"Oh my God! Stop. Stop right now! Mr. Twombley, get off him. I'm calling security!" she wailed hysterically.

"He's on top of me! Are you blind?" Grant said in a

strangled voice. He scrabbled at my hands locked around his throat.

"Oh. True." She paused, confused. "Mr. Shark? Should I call security?"

"Leave. Now!" I barked.

"Oh, okay. But...but...there's blood. Someone's bleeding..."

She covered her mouth with a trembling hand, and the mention of blood made me stop trying to bash my best friend's head into the floor another time.

"Get out, Terryn!" we both shouted from the floor.

Her interruption made us pause long enough to get our heads on straight. We both sat up and brushed off our suits.

The door closed with a quiet *whump*, and I rocked back on my feet, holding a hand out to Grant and helping him stand as well.

"Don't poke the beast, motherfucker," I grumbled, pulling him into a man version of a hug.

"You stupid son of a bitch."

"Me?" I asked incredulously. "Do you want to go again? So soon?"

"Take a look at yourself, Bas. She's got you chasing your tail. Don't you see it?" He shook his head, laughing as he wiped at the blood coming from a crack in his bottom lip with the back of his hand.

"What are you talking about?" I asked Grant, who started digging through his pocket.

"You reacted that way, and all I did was say a few things to intentionally get you riled up. Me." He thumped on the middle of his chest. "Your best friend. Although, that may be up for debate if the blood doesn't come out of this suit. I love this suit." He looked up from rubbing his lapel with the handkerchief from his pocket. "What's it going to do to you to sit at home knowing she's getting boned by some other dude? You're delusional if you think you're going to be okay with that."

"This whole thing is making me insane." I shook my head. Shit, if I thought it hurt before, it was pounding like a bass drum now. "This woman is making me insane. How can a much-too-young redhead be wreaking this much havoc on my carefully planned world? And I've not even seen her pussy? Let alone tasted it, touched it, or fucked it. This is ridiculous. Completely ridiculous."

"My God, your sister would be so proud to hear you right now." He shook his head, smirking.

"Leave her out of this." I pointed my finger at Grant in threat. "Entirely out of this. I'm not joking, Grant. Not a word of this shit to Cassiopeia. She already thinks she has my whole love life figured out with that gloating shit she does. 'Oh, we'll see,'" I mimicked my sister's voice. "Fuck. Fuuuuuck!" I pulled on my hair with both hands. I felt like utter madness was setting in. "There's more. Believe it or not, you haven't heard the worst of it."

"Shit."

"Yeah. Shit." I looked at my best friend, hoping to God he saw the desperation in my eyes.

"Man, what's going on? You look like you did the first time you kicked your dad's ass and came to my house all freaked out."

Odd he'd chosen that memory to recall. I still remembered the day like it had just happened an hour ago. It gutted me to get physical with my own father, but he'd been drunk and started goading me, taunting me about not being man enough to handle the shit life was raining down on us. What a joke. He was the one delivering the shitstorm called life to our front door. No one else. But he wasn't man enough to admit the fault was his own. I'd punched the loser square in the face, grabbed Pia, and fled to Grant's, broken fingers and broken heart be damned.

*Yeah, I thought this pain felt familiar.*

*It's called betrayal, motherfucker.*

"She said Viktor Blake's been sniffing around, and she'd give it up to him if I don't want her." I let my head fall forward until my chin touched my chest. All I felt was shame when I heard the words out loud. Seriously? What kind of man does this to a woman he claims to care about?

"Damn it, Bas. Tell me you stopped her. Please tell me you stopped her. Everyone knows that dude is seriously messed up. I will take care of her if that's the only option you left her with."

I raised my head, growling again. "You stay away from her. I won't say it again."

"But Viktor? You can't allow that, Sebastian!"

"I told her I'd do it."

"Oh, thank Christ. Jesus, why didn't you just say that?"

"Because she told me 'don't bother.' Her words exactly. Then she stomped out of here and has iced me out since. Won't pick up my calls or texts. Nothing."

"So you went home and tied one on instead of tracking her down? Shit. You're losing your edge, man. The Sebastian Shark I know would've been pounding on her door until dawn if that's what it took."

"I guess you don't know me as well as you thought, then."

*My God, I'm exhausted.*

He stared at me. Turned his head slightly and stared some more. As if a different angle would reveal a different truth. "Nah, that's not it. Not it at all," he finally said.

"What the hell are you talking about?"

"It's not you that's different, necessarily. It's this woman. It's your *reaction* to this woman."

"And we've circled the wagon completely. You're a broken record today, Twombley."

"Just speaking the truth, my brother. This one has you all twisted up. It's as plain as the nose on your face." He paused a few beats before he continued. "But you need to do something about it. About her. And before she makes a grave mistake and tangles with that gutter rat Blake. You know it as well as I do. He has a horrid reputation with women. He will break her in ways you won't be able to repair."

The silence that blanketed my office was deafening. Even the streets far below seemed to join in the calm. No traffic sounds. No car horns. Just peace—punctuating Grant's decree with giant exclamation points.

*Or middle fingers, maybe?*

"I don't know how to fix this, Grant." It was the most vulnerable I'd been with him—with anyone—in a long time.

Grant finally spoke. "Sitting here, sulking and feeling sorry for yourself, doesn't suit you. I know that for certain. Call her again. Go find her. Make her listen to you. If she won't listen to you, find her hot little business partner"—he wagged his brows wolfishly—"and talk to her. You have to do something more than this." He waved his hand up and down my disheveled body.

I had nothing else to say. I let my eyes fall closed slowly. I felt worse than I had before. My head was throbbing, my stomach roiling, and now my face was pulsing in time with my heartbeat as well. And I'd thought opening up about this would make it better ... why?

When I finally opened my eyes again, Grant was still just staring at me.

"Well, my job here is done," he said, grinning. "I'm going to head out into the fief and do your bidding for the day, my lordship." He bowed gracefully at the waist, and I was tempted to knee him in the nose while he was in the position.

*I really, really wanted to.*

Instead, I let my hands fall to my sides and my shoulders drop as low as they could go. "Cut me some slack here," I all but begged.

"It's going to be fine. Let it work itself out, Bas. Stop trying to play puppet master to the whole world." His voice was quiet. Gentle. "You like the girl. The girl likes you. Spend time with the girl. Let it happen from there. Stop overthinking everything. You're making it harder than it needs to be."

"You have no idea what you're saying." Things weren't easy in my life. Things were never easy in my life.

"I think I do, actually. But telling you anything when you get like this is impossible." He shook his head sadly. "I'm off to my first appointment. If I'm not mistaken, you have a preliminary with the architect this morning. Let me know how that goes."

Grant gave me a brotherly smack on the back on his way out the door. I could feel a bruise blooming on my cheek where the bastard had landed his solid right hook earlier, but there wasn't much I could do about it at that point.

I didn't have two minutes to myself before Terryn knocked.

*Jesus Christ.*

I put my unbruised cheek on the cool top of my desk and moaned, "Whaaaaat?" I wished I could start the entire day over. Honest to Christ, I did.

My assistant poked her face around the plane of the door rather than coming all the way in. To her credit, it was rare for her to hear my voice in any other version than commanding and authoritative, and it may have thrown her off.

"You okay? I mean, really?" Her voice had a tone I'd never heard before. A day of firsts all around, then. Great.

Without lifting my head or looking at her, I muttered, "I'm fine. If Mr. Cole from Cole Designs arrives, just call me. You don't have to keep coming in here to check on me. Also, see if you can get maintenance up here quickly to clean up this mess."

"Of course," she answered softly. "Uh, umm, Mr. Shark? Can I get you anything? Do you want an ice pack, maybe? Your cheek is swelling up pretty bad." She motioned to her own cheek, pointing on hers where mine was bruised. I just watched her from my one eye, feeling awkward and uncomfortable in trying to cross from a professional to personal demeanor.

"That is all, Terryn." I said flatly after a few odd beats. The last thing I would do was confuse this woman by accepting charity or pity. She had a place in my office, and it would never be more than my executive assistant.

Any peace that could've been found ended ten minutes later. Maintenance bustled in to clean up the mess Grant and I had created with our scuffle. Pia was going to be supremely pissed about the things that were broken. And she would notice the minute she walked in on her next visit. The woman had hawk eyes. She always had, even as a little girl. Probably what made her such a great interior designer, though.

Thankfully, my secretary returned to her duties at the desk outside of my office and became so busy with the day's tasks, she didn't have time to try mother-henning me again.

Jacob Cole arrived a few minutes early, so in typical Sebastian Shark fashion, I kept him waiting outside my office in the reception area until the exact time of our appointment. I didn't like people thinking they could drop in early and take up more of my time than they had scheduled. It was as rude as showing up late, as far as I was concerned. Yes, it was an asshole move. Yes, it was controlling. But if the shoe fit and all that.

The young architect was the hottest up-and-coming designer on the circuit. He came with an impressive list of recommendations from clients and industry professionals alike, and his preliminary sketches really spoke to me. I liked his style, and his laid-back attitude fit well with my uptight one. There couldn't be more than one alpha dog on this project, that was for certain.

"Mr. Shark, good to see you again." He stretched out a hand in greeting. We shook, and I watched him take in the condition of my face and mentally war with himself if he should remark about it or not.

"Alcohol or woman?" he asked with a chuckle, thrusting his chin in the direction of my bruise. I had to hand it to the guy, he had the balls to go for it.

"Probably a little of both," I mumbled, raking my fingers back through my hair.

He nodded slightly but didn't say anything else.

"Didn't expect the truth?" I challenged.

"I wouldn't say that. Maybe a little dance around the edge

at first?" He smiled fully, releasing some tension that had set his shoulders higher than they laid naturally afterward.

"I'm not usually a bullshitter, Cole. Don't have much use or time for it."

"Good to know," he said plainly. "Must be quite a woman."

"Explain."

"To get the all-powerful Sebastian Shark scrapping on her behalf? I'd venture to guess you can pretty much have your pick of the litter, no?"

"Things are rarely what they seem, Mr. Cole."

"Isn't that the truth." He nodded for a few oddly long moments, clearly thinking about something much different than the conversation we were having. He shook his head slightly. "Well, I brought a few sketches for you to look at. Where can we open these up? A bigger space?" He scoped around the room and then headed toward the conference table. "The table here will work, if you don't mind?" He looked back over his shoulder to make sure before rolling out the prints.

"That's fine. Make yourself comfortable." I motioned toward the flat top of the table. "Can I get you anything? Coffee?"

"No thanks. Not really a fan of the way Americans drink it. I got spoiled when I studied in Barcelona. Now I can't stomach the Yankee way, I guess."

"Well, I need the fuel. I'll be there in a second." I made a quick cup of coffee and joined Jacob at the table, where he had opened the prints for the initial phase of the Edge.

I had to step back and take a moment.

Take a moment to absorb the enormity of what I was looking at on the table before me. My dream. My legacy. It was all there in black and white. I closed my eyes and took a steadying breath through my nose, and Jacob Cole had the good sense to let me have the time I needed. I could only assume he watched this same thing happen every time he unrolled his designs for the first time for a client. It was actually difficult to not get choked up. Thankfully, I had years of practice stuffing that sort of shit down.

"It honestly never gets old. I hope it never does," he said when I finally met his wide smile.

"You're in the business of making dreams come true, man. It's pretty heady stuff, I'd assume." I was rarely humbled by another human's talents. This man, however, had it in spades. He deserved my respect because of it.

"If I ever stop feeling the way I just did, watching you experience that? Then I will know it's time for me to retire."

He sobered then, which I also appreciated, because any more gloating and I'd want to punch him.

"So what are your thoughts here?" Cole asked. "Be specific, be honest, be brutal. I have really tough skin, and it's your project. I'm just the conduit from here"—he pointed to my heart—"and here"—then my head—"to here"—and lastly pointed to the drawings in front of us. "You tell me, and we'll make it happen here." He tapped his well-manicured finger on the prints for emphasis.

"First impression? I love it. That's saying a lot. You really listened at the initial meeting, and I appreciate that. Immensely." I looked him directly in the eye when I said that, needing to convey both my appreciation and expectations of the same standard moving forward. The man was both intelligent and intuitive, traits many younger business professionals were lacking, I was finding. It was equally frustrating and infuriating in business relationships.

"Thank you, Mr. Shark. I'm glad you're pleased with the first look. Of course, this is only the design phase. Concept One, as I like to call it. As we move forward, we'll start making changes, and at certain points, the changes will be significant enough to warrant a second rendition. We'll call that Concept Two. For ease of reference, basically." He looked at me to make sure I was following his process, and I gave him a nod, so he continued.

"The design phase, as I'm sure you know, will carry through all the engineering and right up to the construction phase." He stood up tall from where we were bent over the prints. "We have some long days and nights ahead of us until we have the outside and inside of the Edge looking exactly the way you envision it."

"I'm all in on this, Mr. Cole. You have one hundred percent of my focus. This is my priority. You call, I will clear my schedule for you. I will instruct my secretary to ensure it."

"Please, call me Jacob. Or Jake. Whatever works for you. We're going to be spending a lot of time working on this. We don't need to be so formal." His smile was kind, and I knew he expected me to extend the same sort of offer.

But I didn't.

I preferred the higher ground in every relationship, and the formal title was a way to establish that.

Did that make me a dick? *Yep.*

Did I give two shits? *No, I did not.*

If I threw Cole off with my lack of offer to get more casual with the titling, he didn't show it. The younger man was pretty unflappable, all things considered. Maybe I was just off my game because of the hangover and the fistfight with Grant first thing this morning. Regardless, we worked straight through lunch and into the afternoon.

Jacob and I walked out to Terryn's desk just as she was signing something for a courier.

"Please schedule Mr. Cole's next appointment the same time as today's," I said.

Jacob and I shook hands again, and he made his way down the hall.

Terryn stood silently off to the side, awkwardly trying to find something to do while she stared.

"What is it?" I said impatiently.

"This just came for you." She quickly grabbed a letter encased in the overnight sheath emblazoned with the courier's logo.

Taking the letter, I asked, "Did you message Abstract Catering like I asked? I'm starving."

Terryn continued to watch Jacob walk away until he turned the corner to head to the elevator. When she realized I was still waiting for her to respond, she flushed with embarrassment.

"Sorry," she whispered. "Did you notice ... I mean, did he look—" She fumbled with the necklace that rested at the base of her throat.

"Spit it out, please."

"Never mind. He just looked very familiar." Her voice trailed off again as she looked down the hall in the direction Mr. Cole had gone.

"My lunch. Did you tell the caterer?" I was losing patience faster than normal.

"Yes, I did," Terryn snapped unexpectedly, but she quickly steadied her voice. "I forwarded Ms. Gibson's reply to you."

I reached into my pocket and pulled out my phone,

keeping my eyes trained on my impertinent assistant. Deciding I'd had enough drama for one day, I went back into my office and closed the door. I pulled up the app we used for quick office correspondence, and I saw Terryn's response to my earlier request still in the unread messages.

"Ms. Gibson replied to your request. Direct quote: 'I'll get there when I get there.'"

For whatever reason, a wide grin spread across my lips. That little redhead liked poking at me, and she had no idea what it did to me. She'd find out soon, though. As usual, my cock woke up and took notice of all things Abbigail Gibson.

*Not now, man. No time for a quick one in the bathroom.*

She'd pay for all this torment, too. But wait. Virgin. My cock jolted to twice the thickness.

"No," I gritted out. "There is nothing remotely exciting about that." I adjusted myself and grabbed the letter opener off my desk. Grant had given me the pen and opener set one year for my birthday. Both had my initials engraved on sturdy brushed-nickel handles. They had a nice bit of weight in my hand when I used them. Solid desk accessories.

*See? Not thinking about my dick at all.*

*Worked for almost forty seconds that time.*

*A new personal best since meeting Abbigail Gibson.*

Nothing good came by registered mail. That was a given. Certified letters were usually worse. Things sent by courier could go either way since many businesses used couriers to send contracts and other official documents that needed signed originals. I wasn't expecting something unpleasant, necessarily.

I definitely wasn't expecting a handwritten letter. A full page of scrawled handwriting stared back at me when

I unfolded the sheet of paper. Regular, everyday paper. Nothing fancy, nothing noteworthy. There wasn't a monogram embossed on the top or a hotel's logo printed in the corner. No, this was white copy paper, likely pulled from the paper tray of someone's office printer.

*Dear Sebastion,*

Excellent. My name was misspelled. Joyous first impression, dear author.

*You probably don't remember me.*

Nailing it so far.

*I know you have a lot of girls come in and out of your life.*

Jesus Christ, if this was some chick saying I knocked her up, this day was officially the worst day of my life. I. Swear. To. God.

*But ever since that girl, Tawny, jumped off the bridge on the other side of town, I've been doing a lot of thinking.*

Shit, don't hurt yourself with that, babe.

*Maybe she had the right idea, you know? After I met you and danced for you, I thought things were going to change in my life. The way you looked at me like you wanted me. Maybe needed me. Maybe you'd come back and sweep me away from this shitty life I have. So, I waited. Every day I danced, when the door opened at the club and a guy came in, I hoped it would be you, coming back to save me. But it never was. I fell in love with you that day.*

Oh, come on. Are you serious right now, lady?

*But now, I'm saying goodbye. It's time for me to go. To go over the rainbow bridge . . .*

Isn't that what people say about their pets?

*And be with my mom and dad.*

*Goodbye, Sebastion,*

It's an *a*. Fucking t-i-*a*-n.

*Cinnamon Spice*

What was I supposed to do with something like this? I mean, really? First thought, obviously, was the circular file. On any other day of the year, it would've already been in there. However, I already had one woman's death hanging over my questionable conscience. Not sure what a second one would do to my mental state.

Add in the situation with Abbigail. Something about her was gnawing away at the very fiber of my being.

No, not something.

*Everything.*

How could that be? How could she be affecting me so fundamentally when I barely knew her? But I could guess what she would do in the same situation, and every instinct told me it was the exact opposite of my first inclination. Was that a bad thing? Probably. More than probably . . . It was an absolute, resounding affirmative.

I'd never been willing to change who I was. Not for Pia and Vela. Not for Grant. Not even for the memory of my mother. I was proud of the man I'd become. I'd worked hard to get here.

At my core, I was a good man. I did the right thing. Always. People didn't always agree with the route I took to get to the final destination, possibly, but the end goal was always the right outcome. I did what I had to in order to win, and usually that lined up with what was best for my fellow man. I rarely did something solely for myself.

Terryn interrupted my musings with a call to announce Ms. Gibson's arrival. After she rolled in with her stainless-steel cart, I kept my distance as she set up my lunch in the usual spot. If she noticed the décor out of place from my tussle with Grant, she didn't mention it. I waited while she carefully arranged the food and silverware, and then I positioned myself in front of the door. There was only one way in and out of my office, and I blocked her path to it.

"We're going to talk this out, Abbigail. Whether you want to or not, it's going to happen. I tried reaching you last night, as I'm sure you're aware. I don't appreciate being ignored. But that stops now."

She glared at me. That was all. Just glared. No words of protest. No tears for me today. Just an icy stare that would've ruined a lesser man.

Silly girl.

Silly.

Silly...

...girl.

# CHAPTER THIRTEEN

## ABBI

"Damn it."

So much for every precaution I'd taken to banish the word from my mind and lips. For three awesome seconds, I thought I had the self-control nailed—until Sebastian fielded my iciest glower like it'd come from a paltry commoner summoned to court.

Three seconds.

That was really all it had taken.

Three seconds filled with his commanding stance and his steely gaze. I wasn't about to ask about the bruise that swelled high on his cheek, even though I really wanted to. Just one charge in his no-isn't-an-answer-choice baritone, and I'd lost it. Spit the word out with my frustration cranked to max.

But did I really ever have a choice in the matter?

*Rhetorical question.*

I'd been screwed from the second Terryn's order pinged into the online order queue this morning, with the extra details that were always typical for her boss. Sebastian Shark wore his impatience and insolence as perfectly as his bespoke navy-blue suit and dazzling dark-gold tie. It was high fashion, worn by a dark-haired god who effortlessly turned it into his own.

Good *God*. He was so beautiful, it was surreal.

*Damn it.*

At least I was silent about the repetition. Small miracles *were* still possible.

"'Damn it?'"

Or maybe not.

Sebastian's narrowed gaze, on top of his incredulous drawl, confirmed I'd been just as pathetic about spewing the words aloud. He leaned against the door, cocking his head as if to taunt me with the words again, but instead queried, "Is that really all you got for me here, Little Red?"

I would've preferred the profanity again. I think he knew that.

Instead of saying that, I shrugged. At the moment, it was shorthand for my middle finger. I think he knew that too. At last, I summoned up a clenched smile and breezed out, "Fine. Sure; whatever. Let's do this. I'm sure tending bar will be part of owning my own place, so I can use the listening-but-not-caring skills."

One of those weird flashes took over his face, as if he got sideswiped by emotion and had no idea what to with it. "Your own place?" he echoed. "Like a brick-and-mortar restaurant of some sort?"

"Not just 'some sort.'" I fought to make it a snarky snap, but this subject deserved more than sarcasm. "It's going to be a contender, even in this city. Top-shelf, all the way. Edgy décor but old-world service. White linen on every table and tasting rooms for wine *and* whiskey. Classic menu favorites with modern twists. Like the coolest food truck in town colliding with a luxurious restaurant. I'm even thinking of a garden for specialty dessert service. And—" At last, common sense broke in. As my embarrassed flush crept over my cheeks, I slammed my hands over them. "Holy crap," I muttered, able to add in a genuine laugh. "Some epic bartender I'll make, huh?"

A smile spread across Sebastian's face. There was another holy-shit-I-have-feelings flash along with it. "Bullshit. You'll be an awesome bartender," he said, infusing it with the steady confidence he'd learned for Vela's sake—or so I'd thought up until now. "But you'd better hire a team of good backups, because you'll get pulled away a lot to greet VIPs."

"VIPs?" I hated feeling like I was walking into his punch line but couldn't help myself. The fantasy was too enticing.

"It's an acronym." He was still authentic and gentle, as if explaining tax codes to his niece. "It stands for Very Importan—"

"I know what it stands for." Swiftly, I qualified, "I mean, usually. But—"

"So don't underestimate the value of them. Even if someone's a second AD for straight-to-video movies and insists he's a VIP, treat him like one. Of course, the real ones get more than a hug and a free drink."

I hitched out a hip, propping my hand to the same side. "So which one are you, Mr. Shark? An insister or the real deal?"

"Me?" He brushed out a dismissive hand. "*Pfffft.* I'm just an asshole, remember? No freebies for me, though I will insist you keep bottles of all the expensive stuff around for when I stroll in unannounced."

I threw my head back with a new laugh. "Unannounced, huh? You plan on pulling that number a lot?"

"Oh, at least once a week. Because—"

"You're an asshole. Yeah, now I remember."

He pushed away from his spot in front of the door and approached me with steady intent. Once again, I struggled to swallow on an arid throat. Shark did things for cobalt blue that shouldn't be legal.

"But I'm an asshole who thinks your place is going to be insanely successful."

"Well, thank you." There was something weirdly empowering about this. Yes. I actually could form words even with perfection incarnate entering my airspace and turning my knees to gruel. "But that's not what we're here to talk out, is it?" I ordered strength back into my legs and stiffness back into my spine. "You want to drag out the issue of my situation a little more, I take it?"

He halted in his tracks. We were still at least a couple of feet apart, which was fine with me. I could still think at this distance.

"All right, that probably wasn't the best choice of words," he said from tight teeth, and I almost responded with a huge grin. It was likely the closest to an apology he would ever get.

"All right. Pardon me for my forwardness, Mr. Shark, but what did you mean?"

He dragged a hand across his scalp. "That maybe we can talk about this like adults? For once?"

As he dropped the hand to his nape, my attention was pulled back to the nasty bruise below his eye. I fought and failed to ignore the sympathy that hit because of it. *Damn.* What the hell had happened in here? I noticed the two new monitors that replaced the ones he and I had knocked over, but now his desk was the only pristine zone in the room. Everywhere I glanced, there was some toppled or missing décor. And was that *blood* on one of the sofa arms?

*Damn it.* This time, I really kept it restricted to silence. *Don't tell yourself you care about any of this, Abs. And for God's sake, don't show* him *that you do.*

I felt better after the internal pep talk. I was doing well here. Just a few more minutes, and things would be even easier. I'd had twenty-four hours of practice now. My hurt-and-outrage combo had served me well since getting out of here yesterday, acting like an emotional balm on the Sebastian Shark bites. It had even worked on all the fantasies too. I'd gotten a great night's sleep, with no fantasy sex turning me into a sweaty mess by morning.

Now, I was determined to keep that track record going strong.

Even as I followed Sebastian over to the front of his desk.

As he angled a thigh across one corner, I leaned a hip against the opposite one. "All right, then. We're officially in grown-up mode. Speak your piece. I'm all ears."

Without lowering his stare from me, Sebastian leaned over. With a hand braced on his knee, he looked both earnest and empirical—yet completely delicious. Every cell of my senses was rushed by his midnight eyes, his expensive cologne, his fluid power . . .

"Your announcement yesterday . . . Well, it was like a nuclear bomb for me."

"You don't say." I popped my eyes so wide, there could be no mistake about my satire.

He glowered, but as was the case with him so often, the ire only boosted the beauty of his dangerous side. "After you left, I had to ask myself some hard questions."

I leaned against the desk for myself now. Continuing to gaze at him in this new state, still attempting his apology-that-wasn't, had my knees softening by enchanted increments. "And then what? You beat yourself up for it?"

"Right?" He gingerly tapped his bruise. "But in a few ways, yes." He loosely laced his hands in his lap. "Some of this won't be easy for you to hear, but you deserve the truth."

He paused, giving me the chance to say something. But I had nothing.

*His* confession had felt like a compliment but also a warning. Did I thank him or back away from him? I chose total silence, though it didn't feel like much of a choice.

"Taking your virginity is a massive concept for me, Abbigail. It's ground I've never trodden before—or have even wanted to. Since I was young, I was always very aware of my ... preferences ... in the bedroom. I also took the time to identify the desires and needs that drive them. It's never been anything I've had to hide."

"Okay." I sensed there was more, and I didn't want to break his stride.

"It's simply the way I'm wired. My tastes are intense, not wrong. But they do require like-minded partners. Women who don't mind field trips to the dark side. Routinely."

Though he finished that off with a devastating half smile, my heartbeat got erratic for other reasons. I curled a hand to my chest before grating, "So is this the part where you tell me about the kinky dungeon inside your palace?"

He twisted his lips with even more illicit intent. "No, Little Red. This is the part where I tell you that this whole mess has turned *me* into a mess, and I don't know dick about messes or cleaning them up. I've lived unapologetically. I've never cared enough to notice the debris left in my wake. Until now."

"Oh." I pushed back to my feet. "And I assume by mess, you're not talking about the finless shark over there"—I pointed to the glass statue that rested between the coffee bar and the whiskey display—"or the dozen dings in the coffee table?" Or the blood on the sofa, though I couldn't stomach going there.

He took such a deep breath, his chest puffed out by a few inches. "Grant and I had a little…disagreement," he finally said.

"And got messy about it?"

He nodded. "A little."

"What were you talking about?"

He tilted his head. There was new tension in his jaw, emphasizing its stark masculine angles. But robbing my breath the most was the new light in his eyes, like starlight on steel, before he replied without hesitation.

"You."

My belly lurched. My heart leapt. "What about me?"

Shadows fell over his face. He licked the seam of his lips. "He thinks I'm being a fool. About your…situation."

"I knew I liked him." I offered it with a frothy smile. This was exhilarating. There was real liberation in being able to talk like this with him, without tiptoeing around a single subject. Both our cards were on the table, no matter how hard it was to flip a few of them over. I almost forgot that I'd walked in here determined to stay pissed at him.

*Almost.*

It was easier to stay the course on my ire once I circled back around to his first point. Right. There it was. Bedroom preferences. Field trips to the dark side. Desires and needs and drives.

"But I assume our 'hashing this out' doesn't involve Grant." It tumbled out with a harsher edge than I'd expected, but I celebrated the new strength it represented. I was holding my own here, despite his swoon-worthy suit and captivating stares.

"Your assumption would be right."

"All right, so . . . where to from here?" I pressed. "I mean, you don't really want to be regaling me with a blow-by-blow of your sexual history, do you?"

He snorted. "Intentional choice of words, Ms. Gibson?"

"Or not." I scooted off the desk, caving to sudden restlessness. Besides, pacing prevented me from continuing to stupidly stare at the man.

At last, he broke the silence again. "I think what I'm trying to say here is . . . I'm sorry, Abbigail." He punctuated it with a laugh, responding to my instant double take. "I know, I know; alert the press. Shark apologized twice in one week." He glanced up at me through the ungodly thick fans of his lashes. "But I can't help it. You come around, and I want to spill shit out. Tell you things. Things I don't tell others."

I stopped where I stood. Didn't dare venture any closer to him, already knowing he'd turned his freaking magnet back on. Yeah, the crazy-powerful one with all its polarization set to attract all of mine. But I was too late. "*Sebastian*," I rasped as he hooked his hands over my forearms and yanked me three steps closer. "Oh, damn it . . ."

"I know." He held me even tighter. "I *know*. You're running behind, and—"

"No. No, that's not . . ."

And it really wasn't. But how did I explain this? All of this freaking amazement he was drilling into me. This perfect magic . . .

"I'm not . . ." *Ready to let it go yet.*

And how could I be blamed? My knees were melted butter. My ribs were a grill set on high, and my lungs were charbroiled bags of wonder.

And everything in my intimate core . . .

I wouldn't go there. I couldn't.

But there was no place else I craved to think about more. No place I needed him more . . .

"What I'm trying to say is, you need to know that I don't have any special thing against virgins. I'm not hung up or triggered about them. There wasn't any epiphany or heavenly message about the whole issue of you being a virgin." He exhaled roughly. "Just, more than anything, I think it had to do with what happened to my sister."

Since his magnet was clearly on full power now, I surrendered to a little more of its physical pull. I wrapped my fingers around both his biceps as he guided me in between his knees. "Is Cassiopeia a single mom?" I asked, genuinely curious. "I didn't see any 'dad' type at Vela's soccer game—except you, of course."

He nodded. "I've been involved with that child since Pia's pregnancy, which wasn't at all easy. During those months, my knuckles went through a lot of walls—which didn't help Pia's state of mind, of course—but I was obsessed with the injustice that some asshole had fucked her and then left her like that."

I winced. "The guy was her first?"

"And, according to my hopeless dreamer of a sister, her last," he snarled. "The one and only man she'll ever love, forever and ever, as long as butterflies dance and unicorns prance and ponies have sparkles in their manes."

I smiled—who couldn't after a sentence with ponies *and* sparkles?—but understood his bitterness. "No wonder you swore off virgins for yourself."

"Without thinking twice. Until . . ."

His unsteady huff was his interruption. He lowered his

head and hunched in his body. The lean muscles beneath his power suit were coils of anything *but* power. I could feel every shred of tension through his clothes.

"Until what, Sebastian?"

I felt crappy about pushing him. Crappy but doing what was necessary. I needed to hear this answer. Yes, despite how I already knew it. Okay, I *hoped* I knew it. I needed to hear it...because I was damn sure he needed to say it. Out loud. Right now. With the building bustling around us and the city clamoring below, we needed to turn this office into a cathedral and our embrace into a confessional. Safe ground. Total absolution.

He got it too. As he looked back up, I saw the understanding across his carved face. Absorbed it from every facet of his struggling gaze. And heard it in every note of his ragged voice.

"Until you, Abbigail Gibson."

A rush of breath left me. At the same time, he sucked one in. With the slide of my hands up over his chest, I recognized how my pulse matched his heartbeat. But our syncopation went beyond that. Like sun burning through mist, there was a new awareness between us. It was still tenuous and unclear but there all the same. Sizzling through the clouds. Lifting our facades. Our layers.

It thrilled me.

It terrified me.

A million words assaulted my mind, but I couldn't say a damn thing. Nothing made sense. While everything made sense. He had the magnet turned up again—but for the first time, I realized that I possessed a magnet too. One that was drawing him just as hard.

"What do we do now?"

The words alone were unnerving new ground. I had no idea what his answer would be. A wave of strange relief washed in as he cupped the back of my neck to coax me closer and then tenderly bussed my forehead.

"I don't know yet."

The words earned him my huge smile against his neck. Maybe tiny miracles were possible—because his confession officially flushed the anger I'd sworn not to surrender. With his courage, he'd cleansed it from me. With his honesty, he'd stripped me. The nakedness felt nice. My vulnerability felt right.

So beautifully right...

Sebastian hitched away from me. I didn't let him get very far. With a determined tug at his jacket lapels, I pulled him right back in—and then compelled my mouth to dive too. I thanked myself for it as soon as his carotid jumped beneath my tongue. As I kept nipping and nuzzling, he gifted me with a low, lusty moan.

I lifted my mouth up to the crevice of his ear. It was heaven to breathe in the musk of his skin as well as the sage and coconut of his expensive shampoo. The intimate scents gave me the extra jolt of courage to whisper my next words.

"I think I know what we can do."

A new groan poured out of him. His massive body shuddered beneath my roving touch—especially the part of him growing faster than all the rest. "Fuck," he husked. "Abbi..."

"You suggested it just yesterday. Something about a preview of our naughty weekend, right on your desk?"

"Yeah. I—I remember. But—"

"But what?"

"Things have changed, Red." But while he asserted it,

he hardly moved away from my nibbles at his neck and my strokes between his legs. "We've got to acknowledge that."

"Umm ... I think we already have."

His nod, more succinct than I'd expected, preceded his reluctant drag back. The same conflict ruled his face as he set me back at an arm's length too. Though lust still glittered in his eyes, he relented the rest of his features to his CEO scowl.

"Outstanding. Glad we're in agreement, then."

"A-Agreement?" I stammered it, still dizzy from the figurative revolving door into which I'd just been tossed. "What?"

"That I'm not going to handle this issue by fucking you on my desk." He rapped a knuckle on that very surface as he moved to his central location behind all his monitors. Did he have any idea that just by talking about that now while reembracing his dark and imposing side made my sex clench for him in at least ten new ways?

"But you do want to handle it now."

"Never a question of whether I wanted to, baby." He scooped up some loose papers and a courier package in which they looked to have arrived. "It's just a matter of whether I should."

I dropped my hands. Balled them into fists. "How the hell are we back to this already?"

He lifted his head, every crease and furrow once more etched on his bold features, and brandished the sheaf of papers in his tight grip. "Little life lesson number hundred and fifty-three, courtesy of my colorful past." He squeezed his eyes shut as his lips contorted. "People like me don't get to leave the past in the past."

As he spoke, I looked long and hard at him. But more

prominently, at those damn papers in his hand.

The hand that practically shook with tension.

"Sebastian?"

I unrooted myself from my spot and stepped carefully back around the desk. Not that he noticed. Though he dropped the papers back to the desk with a graceful sweep, he stared as if the scribbles on them were rendered in blood. I would have assumed as much when taking in the steel pole of his spine, the tension across his shoulders, and the renewed clench of his jaw.

"Hey. *Hey.* Shark?" As I stepped closer to him, I had the impression of navigating invisible shadows around him. The unease of his aura was that thick and cryptic. "What's going on?" I pressed. "What are you . . ."

He reached up and formed a hand over the one I rested on his elbow. But it was his eyes that wrenched the words out of my throat. I'd expected more shadows in their dark-blue depths. There were none. His gaze was close to black, the color of midnight during the winter solstice.

He was as still and as silent as that long cold night. But he moved at last, sliding the three sheets of paper over to me.

As I accepted them, my fingers trembled. Right before my eyes popped wide with shock. And incredulity. And horror.

"Do you see now, Abbigail?" His words were like accusations. His aura was gallows grim. "Do you see now why I'm not the Prince Charming to give your virginity to?"

I slammed the handwritten note back down. The motion made it possible to move all the way in front of him and then to reach in and grab him by the biceps again. "All right. So that may be the case—but right now, you need to bring your A game to what we've got going on here." I pivoted at the waist to tap on the letter now lying on his desk.

He suddenly jerked as if I'd decked him. "What we've got going on?"

"I said we, and I meant we."

I punctuated my declaration with a solid thump to his sternum. He just glared as if I'd just flung a foam dart at him. "No," he growled. "And I mean it, Abbigail. This is a solo-spun mess. And so—"

"It's going to be a solo-spun disaster, as well. Unless you stop marching in your pigheaded parade and accept a little help from someone who cares."

The way he blinked, then stared, and then huffed out a breath was as though it were the first time he'd ever come face-to-face with the concept.

Through a bemused smile, he said, "Good Christ. Someone . . . who cares."

"That's what I said." I folded my arms and tried to temper my satisfaction. He wanted to like the idea of going at this together as much as I liked the idea of helping him through a crisis.

"I don't know what . . . I don't know how . . . It seems so unnecessary."

"Why? This shouldn't be a shock to you, Sebastian. All you have to do is look around. People probably offer to help you all the time. You just have to let them."

My instincts had my brain bracing for any number of reactions—none of which included his clasp of my body followed by his kiss.

Not that I was complaining. Not one damn bit.

By the time he was done massaging my tonsils with his tongue, I was ready to propose that desk fuck again . . . if it weren't for the glaring pages still centered on its surface.

"How was that?" he drawled, adding an enticing nip at my bottom lip for good measure. "Were you helping me just then, baby?"

The balls of his shoulders got the brunt of my smacks this time. "Well, I'd like to be the only one who helps you that way. But focus. We need your mind in better places now."

His gaze still hinted at mischief, but I didn't waste time on more correction.

Without ceremony, I nodded down at his keyboard in an implied request to access his computer. He swept out a hand, wordlessly granting the permission I sought. I smiled and swiftly typed into the search window.

*Spotlight News Los Angeles*

After scrolling down the news channel's main page, I released a *whoosh* of relief. "All right. We still have time. If she'd really done it and implicated you as this letter states, it'd be the first or second item on the page."

But when I straightened, Sebastian was waiting with a full glower. "We have time?" he charged. "For what? Abbi, what the hell are you—"

"Not me. We. We're in this together, remember? And we need to stop her from doing this." My God. Was I really the cockier one in the room right now? "If we get lucky and find her quickly." But cocky went away when I faced the gritty truth of what I had to say next. "But we have to start at the beginning. Do you remember this girl, Sebastian? What is her name?" I scanned the letter again. "Cinnamon?"

Sebastian pivoted. Stabbed his hand through his hair. Most noticeably, he left the vicinity of my personal space. That alone warned me to prepare for his answer.

"I have no idea who she is."

And thank God I'd prepared.

"Well, if her name is Cinnamon, that means she's probably a redhead." Freaking great. Did this mean he had a type for his one-night stands? One I fit perfectly into? Why was Rio's face popping into my mind so easily? "Does that help narrow it down at all?"

"Barely," he gritted. "Especially because the hair's probably a wig. Strippers change their hairpieces more often than their underwear." He pulled his hand out of his hair and waved it in a dismissive arc. "She's probably the Little Mermaid one night, then a desperate housewife, and a naughty nurse the next."

I dashed my gaze back down to the top of the desk—though for what purpose, I was clueless. I'd already listened to the certainty with which he rattled off that colorful role-playing list—and as a result had already envisioned him being a willing fuck buddy for every one of them. The island prince to her mermaid. The gardener to her bored housewife. The dominating doctor to her illicit nurse.

And I'd just been insisting we do this together . . . why? Or, more accurately, what the hell had I been high on? Yet here I was, still grilling LA's most famous lothario about a conquest he couldn't even remember—less than fifteen minutes after I'd tried seducing him to screw me on his desk.

But I could worry about getting psychotherapy tomorrow. Right now, there were much more dire things to stress about. Like a woman's life.

I pulled out my phone for my next web search. No need for the Shark Enterprises system to see that Sebastian's computer had been used to look up LA's leading gentlemen's clubs. "If there really is any way for us to find her, we have to track down where she might work."

"Now that I can answer." He almost looked proud to be useful again.

I looked up as he slid closer to the monitors. And focused on breathing as he fixed the blue flames of his gaze back on me—

Just before he pulled my phone out of my grip and told the thing to abandon its search for the city's finest strip clubs.

"This isn't necessary. Thanks to someone who didn't bolt from my side over this, I was able to figure some shit out here."

A bashful smile yanked at my lips. Between the intensity of his blues and the strangest compliment I'd ever received in my existence, Sebastian was making it hard for me to figure shit out. But I pulled it together and replied, "Shit like what?"

"I haven't been to a club in at least eight months," he explained. "Between traveling to Europe due to our recent acquisitions and pushing to break ground on the Edge, I haven't had a lot of downtime."

"Guess it's been good to have other . . . resources."

I truly meant it more as a fact instead of a dig, but he side-eyed me for a couple of seconds, as if unsure how to react.

"Damn good," he said, clearly deciding no elaboration was the best elaboration.

Weirdly, I was fine with that. I really didn't need to know why Sebastian booked things with a woman like her. My only concern about it was the safety factor. Undoubtedly, he was paranoid about his personal life, so I was ready to forget it and move on. And he obviously was as well.

"Grant and I used to frequent three places in the city.

One of them, the Gold Rooster, burned to the ground about six months back, so that leaves only two possibilities. Club Delilah in Hollywood or Chemistry, which is downtown." He leaned over and scooped up the courier envelope in which Cinnamon's missive must have arrived. "The origin zip on this is Hollywood."

I pumped a fist. As Sebastian flowed out a smooth laugh, I resisted the urge to jump at him with a congratulatory kiss. One, we had nothing to celebrate yet. If the woman had switched clubs and was now working somewhere else, we'd be at a dead end. Even if it *was* the right club, she might not be there tonight.

And there was third possibility.

That we were already too late.

I frantically opened my phone again. "I just need two minutes to make sure Rio can cover the rest of the lunch run. Can I leave the keys to the van with the security desk in the lobby?"

Sebastian looked over from beside a modern steel art piece on the wall, behind which he had popped open a safe. He yanked out an envelope bulging with cash. I didn't bother asking what it was for.

"Red, you can leave the damn van parked in the lobby if you need to." He walked across the room to the en suite bathroom. Less than a minute later, he emerged with a dark-gray T-shirt in hand.

Which I silently begged him to don slowly.

Over his bared, bronzed, and utterly beautiful torso.

This was insane. The man belonged up on stage in a strip revue of his own, sharing with the world the glory of those veined arms, that rippled abdomen, and those serving platters being passed off as his pecs.

But for right now, I was happy just letting the magnificence fill *my* world.

Unfortunately, he didn't hear my plea about taking his time with the more club-worthy outfit. Within seconds, he had the tee on and was replacing his polished Ferragamos with a casual pair of ankle boots. As he did that, an incoming text buzzed at my cell. "Rio, I hope?" he queried.

"Uhhh . . . yeah." His muscles still had me at a stammer.

"Outstanding. So we're set?"

"Uh-huh."

"Ready whenever you are, Ms. Gibson."

"Sure. Okay. Just as soon as I pick my tongue up off the ground."

His smile was sultry, secretive, and sexy as hell. "I'm glad you like what you see."

"Like? Mister, you owe me a massive apology for having to deal with this case of 'like.' You might possibly owe me one tomorrow too. And the next day."

Sebastian snickered. "All right, then. Sorry . . . not sorry."

I rolled my eyes and giggled. "I don't doubt that for a single second."

★ ★ ★

Club Delilah was located in a part of Hollywood people drove through without truly seeing—the "real life" on the way to the flashy dream. The horizon was a block-shaped collection of big and small sound stages, punched by a bright glow from where some movie shoot was being set up.

We drove past a strip mall with a tattoo parlor, laundromat, threading studio, hookah lounge, and pho restaurant—the last one prompting my stomach to growl on cue as Joel, Sebastian's driver, guided the car toward a garish neon sign planted atop a surprisingly stylish building.

Surreal. It was the only way I could describe all of this. Surreal. Was I really being chauffeured in Sebastian Shark's private town car through a NoHo strip mall, on my way to find a dancer before she committed suicide? Because of the man I was still seriously thinking of giving my virginity to?

But sure enough, this was really happening. I couldn't deny it, despite my knees wobbling like the club's velvet ropes in the brisk Santa Ana wind. As Sebastian exited the car and then reached in for me, I was at eye level to notice the stanchions for the ropes, designed like curvy women. The same design was repeated in the frosted glass cutouts in the club's ornate purple doors.

Approaching, I was so confused, so out of place, and the experience in my mind so at war with the actual one playing out before me. We were less than ten feet from those bright-purple doors, but the scene was quieter than a church. I was actually reassured to feel faint thumps under my feet that were matched by discernible vibrations on the air, hinting at the music inside.

My face must have reflected my bewilderment, since Sebastian's brief smile was the only break in the tension that had engulfed him during our twenty-minute drive. "City ordinances," he said. "The club is their golden goose for tax revenues, but nobody in the neighborhood wants to know about it. Besides"—his lips twisted into a damn cute grimace—"the music usually sucks ass."

I cocked a brow. "But isn't 'sucking' and 'ass' the name of the game here?"

Sebastian rolled his eyes. "Come on, smarty-pants."

He laced his fingers through mine and clutched hard. I hung on with equal force. Okay, this really was going to happen. Not anything close to what I thought the day would bring when waking up this morning, but life taught me a long time ago that it rarely went as one expected.

And sometimes, it fit expectations in scarily accurate detail.

As soon as Sebastian paid our entry fees—along with generous advance tips for all the dancers—the doorman dipped a respectful nod and then swung the door open. At once, we were blasted by a nineties grunge tune blaring over warbling, fuzzy speakers.

I could safely check off the box for strip club expectation number one.

As a second bouncer opened a set of interior doors for us, Sebastian tucked my hand all the way under his arm. The next second, I knew why.

In this big room, with my formfitting white T-shirt and my skinny jeans beneath these unforgiving black lights, I felt like the object of the whole room's leering curiosity. Checked out and assessed from head to toe.

This was an expectation box I'd hoped not to encounter.

But thanks to Sebastian's bared snarl and malignant glower, it was checked off with merciful speed.

Boxes three, four, and five happened in rapid order as well.

The big room smelling like booze, weed, cigarettes, and sweat? Check.

The soundtrack consisting mostly of that nasty Nine Inch Nails song, woven with subdued conversations and appreciative male growls? Big check.

A profusion of female flesh everywhere I looked, from the topless waitresses to the pair of beauties in G-strings twirling around poles on the stage? Bold-marked check.

Yet despite my wide-eyed scrutiny as we moved through the room, nothing about this was as intimidating as I'd spun it up to be. I was clearly here with Sebastian, so aside from the awkwardness during my initial entrance, I was left alone. And as my eyes adjusted to the dimness, I noticed I wasn't the only female guest in the crowd. Everyone was just as deferential to the other women. They displayed even more "church manners" for the women up on stage—one of whom had just peeled her panties all the way off. There was a smattering of applause for her elegant move, along with a flurry of tips being pulled out to show real appreciation. But all the money was tucked into collection boxes attached to stanchions placed six feet from the stage. Not once did anyone throw their money at her. Nor were there any shouts, catcalls, or lascivious whistles.

"Whoa." I actually stopped in place while vocalizing my reaction.

Sebastian pushed in close to me. "What? What is it? Did someone paw you?"

"Easy, there. I'm just recovering from my own blown mind."

"Explain."

I let out a wry laugh. "You've clearly never been to this kind of thing"—I searched for the right wording—"in reverse? Male strippers, female audience?"

"Ah." He straightened his stance. "Chippendales? Magic Mike? What's the other one? Thunder from Down Under?"

"Yes!" I commended. "A real tribute to the Outback, that

one. But seriously, the women all but climb over one another to get up close, and the performers take a select few on stage, grind on them with oiled body parts." I widened my eyes, thinking of the memory. "And those tiny, tiny G-strings being tested to their limits by both the dude's junk and all the money that's been stuffed inside."

"Huh. Sounds like fun."

Blank stare.

For such a territorial alpha wolf, he completely threw me off guard with that answer. While I tried to reorganize my thoughts, a special security guard approached us. He was dressed differently than the doormen, in basic black utility pants and boots, but his block-lettered T-shirt and shiny name badge seemed legitimate. A close-cropped haircut screamed ex-military.

"Good afternoon, sir." The guy greeted us like a soldier at his post.

"Hi there"—Sebastian lowered his eyes to the guard's name badge—"Hank. What can I do for you?"

Hank nodded and folded his hands over his belt buckle. "The door radioed back to me at your request. They said you were interested in talking to Cinnamon?"

Sebastian subtly swept out a hundred-dollar bill between two fingers. "And would make it worth your while to facilitate the meeting. Yes."

Hank flicked a suspicious glance between the money and Sebastian's face. "Can I interest you in another one of our girls?" he finally said. "Cin doesn't enjoy being a third. She's into guys, period."

"Yes." Sebastian dragged up a smile. "I'm aware." As soon as the man scowled, he added, "We really just want to talk to her."

Hank stared as if Sebastian had suddenly dropped trou. "And you're paying *that* for it?"

"It's important."

His gaze bugged. "No shit."

I swallowed hard, reining in my gasp of relief as the guard snatched the money from Sebastian. Hank lifted a finger, indicating we should wait for his return.

"She's here." I hugged the crap out of Sebastian's bicep. "Holy shit, Sebastian. We did it. She's here and she's alive!"

"Thanks to you and that persistence that drives me crazy."

He tilted his face lower as he murmured it. There was an impending kiss in his eyes, but he didn't act on it. The tension in his form told me it killed him as thoroughly as it did me.

I hoped he could see the same need in my gaze before I whispered, "Crazy good or crazy bad?"

"Both. Which drives me even crazier."

"Hey. Summer Lovin'." Hank called us over with a brief head jerk. As we got closer, the guy said, "Cinnamon is on a short break. She can squeeze you in now. You ready?"

"As we'll ever be," Sebastian said. It was the last comment of the exchange until we were about halfway down a cinder block–lined hallway smelling like a locker room badly in need of a hose-down. With fifty gallons of bleach.

I seriously prayed this intervention didn't take very long.

Just as I started the silent beseeching in earnest, Hank hitched a look at me over his shoulder. Okay, not quite at me. His examination was more about the . . . assets . . . he saw in me. "You here to get some dancing tips, sugarplum?" he drawled.

"She's not interested," Sebastian cut in.

"Because Cin is one of the best. She could show you some moves. Then make sure to audition for George, our owner.

He really likes redh—"

"I said she's not interested."

So much for picking up my prayers where I'd left off.

Inside a heartbeat, I was back to questioning the stability of my reality as I watched Sebastian transform from casually dressed billionaire into badass barroom brawler, as he grabbed Hank by the neck, slammed him to the wall, and lifted him several inches off the floor. As the bouncer fought the hold, his eyes bulged and his teeth clenched. Both were weird shades of yellow—an observation I couldn't believe I fixated on until realizing I was watching a human male pissing match that was going too far.

"Sebastian!"

I grabbed the back of his shirt. He shirked me off like the rabid wolf he was channeling.

"*Sebastian!*"

A woman appeared from one of the closed doorways along the hall. She strutted out of a room in stars-and-stripes stilettos, a red glitter G-string, a flowy blue silk robe, and nothing else. A shit ton of stage makeup highlighted the best parts of her perfect bone structure, and her stunning red hair was curled in a forties-style hairdo.

"Boys?" she crooned, though she directed her gaze my way. She doled out a commiserating eye roll, as if she'd just witnessed my futility at breaking this crap up. When it was clear they weren't listening, she strolled over and leaned down.

And then grabbed Sebastian from behind.

Yep, right *there*. In the juncture that would definitely get her some attention.

He snorted violently before breaking away—but not before landing one last jab to Hank's chin.

I whipped a hand around his wrist and openly seethed. "Enough."

The gorgeous woman shrugged. "Or they can decide that it's not and I can bring out the tranquilizer gun."

Hank stepped back while lifting both hands. "She's really got one," he muttered. "And it works."

"And it's really cool. I use it for my lion tamer routine."

Just when I thought this scenario couldn't get any crazier, Sebastian threw back his head on a good-natured laugh. "I remember that routine. It was damn good."

"Still is," quipped the redhead. "But not on the schedule tonight, big boy. You should come back over the weekend. I even use the gun." She waggled her overly made-up brows at the men.

I scooted around, moving to scrutinize the glamorous stripper a little closer. Now that I had better proximity, I noticed the layers of makeup were really necessary. She was a wan thing, with eyes that were hollow and world-weary. Beneath the robe, her breasts were abnormally large compared to the rest of her frame. The fake nipples on top of the equally fabricated swells were colored with red lipliner so they appeared more aroused. But unlike what Sebastian had told me earlier, her hair was definitely all hers. No way could that lustrous red color come out of a bottle. At least she'd been blessed in that department.

"*You're* Cinnamon Spice." I was that sure of the fact. Sebastian's line had helped me get there too. He recalled her dance routine from nearly a year ago. This *had* to be her.

The stripper swiveled my way. She checked me out from head to toe before responding, "Who wants to know?"

I deflected my nervousness by channeling my professional

persona. If I pretended I was simply visiting a new vendor, I could get through this without envisioning the woman—and her naughty smirk and playtime boobs—in bed with the man next to me. We were here to help her, after all.

"We're just hoping to talk you. We only need a few minutes."

"Okay. Cool."

She flowed out a hand, directing us toward her door—but before Sebastian could lead the way inside, Hank pulled at his shoulder.

"Yo, dude. Are we cool, man? I didn't mean anything toward your woman."

"Oh, I'm not his—"

Sebastian sliced me short with a fierce glance. "It's fine," he said to Hank. "We're good."

"But you can't blame me for looking, right?" The guy flashed crooked teeth with a fresh chuckle. "I mean—"

"Hank." Cinnamon glared like a mother who'd caught her kid licking a frozen pole. "Do you seriously have a death wish?"

After Hank turned and returned to the main showroom, the woman shook her head and shot a rueful gaze at both of us. "He's got a heart of gold, fists of steel, and the brain of a Muppet." After she entered her dressing room, she whirled around and snapped her fingers. The action made her robe sweep outward, affording an extended view of the curves that made her a star on stage but did nothing for the butterflies in my stomach. "But hey! He did just help me remember you!"

I plopped down onto a chair that wasn't covered in costumes, accessories, or thigh-high boots. My timing was perfect, since I was struck hard by a jolt of astonishment.

"Wait." I bit hard into my bottom lip. "You— You just

remembered him?" I asked while pointing to Sebastian.

The puzzle pieces of this thing were getting drastically rearranged by the second, and I still didn't know where they were all going to land—if at all. A quick glance at Sebastian wasn't any reassurance that he knew either, especially when he added his own query to Cinnamon.

"But...you do know who I am?"

Cinnamon slinked into the fancy vanity chair in front of her wide makeup mirror. "Yeah. Sure." She flipped a switch, illuminating the big round bulbs bordering the glass. "I think so...Sebastian, right?" Via the mirror—which seemed the best way to communicate now, since those bulbs could probably be seen from space—she inserted a saucy wink. "But as I'm starting to recall, you really like being called Sir."

Sebastian shifted his weight and inhaled through his nose.

I shifted my own weight and asked, "As you're starting to recall? You mean...just now?"

"That's right." She lifted a friendly smile my way via our reflections. "But it's been quite a while since that fun-filled night." And then she flicked her gaze Sebastian's way. "Right, Bas?"

"Sure," he spat. "Fun. Loads."

Cinnamon straightened with an affronted pout. "Gee, don't get too excited on my account. I never send a client away unsatisfied. Ever."

"Oh, I'm sure he was satisfied."

Both sides of my jaw were aching from tension now—but I wasn't relaxing them anytime soon. Cinnamon picked up on that message fast, making a concerted effort to address me first when she swiveled back around.

I was appreciative, and noticed Sebastian was too—

but now I was more baffled than ever before. This was the woman who'd scrawled that desperate letter to Bas? This bright-eyed bombshell with the va-va-voom one-liners, who claimed she only recalled him five minutes ago?

And yes—this woman who now took one look at my face and perceived the bewilderment likely painted across every inch of it? To the point that she finally glanced at Sebastian and asked, "But reminiscing over the good ol' days isn't why you've come to see me . . . is it?"

There was a long pause. I didn't answer her question, and neither did Sebastian. Instead, he dipped his head and then quickly straightened, seeming to have come to a major decision.

He pulled out the letter I'd read back in the office.

Quickly yet carefully, he unfolded the paper.

But he didn't hand it over to Cinnamon yet. He seemed to be assessing her . . . maybe wondering if the woman's flippant attitude was as fake as the glitter on her face and the breasts on her chest.

Through the closed door, we could hear a Prince medley cranked up to full volume. So, at least all the music didn't suck in this place.

"Hey, Sebastian?" The prompt came from the woman with her legs now crossed, one stilettoed foot jiggling with an impatient rhythm. "You hear that? It's the middle of Contessa's set. That means I'm up next. Shoot your wad now or forever hold your peace."

In another time, under other circumstances, I would have given in to a good laugh at that. Sebastian didn't seem to share my demented mirth. But he was the one still holding the letter that this crazy-pants had written.

Or so we'd thought.

"Cinnamon…" His tone was a perfect blend of understanding and firmness, but he only got one word out before stopping and grimacing. "Can I just get your real name?"

Now Cinnamon looked like the one debating if she sat here opposite a dangerous creeper. After a nervous side-eye, she replied, "Sarah."

"That's so pretty." I meant the compliment, but Prince was jamming even louder out in the showroom. I deferred back to Sebastian.

"Sarah," he echoed, finally holding out the letter to her. "Why did you write this and send it to me?"

The woman quit rocking her foot as soon as her gaze got deeper into the note. "What…" Then she uncrossed her legs. "The…" Then lurched all the way to her feet. "*Hell?*"

I rose along with her. I was a freshly melted puddle as he stared at Sarah with a mix of firmness and compassion. "We're—I'm—just here because I want to help, okay?"

"Why?" she shot back.

"Because this letter is a cry for it."

"Dude." She spurt-laughed it. "Are you serious?"

"Uh, yeah." His glower was as raw and dark as a Prince guitar riff. "I am. I mean, if you feel like things are out of control, or like you've got to talk to someone, or even need deeper help than that—"

"Stop." The stripper backhanded the middle of his chest, giving back the letter as if the thing had caught fire in her grip. "Just freaking stop, okay?" She flung off her robe and started rubbing glitter gel across her breasts and stomach. "Bas, baby, I'll try to be gentle here. I mean, you're hot and all"—she glanced over at me—"Sorry, chica. He is a fine, fine man and fucks like a machine, but no way in hell does that mean I've been pining away for him like Little Miss Lost Lamb here." She stabbed a finger toward the letter. "Look. I'm supporting my little boy and trying to get my own degree at the same time. I don't have the time nor the inclination to mope over the guy I screwed last night, let alone last year."

"Wow." I didn't try to hide my surprise—or honestly, my awe. "What are you studying?"

"Environmental Science—which is not a cheap field of study, especially at Pepperdine. But this job is paying for it." As if summoned by her perfect invocation, there was a rap at the door and a voice giving her the five-minute call for her performance. "So, if you both don't mind, I've got to go make sure I can buy my books in September."

As soon as she clacked out the door and down the hall, Sebastian and I stood mute and motionless inside the tiny dressing room. As the final strains of "Let's Go Crazy" filled the building, we finally looked back to each other again.

And recognized one distinct fact again.

We were in a deeper hole of *what the hell* than ever before.

If Cinnamon hadn't written the letter . . . who had?

And if this letter was fake, was Tawny Mansfield's suicide note fake too? If not, then what had happened behind the woman's suicide? Was it a suicide?

Most urgent, why was Sebastian getting pulled into these occurrences? I was broken out of my perpetual questions loop when Sebastian finally stashed the letter into one of his back pockets. He swept his phone out from the other one.

"What are you doing?" I asked softly. Was I overstepping by asking him who he was calling? Everything was so undefined.

"Sending a note to Elijah that Sarah needs a shadow

ANGEL PAYNE & VICTORIA BLUE

bodyguard for the next few weeks. Now that she knows about this—about someone using her persona and name—she might be a target." He hit Send, and I was grateful to hear the little *bloop* of the text message shooting into the atmosphere.

"And now," he continued, "a second message for him to find out her last name so I can cover the rest of her tuition bills."

I couldn't launch myself at the man fast enough or get my lips back on his soon enough. And I really, really couldn't believe that less than eight hours ago, I'd planned to stay mad at him for the rest of my life.

Such a silly, silly plan.

So useless against this amazing, dazzling man.

At last, after I'd ravished his lips and tongue and mouth through the first few stanzas of Sarah's routine—she was dancing to an "updated" forties medley with synthesizers and guitars—we reluctantly drew apart. Sebastian's stare was full of light-blue fire but dark-blue regret, as if this was the hottest kiss of the night and couldn't be topped.

Well, it was time to show him differently. In a lot of different ways.

"Mr. Shark?" I pleaded, hovering my face just half an inch from his.

"Yes, Ms. Gibson?" he flowed out.

"Please, would you be so kind as to get me the hell out of this place?" I slanted another long kiss across his eternally stunning mouth and then tugged him toward the hallway. "Before Hank finds out I'm still here and drafts me to dance to something like *that*."

I was deliberately goading him, but my teasing laughter got drowned out by the deafening music in the hallway. The tension in his neck and the ferocity in his eyes told me that he probably growled, but there was no chance for a repeat of my answering giggles. They were replaced by a stunned shriek when I was hoisted off my feet and then all the way over the muscled plane of his right shoulder.

"Ahhh! What the—"

"Just a little preview of what you can expect if you ever get up on that stage, young lady."

"You have an odd way of defining little, Mr. Shark."

"Just be thankful I haven't imprinted my hand on your sweet ass yet, Ms. Gibson."

Sharp gasp—mostly as an effort to diffuse the new zing of heat to my pussy. "You. Wouldn't. Dare."

"Just try me, baby." To rub that in, he did the exact same with his forceful fingers across my backside. "Oh, how I'd love you to try me."

I was a new collection of both sighs and snickers as he walked through the club, continuing to possessively palm my upended butt.

By the time we hit the front doors, I wondered if I wanted him to put me down again. Ever. Dear God, what he was doing to me with the take-no-prisoners treatment. I was becoming just that. A hostage of his aura and power. A willing captive of his protectiveness and passion. If Sebastian wanted to haul me all the way back to downtown like this, I was pretty sure I wouldn't complain.

"Okay, there are no dance poles in sight anymore. I'm fairly sure I can walk the rest of the—oh, holy shit!"

I almost chastised myself for being melodramatic but realized Sebastian had yelled out at the same time—and his words matched exactly what had exploded from his driver's lips.

"Get down!"

A person shrouded all in black had seemingly manifested out of nowhere. Or the parking lot pavement. Or maybe straight from hell. None of us had any way of knowing, since the invader raced up to us so quickly and unexpectedly.

Sebastian pulled me down beside him and then pressed me to the side of the town car. He wrapped himself around me, his hands covering mine and his breath a frantic firestorm in my ear. I was breathing a similar cadence. My lungs pumped with dread.

Was this the same lunatic who'd sent the bogus suicide threat from Cinnamon? If so, were they also connected to the food poisoning? What if this was something new? A desperate street punk who figured the guy in the town car had some major flow—or, *holy shit*, a holy extremist ready to take down one of the "infidels" who'd been at the sullied strip joint? What if we'd been caught in the middle of a gang turf war? Or what if—

"Mr. Shark? Oh, dear God, Mr. Shark, are you okay?"

A second of total silence passed.

Then another, not so quiet—because the chaos in my head had turned into a rushing din of disbelief.

Then a third, filled with Sebastian's growing growl.

He exploded with the sound as he shoved to his feet. At the same time, Joel rose from where he'd been crouching against the town car's back bumper. Neither of them looked at each other. They were too focused on the owner of that voice.

My brain refused to recognize it, but my gut knew—and was twisting back on itself because of it.

"Terryn?"

Joel actually got it out before Sebastian. He finished his question—his accusation?—with a *whomp* of a hand atop the car's trunk.

After a long, labored inhale and exhale, Sebastian got out intelligible words between his teeth. "What. The. Fuck?"

"I—I couldn't believe it when I saw that you were in this part of town," Terryn said. "I panicked. I knew I had to make sure you were okay. This is an awful neighborhood. With all of the weirdness going on lately, I thought you'd maybe been taken by bad people or ended up somewhere you didn't mean to be. And if you needed help, I wanted to be here to ... umm ... well ... help."

"To help," Joel deadpanned, as if she'd shown up in a plastic Halloween costume with a toy gun and a spy decoder ring. "To help ... how?"

But in my gawking and humble opinion, he was missing the more important point here.

"With a situation you even knew about ... how?"

That point. One that Shark didn't sound even one molecule happy about.

"I have to admit, I'm a little curious about that one myself." Voicing the sentiment lent my knees the strength to support me again. Though I felt fairly stable, I was still quietly tickled that Sebastian kept our hands entwined after he helped me rise.

Terryn, on the other hand, was not tickled about it. Or about seeing me at all. "*You*," she practically seethed, though she recovered with agitated speed. "I—I mean it's n-nice to see you, Miss Gibson. Especially at such an odd place and time."

"A fact we could point out about your drop-in, Miss Ramsey," Joel said.

She whipped a burning glare his way. "I already told you. I came because I wanted to help!"

As wrath began coursing off Sebastian like heat waves, he

let me go and stepped away. His tight stare told me he didn't want to, but I sensed things were about to get really ugly.

"You wanted to help." Every syllable he gritted was clipped, terse, terrible.

"Yes!" Terryn exclaimed like an exonerated murder suspect.

"And you just knew where to come and help . . . how?"

As swiftly as the woman's celebration had begun, it fizzled. She gulped, clearly panicking now. "Well . . . I . . . uumm . . ."

"Terryn."

"Y-Y-Yes, Mr. Shark?"

"Have you been tracking my phone?"

She frantically licked her lips. "Well . . ."

"Answer me!" His voice echoed off the stucco walls of every shop in the adjacent strip mall, ringing back to us with exceptional clarity in the early evening air.

Her eyes were huge buckets of unshed tears. "Y-Y-Yes, Mr. Shark."

"Give me your fucking phone."

# CHAPTER FOURTEEN

## SEBASTIAN

"Start the car," I said evenly to Joel as I strode past him and closer to Terryn. This entire situation was going to end, one way or another. I thought it would be as simple as going into the Find my Friends section of the system file of her phone and deleting my contact. But when I found the utility, no contacts were checked off. Icy fingers crawled up my spine as I raised my eyes to my assistant's expectant ones.

I only held her gaze for a short second. I made the motion of deleting a few things—moving things around, pressing buttons, and so on, but really, there was nothing I could do.

"Abbigail, get in the car."

"But I want to—"

Of course she had to argue.

"Now!" I barked. Much more forcefully than I wanted to. *Damn it.* Another apology was on the horizon. Three in one day? Hell was going to freeze over.

I waited for Abbi to be safely inside the car before I turned back to Terryn. "Do you have your car here?" I asked, my tone of voice giving nothing away.

"Yes. Of course. Do you need a ride somewhere? While Joel takes her home?"

I really didn't care for the way her voice shifted every time she spoke to or about Abbi. This woman was unstable at best, a real danger to herself and everyone around her at worst.

I tapped on the front passenger window, and Joel lowered it. "When I give you the cue, I want you to drive forward about eighteen inches and then stop. Back up about eighteen inches and then repeat that about three times."

"You got it, Mr. Shark," Joel replied.

I bent down and placed Terryn's cell phone right in front of the tire of the town car, and when I was clear, I gave Joel the signal to carry out my instructions. A satisfying crunch could be heard as he drove over the cell phone repeatedly.

Terryn's gasp was even more satisfying. I spared her about five seconds more of my time before joining Abbigail in the back seat.

"Run along, Terryn. I hear this is a really bad neighborhood. We'll wait and watch to make sure you get in your car safely and drive out of here. The freeway onramp is right there at that intersection." Hands casually slung in my suit pants pockets, I pointed with my chin in the general direction to get on the 405.

From the back seat of the town car, we watched Terryn skulk back to her entry-level Toyota and speed off into the night. I let my head flop back into the curve of the seat before looking at Abbigail.

"I'm sorry I raised my voice."

"I'm sorry I questioned your judgment," she said at exactly the same time.

We both took deep breaths and sat quietly for a few minutes. I had no idea what to do with the mess that was unfolding in front of me.

Finally, Abbi spoke up. "What did you see on her phone?

You stiffened like you'd seen a ghost."

I rubbed my throbbing brow bone. "I don't really know what to make of that woman right now."

"It seems pretty obvious to me."

"Explain."

"Well, it seems like she's carrying a torch for you, Sebastian."

"This has moved into creepier territory than a harmless crush. When I looked on her phone, not only was my contact not checked in the Find my Friends app, but also there were no other apps like that on her phone. At all."

Abbi nodded. "My brothers have warned me about people having cloaked apps on their phones that appear to be something innocuous like a calculator or a stock ticker but are actually a tracker or a booty call app. She must have had something like that."

"That's what I was thinking, too. Or something more sophisticated. Either way, that's why destroying her phone completely seemed like the best option."

"Aren't you worried about owing her a new phone? Although"—she laughed in the middle of her thought—"like that matters to you, right?"

"I have a legal department filled with lawyers who live and breathe to pursue and prosecute idiots like Terryn Ramsey."

"So why didn't you just fire her? Right there on the spot?"

"You know the saying about keeping your friends close and your enemies closer? I'm still trying to figure out which one she is. With all these other unanswered questions floating around right now..." I ticked them off on my fingers while listing them. "Mysterious food poisoning, a dead woman, and a letter hinting at suicide not written by the supposed author. If

Terryn is the one who can provide the answers, I want to keep her close at hand."

"It makes perfect sense when you take all of that into consideration. So now what do we do?"

"I need to drive you home. I'll have someone bring Rio's vehicle to her home as well."

"No, that's ridiculous. We live in opposite directions from your office, and the traffic will be a nightmare at this hour. I'll be fine on my own. Honestly."

I could've bet a month's salary on this being an issue.

"Well, according to Grant, anyone with half a brain knows you would be a good place to strike next," I said, turning to stare out the window. I couldn't meet her gaze after having to admit that information to her.

"Huh?"

"My best friend seems to think I'm wearing my heart on my sleeve these days where you're concerned." I turned to face her then. "My sister seems to share his opinion. Therefore, if someone is trying to fuck with me, they've probably put the pieces together to connect me to you. I'm sorry to involve you in something you don't necessarily want to be involved in. But . . . well . . . here we are."

"I'm not completely sure I'm following this whole last part." She waved her hand through the air, confusion wrinkling her brow. "I don't mean to sound dense, but I have conversation whiplash."

"Conversation. Whiplash." I chuckled as I tried the words on for size. "I don't think I'm familiar with that injury. Sounds serious." I laced my voice with mock concern to attempt to lighten the mood.

"It can be. I'll explain." She sat up taller, taking an

authoritative mien before starting.

*Damn, this girl makes my dick throb for the oddest reasons.*

"It's when a person—you, in this particular case—changes their position on a topic—me, in this case—so rapidly that the people involved in the conversation—us, in this case—get whiplash."

I couldn't take it. Not for one. More. Fucking. Second. I unlatched my seat belt and slid across the seat until I was right up against her. Her already huge green eyes grew impossibly larger.

"Do you know what I think, Ms. Gibson?" I said right into her ear in a register so deep, it all but vibrated the windows. I was sure she could feel my warm breath on her skin, my need pulsing through my system where our legs touched.

"What?" Her breathy whisper felt like fingers strangling my cock.

"I've decided I like hearing you say the words *you*, *me*, and *us* in the same sentence. I like it a lot."

I couldn't stop myself from tasting her. Being that close to her, smelling her, feeling her heat. I kissed her neck. Just leaned my head onto her shoulder and pressed my lips to her silky skin. Perfection. Fucking perfection. How had I forgotten since the night at my house? How had I forgotten how right she felt against my mouth? I reached my arm across her chest to fan my fingers against the column of her throat on the other side. I could feel her throbbing pulse beneath my touch.

I ran my tongue up to her ear and back, and when she gave me a little moan, followed by a little sigh and shift in her seat, I did it again.

"Do you like that, Abbigail?" I said beside her ear and pulled back just far enough to watch her reaction.

Her hand flew up so fast I thought I might be slapped, but she clutched my face so I couldn't move far. "Yes. Yes, I do. I'm an idiot for it, but I do."

I threaded my fingers through the loose strands of hair that had worked their way free of her work-required ponytail and rubbed firm fingers along the base of her neck. Long days on her feet and lots of lifting and carrying had stored tension in the muscles of her shoulders and neck. Of course, I might have had something to do with the fatigue as well.

"Oh, that feels good." Her eyes fell closed while I stroked her. Over and over, long caresses to ease the day away. Any reason to keep touching her.

When she seemed relaxed and hopefully more agreeable, I asked quietly, "Will you let me make sure you're safe? Please? Just let me take you home tonight?"

After a few long moments, she answered. "Fine. But why don't you just follow me? I'll take Rio's car home tonight." Her eyes popped open, and she sat up taller again, the spell from the massage broken with the conversation. "But why would you drive all the way across town? Do you see how ridiculous that is? Traffic is horrible at this hour."

I pulled back a bit. "But you should have to do it? Alone? Because I've kept you on this side of town long past the time you normally are? How is that fair?" She would never win an argument with me. We could do this for the next hour. Every point she could think of, I'd have a counterpoint. It was one of the many reasons I was so successful at my work. I whittled people down until they just gave in. I could verbally beat someone into submission within minutes.

"Sebastian," she said plaintively.

I picked up her hand and kissed her knuckles. "What is it, Little Red?"

She just whimpered. Whimpered in submission.

I was the master, ladies and gentlemen. It was the plain and simple truth. I mentally took a deep bow in the middle of a stage, spotlight focused directly on me.

"Are you hungry?" I asked her, hoping to redirect the tired subject of car relocating.

"No, not really. Are you?" She rested her head on my shoulder, and it felt so nice.

*So right.*

"I had lunch really late." I smiled and tapped her nose with my index finger. It had been one of the longest days I could remember.

"Do you want to come up or wait in the car? I'll just be a few minutes."

"I'll come in, if you don't mind? I'd like to use the restroom. I didn't dare go at that club."

"All right. And that's a very clean establishment, I'll have you know. They have very high standards there. For the employees and the facility."

"I'll take your word for it." She rolled her eyes at my defense of the club, and in the interest of not going back down that path, I dropped the subject altogether.

We were in and out of my building within fifteen minutes and back on the freeway heading to her place in Torrance. Since Rio had left her car at my building earlier in the afternoon and taken the catering van, we drove to Torrance in her car with Joel following behind to bring me home afterward.

"This still seems ridiculous. I drive all over this city by myself all the time."

"It makes me feel better knowing you're safe. That's not ridiculous. And Joel gets paid very well to do what I ask him to do. All of my employees do."

"Oh. Good to know, I guess." She frowned and concentrated on the road.

"Explain."

"Well, technically, I work for you, Sebastian. Do you expect me to just always do what you say?" She glanced between me and the road again.

"Ms. Gibson..." I shook my head. "Do you really think any of my regular rules apply to you? I mean, really? Do you still think that at this point?"

She smiled slowly, but as quickly as the smile appeared, it faded. "There are times I think no, but then something happens and I'm completely thrown off guard and you treat me like everyone else. So, to be honest, I don't know what to think."

She had a valid point. I hadn't been entirely fair with her or with the way I'd been treating her. "I've been... I'm trying to think of the right wording here because it's important to me."

She sat in silence, waiting for me to explain.

"I think I've been unfair. Maybe that's accurate? I've been inconsistent with my... This is harder than I expected, Abbigail."

It felt like the temperature inside the car spiked by about ten degrees.

"Why don't you just speak from your gut? Or your heart or wherever it is your words are coming from? I'm not going to judge you or tell you it's wrong," she said gently, putting a hand on my leg.

"I'm in uncharted waters." There. Perfect. That was exactly what I needed to say, and it felt like the weight of the entire land lifted off my chest.

"Okay..."

She didn't look any more enlightened, even though I felt like I just told her everything with that declaration. More explanation was needed, apparently. But it just about killed me getting that one sentence out.

*Definitely not cut out for emotional engagements. Of any sort.*

"I've been accused of being emotionally unavailable before." Deep inhale. "That being said, I feel things where you're concerned that are..." I looked heavenward, searching for the best word again. "Different?" I nodded. "Yes, different from what I'm used to experiencing."

"I'm not going to put words in your mouth, Sebastian. Or try to read into what you're saying. So I'm going to take what you tell me literally. I won't get hurt in this, whatever this is or isn't, by making up some sort of fairy-tale romance that doesn't exist." She looked over to me while traffic was steady. "You already know I don't have time for that in my life. Okay?"

"Yes." I nodded firmly.

"That's it? Just yes?" She looked at me expectantly. Hopeful, even.

"Should there be more?"

She just stared at the road, gripping the wheel with both hands again.

*Did I say something wrong? Am I fucking this up?*

"No. Not necessarily. I just thought that would encourage you to say something more. Maybe?" She still had that hopeful look in her eye.

Time for a different approach.

"I think Grant gave me some decent advice this morning. After I smacked his head into the floor a few times, but that's beside the point." I grinned, thinking of the blood on his favorite suit. Dickhead.

"What did he say?" she asked after a few long, quiet beats while I daydreamed about the rumble we'd had on my office floor.

"He said I should stop trying to manipulate everything where this is concerned." I motioned between us. "Just let it do what it's going to do."

She nodded. "That was good advice."

"I like you. I think you like me. Shit, I sound like I'm in junior high right now." I shook my head, feeling so foolish.

"I do," she said quietly.

I snapped my head left to meet her gaze.

"I do like you, Mr. Shark. Very much, in fact."

A rush of air escaped me.

"Why don't we just see where things go between us, then? That's what he said. Let it do its thing." I shrugged. "I haven't dated anyone or been in anything even closely resembling a relationship, since—okay, ever. I don't even know what that means. But I know when I think about you with another man, I see red. An actual red haze clouds my vision, and I want to hurt people and break things. I haven't felt like that before. Outside of Cassiopeia and Vela. Grant to a certain degree."

"There's more to caring for someone, though, than jealousy and control. You understand that, right?" Legitimate concern etched her face.

"Of course I do," I said as if she were absurd.

I mean, I thought I did.

The drive from downtown to Torrance took over an hour. I knew it wouldn't be pleasant, but I had no idea just how bad it really would be. When we finally got to her place, I wanted out of the car so desperately, it wouldn't have mattered if we were in front of a crack den. I would've still been happy to bail out of the passenger seat of the car.

"I'm a little embarrassed. I mean, it's nothing like your house. Really though, what is?" Abbigail stalled at the end of the winding walkway that led from the street to the multistory building before us.

"Stop. I love it already. Because it's where you live. Where is your condo?" I took in the expanse of the complex, surprised something like this popped up in this neighborhood. "Has this always been here? This complex, I mean?"

"I'm not sure when it was built, but they were recently renovated, so it's like brand-new inside. I'm really enjoying the place. I'm on the third floor, so grocery day sucks a bit, but other than that, I love it."

We walked around the building to the back and up the flights of stairs to her door. I stood behind her while she dug through her bag for her keys. I couldn't help touching her though, and I knew it was making the door-opening process take that much longer.

"Some of the residents own, but I just rent because I've been saving to expand the business." She fiddled with the key and the lock. "I spend so much time at the kitchen and at my brother's." She sighed and let her head fall to the side while I kissed my way up her neck, nipping the smooth skin.

"Jesus, just let me open the door. I can't think straight." She was breathy and flushed.

"I find it very difficult to keep my hands off of you." I tugged her backward into my groin by the pockets of her jeans. My erection pressed into her, and she moaned.

"My neighbors are going to be wondering why a man is

groping me on my front doorstep."

"It's pretty obvious why, Ms. Gibson. You're sexy as hell. What they're wondering is why I'm so lucky and they're so sad."

Finally, she opened the lock and pushed the door forward, the cold air from inside washing over our overheated skin as we entered.

She turned to face me, eyes glittering with lust. "Well, I guess—"

*Shit.* I was supposed to bring her home safely and then leave. That was as far as this plan went. I didn't want to leave, but now I had to face the whole virgin-shaped elephant in the room.

"Tell me what you want, Abbigail," I said, voice low and lust filled. I held on to her hips but kept her body away from mine. I couldn't think clearly when she was against me.

She stared, eyes burning with need.

"Be honest."

"Will you stay?" she whispered, husky and low.

"If I stay, then what? What do you want from me if I stay?"

"I want to . . . I want you . . . to . . ."

"Baby, if you can't even say it, how are you going to follow through with doing it? We don't have to rush into this."

Rays from the setting sun filtered into the condo through slanted wood shutters. Shadows danced across her face while she spoke.

"No. I want to. I want you to make love to me." She rushed the words out.

I shook my head slowly. "We've been over this before. I don't—"

"I know. I know."

I pressed my forehead to hers and rolled one side to the other. "You don't know. I don't want to hurt you. I will never forgive myself if I hurt you. But I don't know how to be gentle. The way you need to be treated your first time. It's not in me to be gentle, Abbigail. You don't understand what you're asking me to do."

"Is this why you pay women to have sex? So you can hurt them?" she whispered, still with our foreheads pressed together.

"No. No. Not at all." I straightened up and let my hands fall from her body. She thought I was a monster. What was I supposed to say to that? How did I explain rough sex to a virgin, for Christ's sake? How did this woman reach her fucking twenties and not know the difference between consensually being dominated versus being abused?

"Fuck me." I scrubbed my hand down my face. "Can we sit down?"

"Yes, of course." We moved to her open-concept kitchen-dining-living space. Two slightly opened pocket doors were visible, showing where space could be divided if you were looking to section the area off. A sofa was against one of the crisply painted walls, and Abbi motioned for us to sit.

Jesus Christ, this place was small.

"I'm just going to get right to it. I don't know how to tiptoe around all of this, but we're going to have to talk about what experience you have and don't have."

She just nodded. One quick nod.

I took her hands in mine and rubbed my thumbs over the tops of her fingers. "For starters, I don't pay women so I can physically hurt them. Ever. I have issues with being in control, I guess you could say. I typically find . . . partners . . . who like being controlled. Does that make sense?"

"Do you mean dominated?" She sat up a bit taller, like an eager student who knew the right answer to a question asked in class.

I grinned at her enthusiasm, still rubbing her fingers with mine. "Yes, that's another way of saying it. That doesn't always mean with toys and tools and all that 'Fifty Shades' bullshit. What it does mean, however, is I say when. I say how. It's that simple. I have to work and bargain and negotiate all day long. In bed, I don't want to. I want things to happen a certain way."

"Your way," she added, not in question but in confirmation.

"Yes, my way."

"All right, I understand that."

"Good. This is not negotiable for me. I've always been this way. I don't foresee it changing. My concern is that for a first time—*your* first time—my patience will wear thin and I will become too demanding and frighten you."

"That doesn't make sense, though."

"Abbigail." Her name came out in a huff. Already the frustration of the situation was leaking from the cracks forming in my control.

"No, Sebastian, you just said you don't like hurting women. So why would you scare me?"

"I said that's not the reason I pay women to have sex—so I can hurt them. The two things are not related."

Her face screwed up in the most adorably confused way, and I couldn't help but chuckle.

"I know this is hard to understand, and I think it will continue to be until you have more experience under your belt. Quite literally. The only thing I can keep emphasizing is my concern for my ability to handle things the way they need to be handled."

"Let's skip over this for now. We can circle back if you still feel like you need to." She switched to a playfully hopeful look before saying, "Unless the interview portion is over and we can get back to the kissing and good stuff. I'd much rather be doing that anyway."

Only a fool would turn down the chance to kiss this woman. Touch her. Stroke her.

I held her face in my hands while I explored her mouth. Kissed her lips and jaw and then journeyed back to her ear, marking her with nibbles that made her moan softly when I nipped the skin just beneath her earlobe. I soothed the spot with my tongue and then bit again, harder the second time, until she groaned louder.

"You like that, Little Red? Do you like it when I can't get enough with just kissing? That I have to bite?" I pressed into the spot with my thumb while I watched her process what I was asking her. I didn't really need an answer. Her body was telling me how much she loved what I was doing. But making her admit it just added to the heat.

"Have you touched a man before? His cock?"

Her green eyes grew impossibly wider.

"Tell me."

"I've touched a man before. Through his jeans, I mean." She swallowed hard, her slender neck flexing and undulating like she was moving a golf ball down to her belly instead of a knot of anxious need.

"Feel me." I shot my stare down to the obvious outline of my erection in my slacks. While suit pants looked sharp and appropriate for business hours, the material did nothing to hide a man's arousal. "Feel what you do to me."

Her eyes dropped to my lap. I wanted to grab her by the

wrist and force her to wrap her fingers around my shaft while I thrust my hips up to meet her touch.

Instead, I inhaled sharply through my nose and all but begged, "Feel the way my body responds to you. How I want you. I'm so fucking hard every time you're in the same room, Abbigail. Fuck, the same goddamn building."

She was taking too long. Too much hesitancy. It was the perfect example of what I had been trying to explain to her. Maybe if I showed her, she'd get my point and abort the notion I was the man for this crucible after all.

Acting on my carnal instinct, I lunged toward her and grabbed her wrist, exactly as I'd been picturing. She gasped sharply, and I knew I'd startled her. But I didn't relent. I couldn't. Taking control turned me on that much more.

"I said touch me, Little Red. Don't make me repeat it. Wrap those sexy fingers around my dick and feel how stiff I am." I put her palm against my cock and rocked my hips into her touch. "Christ Almighty, yes."

I let my head fall back and just sat like that for a few moments, enjoying the feel of her trembling hand over my crotch. "God, so good, baby. Squeeze me. Mmmm, more." I said the words while still looking heavenward. I loosened my grip on her wrist, and my good little girl continued stroking me on her own. I wanted to rip my belt open, pull my zipper down, and free myself so we could be skin to skin.

"Oh, good girl. So good, Abbigail. Did the last cock you touched feel like this?" I brought my head forward to meet her gaze with the question.

"No," she whispered. "Not at all."

"What was different?"

"Sebastian…" She moaned my name, but when she

moved to stop touching me, I growled low in my throat.

"Don't you fucking stop. I'll say stop when I want you to stop. Remember what I said? I say when. I say how. That's all you have to remember in all of this. It will always be amazing for you. Hand over everything to me, Abbigail."

"You're very sure of yourself." She reverted to flippancy when she was out of her comfort zone. I'd have none of it. Especially right now.

"Is your cunt wet, Abbigail?" When her eyes widened at my boldly worded question, I pressed further. "Answer me."

She nodded. Just the slightest dip of her head.

"Tell me, or I'll put my hand into your panties and find out for myself."

"Yes." She huffed lightly. "I said yes. Jesus."

"Is it too much? Already too much?" I challenged. "This is about a two on a scale of ten. It won't lighten up from here, Abbigail. This isn't a game for me. It turns me the fuck on to be touching you and for you to be touching me." I leaned closer and kissed her mouth. Slowly but firmly. When she attempted to deepen the kiss with her tongue seeking mine, I pulled back. "This is all I've been thinking about for a very long time," I said in a low, husky voice.

She watched me intently as I spoke.

When she didn't respond in kind, I had to ask, "Is this still what you want to do? Am I still the one you want to be doing it with? It's not too late to say stop. Until the literal moment my dick is inside you, it won't be too late to say stop."

"Yes. And yes. This is what I want. You are the man I want, Sebastian." She reached for me, and I took her hand, kissed the back first, and then I turned it over to kiss the more sensitive inside of her wrist. Her eyes grew hungrier with each brush of my lips.

"This is all I've been able to think about too. I don't have the confidence you do, true. I'm nervous. I'd be lying if I said I wasn't. But I like what you've been doing. It doesn't feel anything other than amazing—and right. I'm not scared of you, if that's what concerns you." She paused then, waiting for something, but I wasn't quite sure what. Maybe for me to tell her she should be or something predictable like that. Instead, I continued stroking her hand, giving her time to work through what she needed to say.

"I'm nervous, but it's excitement. Like, I don't know . . . the top of the big hill on a roller coaster? You're excited and scared, but it's a happy kind of scared, not a terrified kind of scared." She looked at me carefully and offered a self-deprecating chuckle. "Am I making sense at all?"

"Yes, it makes complete sense. But you must realize"—I surged my whole body forward, pressing her down into the seat cushions of the sofa so she lay beneath me—"like the first drop on that roller coaster, I'm going to push you over the edge." I loomed above her, not letting my full weight on top of her but enough that she was pinned.

*Helpless.*

"You are so fucking beautiful. Have I told you that?" Supporting myself on elbows along either side of her face, I stroked my fingers through her silky hair.

"No. I don't think you have." She smiled in a way I hadn't seen before, enjoying the compliment straight through to her soul. I could only guess in a house full of brothers, she didn't hear that enough. I made a mental note to tell her every single day from now on.

"Is this the night you want to do this, Abbigail? We don't have to rush this. I'm not going anywhere."

"Yes. Tonight. I don't want to wait any longer."

I'd had a feeling that would be her answer, but I would continue to give her the option to tap out until the very last second, as I'd said I would. But kissing her when her mouth was this close to mine couldn't be stopped. Our lips came together with need and hunger while our tongues danced with one another's. Slow and soft and then harder and more insistent.

"Well, it's not going to be on your sofa the first time. Where's your bedroom?"

With the will of twenty men, I dragged my body off her very pliant one and helped her stand. I motioned with a sweeping hand for her to lead the way, taking the opportunity to gawk at her ass while we went down the short hall to her bedroom. The smooth concrete floor carried through the entire condo, including the bedroom, where another colorful area rug covered most of the floor not occupied by furniture. The en suite bathroom light cast a soft glow over the room, and I excused myself to freshen up—and, honestly, to gather my wits for a few minutes.

How in the actual fuck was I going to deal with this? My own ancient history and enough horror stories from other men—urban legends, hopefully, about blood and tears and horrible pain ruining the whole experience. Granted, blood and tears didn't usually deter me in the bedroom. Quite the opposite, usually. But in those cases, it was intentional and consensual and not because the woman was untried.

*Pull on the man pants, Bas.*

A quick text to Joel that I'd be here a while and then a check of my wallet to make sure I had a few condoms. I couldn't remember reloading after the last time I'd used the usual stash I'd kept in there, and a surge of panic had me whipping through the billfold like a teenager on prom night.

I splashed my face with water and dried off. Gave myself a once-over in the mirror...for what? Not really sure, other than I was stalling. That was all there was to it. If Grant saw me right now, I'd never hear the end of it. After a deep, fortifying breath, I opened the door to go back into the bedroom.

*Beautiful. Just beautiful.*

My God, this woman. She lay on her bed, covers pulled down to the foot of the mattress. She was a goddess. A perfect female offering of bare flesh and flowing red hair. Positioned perfectly on the center of the platform like a sacrificial lamb to a lustful god.

Yes. Sign me up. I'd be that god tonight. My fingers tingled, and my cock jerked. My mouth watered—actually surged with saliva as though I was approaching a buffet of my favorite delicacies.

"Oh, Little Red," I groaned. "Look at you, pretty baby." I stood and stared at her, holding her gaze with mine for several long moments. She transfixed me. Incapacitated me with need.

I had come out of the bathroom with my belt and slacks undone, so my pants rested low around my hips. The top few inches of my erection were exposed. I was so thankful I wasn't completely confined by material as I swelled even more from viewing her.

So available.

So perfect.

So mine.

*Pump the brakes, chief. You haven't even touched her yet. Or tasted her.*

I unbuttoned my dress shirt and prowled toward her. Slowly. One button, one step. Never losing the eye contact that was anchoring me to her. To the moment. One button. One step. No rush.

"Sebastian..." My name sounded more like an entreaty. An appeal to the merciful man somewhere inside me.

A laugh threatened to spill free. Silly girl. A man as such didn't exist inside this shell. Never had. Likely never would. "What is it, baby?" I untethered the last button and let the shirt hang open on my body as I stood right beside the bed.

Abbi reached a hand up to touch me, but I stopped her by backing just out of reach, tutting a reprimand.

"Ahh-ahh. You keep your hands by your sides for now, Little Red."

"What? Why?" she implored softly.

I shrugged carelessly. "Because I said so."

"That seems terribly unfair, don't you think? Very one-sided."

"Hhmmm." I pretended to consider her question. "Give me ten minutes. Fifteen, tops. Then we'll check back and see if you think the plan is unfair. Deal?"

"Why do I have the top-of-the-roller-coaster feeling again?"

"Because you're a very smart girl." I lifted my shoulders and let my shirt slide off my torso and fall to the floor at the side of the bed.

"Turn your hand so your palm is facing up." After she did, I ran my index finger from the tip of her middle finger, across her palm, over the inside of her wrist, and trailed my teasing touch up her forearm. My path continued up her arm, skated over her armpit, and continued across her chest, just under her collarbone, and then down the other side to end on the tip of that middle finger. Goose bumps covered her skin everywhere

I surveyed. On the tops of her thighs, both arms, even on her chest and belly.

Her nipples were tight and inviting, and I wanted to feel them under my tongue. No. I needed to feel them. "Oh, baby. I don't know where to start with you." I blatantly drank her in. "I want to be everywhere on you and in you all at the same time."

I climbed onto the bed, straddling her hips with my knees. While she watched, I took the wallet from my back pocket and fished the row of three condoms, still strung together, from inside. I tossed them onto the mattress beside her shoulder, both so I could grab one when the time came but also as a mind fuck of a reminder of what we were about to do.

I didn't miss her sharp little inhale when the packets made a little *thwack* sound as they hit the sheets. I also didn't bother to hide my grin from her reaction. Such an innocent little bird. I positioned my body over hers, holding myself above her and nudging her knees apart with mine so I could settle some of my weight on the bed between her thighs. Our stomachs touched, and I lowered down even more so my bare chest rubbed directly against hers, sending bolts of electricity straight to my dick.

"You feel so good under me, Abbigail. So warm, so pliant. Your skin is like silk." I ran my hand up the side of her rib cage to palm her breast fully. "God, these tits, baby. So perfect. So fucking pretty." I pushed up to sit back on my heels to use both hands to knead and plump her mounds. But also so I could stare at her again. There was something transfixing about this woman. Something I couldn't put into words. Her beauty—so pure and natural. Was it because I usually bedded women who were a certain percent plastic and polished and very practiced? Maybe.

*Probably.*

It made the moments with Abbigail poignant. Sublime, even. I wanted to simultaneously take my time and rush. Ridiculous, I knew. But she had me so turned around. I never wanted to stop and look at a woman for anything more than the physical, reactionary need. The required stimuli to become aroused. Yet here I hovered, positioned above a very willing, wanton virgin. And all I wanted was to savor and linger. To appreciate and catalog her every pant and rush of needy breath.

What in the actual hell was happening?

Her soft moan brought me back to the same mental dimension with her, and with each pass of my hands over her body, I grew rougher with my groping. I rubbed over her nipples with my thumbs, massaging her breasts so firmly, her body was rocking in a steady rhythm on the mattress. A light surge forward and then back. Quite similar to what it would be like when I was finally pumping my cock into her.

"Fuck me," I gritted, leaning down to cover one of her tips with my mouth.

"Yes, please. Please, I want that too." Abbigail moaned up to the ceiling while fishing her fingers through my hair and holding my mouth to her.

I licked around the tight bud of her nipple several times with my tongue before sinking my teeth into the flesh on the underside. Her skin smelled so divine. Feminine and arousing with a spicy flair, echoing her personality perfectly. An enticing combination of sage and mint or some sort of invigorating eucalyptus. It was hard to identify precisely, but the appeal kept me pressing my nose and mouth to her skin as if I would be able to take a part of her with me when I finally had to drag myself away from her.

Because I would have to. Eventually. I knew it more positively than I knew my own name. Even if it killed one of us. And at the rate I was kissing and sucking on her, it would be yours truly.

I worked both breasts with equal fervor—kissing, licking, devouring. Abbigail writhed and moaned under my body, adding delicious friction to the swell in my slacks with every move. I sat back and looked at her, pale skin flushed with excitement, red hair in a messy tangle on the pillow beneath her head.

"So sexy, baby." I traced my finger down her jaw, and she leaned into my touch, eyes drifting closed. "Pretty little baby." She soaked up the praise as I traced my finger lower, down her sternum and over the swell of her belly and then back.

I'd been avoiding her pussy up to this point, but I couldn't for another second. I backed down her legs in a crawl, kissing my way down her body.

"Little Red?" I asked in a gravelly whisper, hovering above her mound. My breath fanned over the slickness on her cunt, making goose bumps break out once again.

"Ooohhhh, God," she stammered, making to sit up, but I halted her progress with my full hand across her torso.

"No. Stay." I waited for her to relax back on the bed before continuing. "I have to taste this pussy. I can't be this close to you and not put my mouth here." I ran my fingers across her pink slit, and she bucked into my hand. "Already so wet. So ready." My index and middle fingers formed the slight vee of her petal-soft lips as I spread her pussy open a bit, releasing more of her addicting scent into the air. I inhaled through my nose so I didn't miss a bit of it while I pressed her clit like the needy button it was.

"What do you mean 'already'? It feels like I've been waiting—fantasizing—about this for months."

"Is that right? I asked, dangerous delight in my tone as I looked up the length of her body. And now that I'd done that, I was distracted all over again by the incredible sight she presented. Flushed, naked, and aroused. Maybe it was her inexperience—her innocence—that made her so appealing? I didn't want to ruminate over it for another second. Whatever it was. It was time for action. Time to make her fantasies reality. Replace the dreamscape with actual memories.

"Spread your legs wider for me, Abbigail."

She propped herself up on her elbows, swallowed hard, and whispered, "Whaa...?"

The big bad wolf inside growled. "You heard me. Show me your cunt. Show me more."

"Sebastian."

I held her evergreen gaze in mine. "Last time I'll say it nicely. I'm not playing games, girl. And I'm not used to saying things more than once. Now open your legs wider and let me see that wet pussy."

Slowly, she moved her leg toward the edge of the bed. I tilted my head slightly, and she pushed it farther. "Good. Now, watch me."

"I don't—what—" she stammered before I started moving to get comfortable between her thighs. The questions she wanted to ask, but couldn't organize, were answered with my position.

"Keep your eyes on me, or I stop."

Her breaths came in quick jerks, and I chuckled. I hadn't even put my mouth on her yet, and she was all but hyperventilating. "Breathe normally, Abbigail, or you're going to pass out and miss all the fun."

"You're not very nice," she barely more than mouthed.

"I think you're going to change your mind in a minute," I said almost against her mound, still with her gaze captured. Her thighs trembled, skin pebbled with chills, even though heat radiated from her core—so much so that I felt it before I took the first long swipe with my tongue.

"Fuuuccckk," she moaned, letting her head fall back on her shoulders.

"Oh, baby, already?" I *tsked*.

It took a few seconds for her to realize I was waiting for her to bring her eyes back to me. When the little rule I issued was recalled in her mind, she leveled her stare back to my waiting one.

"Don't tease me again, Abbigail. Do you understand me? I need more than one taste at a time. Show some control, girl."

She widened her eyes at me.

"Watch yourself, girl." I dug my fingers into the soft flesh on the inside of her thighs to hold her still while I licked her again. She watched me without looking away, like a very obedient girl. She watched me trace her pussy up and down, inside, outside, every delicate inch I could stab and flick my tongue while she bucked and moaned in response. Her sweet juice coated my lips and chin, even the tip of my nose from when I got extra ambitious and fucked her hole with deep thrusts of my tongue.

I took Abbi by surprise, surging up her body to kiss her mouth. It made me so fucking hot when a woman licked the taste of her pussy off my face or hands, or . . . fuck . . . my cock. "Taste your cunt on my mouth, Little Red. Taste how fucking sweet and tangy you are."

My cock leaked from the tip when she attacked my mouth, groaning and eating my lips, greedily licking my lips like she'd be happy to eat pussy if given a chance.

*Hello, idea. File that away for another time.*

"I think there's a dirty little girl in here. She's been hiding away, waiting to be set free, hmmm?" I taunted between openmouthed kisses.

"Who says I've been hiding? Maybe the right person just wasn't looking," she said with a sassy little shrug.

With her knees bent and her heels about twelve inches from her ass, I had a delicious view of her cunt. My cock had made its way out from my boxers so far, it was almost pointless to still have pants on.

"Stay right there." I backed off the mattress to undress fully. I was out of my pants so quickly and back on the bed, it was like I had never really gone. "Drop your knees out to the side. Leave your heels right where they are." And this time, she did exactly as I said. No hesitation. No argument. Not even a questioning look.

*Oh, fuck yes.* I went right in for the treasure I was seeking. The swollen pink fruit, so ripe and ready, the juice was running down the crack to her ass. I swiped up the trickle of moisture with my finger and brought it up between our faces. The gooey substance stretched between my fingers when I touched them together for her to see.

"Do you want me to fuck you yet, baby?" I stuck my finger in my mouth. I knew the answer. I wanted her to be begging me for it by the time it happened. I wanted her to want it more than air, so no matter how badly my big cock hurt her, the memory would always be a good one.

"I do. I want it so badly, Sebastian."

I found her pussy again while she spoke and stuffed a finger inside. She was so fucking wet and, goddammit, so tight. The invasion took her by surprise, but she moaned in pleasure, not in pain or fear.

"Oh, baby, you feel so good. So fucking tight here." I got closer to her, pushed my way between her feet with my knees so I was sitting back on my heels between her bent legs. I leaned forward to take her mouth in a deep, demanding kiss.

In and out, working my index finger until she was completely accepting. I moved my kisses down her neck, roughly biting and then licking where I had tasted. I was working us both into a frenzy.

"More, Abbigail?" I asked. Demanded, really.

She looked at me, dazed with lust.

"Do you want another finger in your pussy? Do you want to feel fuller?"

"Yes. God, yes!" she answered easily. And thank God for it. My cock was much bigger than one of my fingers. If she begged off after one, we were going to be in for a really long night.

Her pussy was so wet, the noises coming from my fingers pumping into her were lewd and erotic. "Fuck yes. I love that sound. Feel me, baby. Feel what you're doing to me."

Fuck, I was so wound up, I wanted to explode. I was afraid when I did finally get inside her, I'd last for only a few strokes. Abbigail wrapped a tentative hand around my erection, and I hissed.

"Did that hurt you? I'm so sorry."

"No." I tried to laugh, but I sounded like an injured farm animal instead. "No, I'm so jacked up, it feels like electricity," I said in a strangled voice.

"Oh. Ooooohhh," she responded when I added a third finger.

"Take it, baby. Take it for me. You can handle it, can't you?" I chanted and then challenged.

She nodded quickly. Short, jerky nods.

"That's my good girl. My cock is bigger than my fingers, baby. Think of how good you're going to feel stuffed full of my dick." My praises and taunts were tangled with our kisses and tongues' choreography.

"See? Your body likes that idea. I felt your cunt gush more when I said that. Dirty girl. You want my cock so bad, don't you?"

"I do. I do, Sebastian. Please. Just fuck me now. I'm ready now. Please." Abbi whimpered and begged, and I knew it would play on a continuous loop in my memory for a very long time.

"I think you are too. Lie back, baby. It's time. Is this how you want it? Missionary?"

"I don't . . . I don't know? Can you just decide that part?"

Record-setting condom donning time clocked after that, and then I was positioned at her entrance, Abbigail's extra-large emerald eyes riveted to mine.

"Relax, baby. Just relax. It just felt so good with my fingers, right?" Where the scholarly patience came from was beyond me.

"Yes." She nodded quickly. "Yes, so good."

"Okay, so just remember that. This is going to be amazing too. I'm going to try to go as slow as possible. God fucking help me. Because I want to ram straight in and get the bad part over with all at one time."

Her eyes somehow went wider still with panic.

"I won't do that. I wouldn't betray your trust like that. Now kiss me; kiss me and feel me here." I rolled my hips so the head of my cock rubbed on her clit. Even through the condom,

I could feel her heat.

Bit by bit, I eased my cock into her. It took every shred of control I could muster to not just give in and pound into her. When I felt the resistance of her virginity fight back, I buried my face in her neck and crooned, "Baby, baby, I have to do it. It's the only way to get it over with. This is what you wanted. Forgive me. Forgive me."

I surged my hips forward, and Abbigail wailed, her back bowing off the bed in pain.

*Monster.*

*I am a fucking monster.*

I went to pull out of her, but she stopped my retreat with surprisingly strong grips of her thighs around my waist and arms around my neck.

"Don't you dare leave me now."

"I hurt you," I said into her neck. I couldn't look into her face, not with the sound she just made still so fresh in my ears.

"The only way you will hurt me is if you bail on me right now. My body is already adjusting to you being inside." She rolled her hips slightly under mine, and I groaned low in my throat. My cock was still very hard and very needy from all the foreplay.

"Move, Sebastian." Abbigail dug her fingertips into my ass, pulling me into her. "Don't start something you're not going to finish, damn it."

I pulled back to give her a look of warning, sliding out of her pussy very slowly while doing so. Just a bit at first and then back in, my stern expression locked on her the entire time. Somehow holding on to the obligation helped me manage the feat. Gripping on to the mental bubble of duty didn't override the physical feeling, though. Nothing could've done that. Her pussy was heaven. Fucking heaven.

"Okay? Better now? Tell me, Abbigail. How does my cock feel inside you?" Yes, I was goading her, but I needed her feedback. Needed her to stay right in that glorious moment with me.

"Oh shit, Sebastian. It's so good. So . . . so . . . I don't know. I can't think right now. Just"—*gasp*—"want to"—*gasp*—"feel it all."

*Hell yes, baby. Feel it all, indeed. Feel me. Me. Me. Me.*

It was all I could think of on repeat. It was me inside her for the first time.

*Me.*

"We'll go nice and easy this first time. Yes?" My own voice was as choppy as hers. I was gripping on to my control by a thread.

"Okay"—*pant*—"okay. *Shit*, oh shit, that's so good. I didn't know. I didn't know . . ."

She was so amazing. So amazed, too. Adorable and stunned with the wonder lacing her words as if she were discovering a new constellation or seeing a shooting star for the first time.

I tried to move at a steady pace. I occasionally changed the angle of my hips and toyed with her clit and nipples to see if either appealed to her as I slid my dick inside her pussy. The familiar pull gathered low in my stomach, and I bit into the inside of my cheek to distract me from my impending climax. There was no way I'd come before she got off. If I could just fuck her in earnest, she'd hit the right pleasure combo to rocket to ecstasy.

"Baby, I need to fuck you for real. I can't hold it back. This is what I knew would happen. I can't . . . I don't . . . I shouldn't . . ." I couldn't finish a damn thought. My body was taking over, warring with the carefully knitted control I had woven to handle her properly for her first experience.

But it was all falling apart. One more pump . . .

One more throaty, sexy sound from her . . .

"Fuck, Bas, just do it. Fuck me. Do it, please. God, yes."

My hips started driving the moment she called me Bas. Something about the more intimate moniker coming off her lips. What a bizarre thing to flood me with desire. But once again, Abbigail Gibson slew me with a secret weapon I didn't expect her to wield. Her final affirmative plea was all I needed to hear to cut the tether that had bound my primal urges.

Fisting my hands into her long red mane, I anchored myself to her and thrust. My hips punished as we smacked together. Again. Again. Again.

"Yes, God, yes!" she shouted. My name, God's name, random exultations, and pleas, pants, and moans. All provoked me onward as I chased our mutual release.

"Come, Abbigail, fuck! Give it to me, baby!"

"I'm so close, so close, so close."

I yanked myself free from her body, flipped her onto her stomach, and quickly pulled her back so her ass was raised into the air. I knew I'd berate myself as soon as we were done for treating her so roughly, so crudely. The exact way I'd handle any other fuck. But I needed to drive into her deeper. I wanted her to feel me in her womb, taste me in her mouth, smell me when she inhaled.

Abbigail scrambled to support herself on her arms, but I pushed her back down so her face was to the side on the mattress and her chest lay flat. "Stay there. Keep your ass up high where I put you in the first place, damn it."

My hips slapped her ass with each thrust forward, filling the room with an erotic echo of flesh.

*Smack. Smack. Smack.*

"Rub your clit while I fuck you. You're going to know who was in this pussy every time you move tomorrow, won't you?" She didn't answer me at first, so I pinched her ass, and she yelped. "Answer me!"

"What? I can't think straight. What?" Her sex-roughened voice was muffled by the bedding.

"Are you going to have a sore pussy tomorrow? Do you hear how wet your cunt is? For me. Just for me! Naughty girl."

*Smack. Smack.*

"Yes. Definitely sore tomorrow," she said between breaths.

"You like being fucked?" I raked my nails down her spine, just firmly enough to leave light marks and make her arch deeper and thrust her ass toward me more.

"Yes!" She moaned. "Gooood, yes!"

"By who, Abbigail? Just anyone?" I reached between her legs and batted her hand away from her clit where she'd been rubbing herself and pinched the swollen bud until she shrieked. "Answer me, girl. Do you let anyone else touch this pussy?"

"No! Nooo. No!" She was so worked up, it was killing me to hold on.

"No what?" I leaned over her and growled, pressing my cock so deep into her she yelped.

"No. Just you, Sebastian."

"That's right. Just me. This is my pussy. Mine. Say it, baby. Tell me!" I fucked her so hard she gasped for air and the bed started banging into the wall.

"Fuck, I'm going to come. God, Bas. Please, God, fuck, yes."

"Say it!" I bellowed, pounding her like a crazed man.

"It's yours. It's just yours! Fuck! Yes! Goooooooddd!"

"Oooohhhh, Abbigail." I went completely still, but my cock pulsed and jerked deep inside her, doing its very best to blow through the end of the condom with hot jets of semen. Over and over, I felt the pulses fill the rubber.

I pressed my forehead between her shoulder blades, and we lurched forward onto the bed, me on top of her, two very overheated bodies thrumming together as one.

"Fuck, baby. What are you doing to me?" I whispered, trying to regain a regular breathing pattern.

"Me? Doing to you?" She laughed lightly, seeming completely boneless beneath me. I knew I needed to roll off her, but I wasn't ready for it to end. The moment I pulled out of her, it would all come to a screeching halt, and the self-recrimination and loathing would begin. Just another moment or two wouldn't hurt.

"Don't do it, Bas," she said quietly, trying to move below me.

I rolled to the side and then off the bed to deal with the condom. I went to the bathroom and returned quickly, pulling her into my arms on the rumpled, sex-mussed sheets. I didn't bother reigniting the spark of the conversation she attempted to start before I got up, however. I wasn't about to douse the flames of the experience we'd just shared with psychobabble so soon.

With her back against my front, I nuzzled my face into her hair, loving the smell and feel of her on my face. I wasn't usually a post-fuck cuddler. Another Abbigail-only habit, apparently.

"How are you feeling? Are you hurting?" The least I could do was check in with her physically. "I tried to keep some sort of control. I swear I did. I apologize if I hurt you. I had a feeling I wouldn't be strong enough. I know this probably isn't the ideal time for an 'I told you so.'"

"Please don't ruin this. Seriously. If that's the path you're going to wander down, just stay quiet. I'm fine. Physically, I'm fine. Yes, I'll be sore tomorrow. Twenty minutes ago, that seemed to be some sort of fuel on an open flame to you. Forgive me if I'm having trouble believing the doting lover routine now."

I pinched the nipple I'd been petting.

"Hey! What was that for?" she whined, and I hid my grin in her silky hair.

"Watch the sassy mouth, Abbi. I am concerned about your well-being. Don't question it again." I wet my fingertips and rubbed her where I'd just pinched, letting the cool air pucker the sensitive tip to a sharp point. "I'm trying not to mentally drag myself through the fire here for the way I just fucked you like an animal."

Abbigail turned in my arms so we lay nose-to-nose. Her soft lips were just a whisper from mine, and I couldn't resist the chance to feel them beneath mine again. We kissed a few times softly before she pulled back.

"Sebastian Shark, listen to me right now. I wouldn't change one single minute of what we just shared. Okay?" She waited until she was entirely sure she had my full attention, and I wasn't going to object. "Not. One. Minute. Please don't trivialize it again by apologizing or feeling bad about it. That's all I'm going to ask of you regarding this." She ran her fingers through my thick hair, scraping her fingernails on my scalp while she did. "I know it wasn't something you wanted to be a part of in the first place. You didn't want me holding some romantic notion about you or you and me afterward. I get that. But I'm asking you to not cheapen what just happened by saying any more of those things. Deal?"

I gave her my acquiescence in the form of a very urgent, seductive kiss. When she parted her lips for me, I thrust my tongue in and out deeply, reminding her of the way I had just mastered her body with my cock. We moved apart, and her eyes were glassy and full, no longer questioning how I felt about the evening's activities.

"Can we have sex again?" she asked, her green eyes all but glowing in the dimly lit room.

"I think that can be arranged. But let's shower first. Then I'm going to eat your pussy until you can't remember your own name."

"Oh," she croaked.

I chuckled and pulled her up from the bed. My dick already stood at full attention.

But then the sound of my cell phone interrupted all thoughts of naughty-shower-time fun.

"We need to learn to put our phones on silent when we're together," she grumbled, walking into the bathroom and turning on the water for our shower.

At the same time, I stomped to where my pants lay in a heap on the floor and fished out the offensive device, stabbing the green key to answer.

"Shark."

"Hey, man."

"Twombley, this better be important. And why aren't you calling from your phone?"

"Not important," he said without a pause. "And I wouldn't call you at this hour if it wasn't important. We've got a big problem with the city. We need to brainstorm, and fast, or the groundbreaking isn't going to happen on schedule."

"Fuck me! Goddammit, Grant! We have the press lined up. It has to happen." I scrubbed my hand down my face and around to grip at the back of my neck. My patented stressed-out move.

"I understand that, Bas," my best friend said with patience I probably didn't deserve. "That's why I'm calling you."

"Fine. Where?"

"Your place?" he asked, sounding as tired as I suddenly felt.

"Fine." I checked the time on my phone's screen. "I'll be there in thirty minutes."

"Where are you?" he asked, merely being a nosy shit.

"Goodbye, Twombley." I ended the call and let my head fall forward until my chin hit my chest.

*Motherfucker!*

I didn't want to leave, but I didn't have a choice. I needed to fill Grant in on all the shit that happened with Terryn and Cinnamon too. Outside of the amazing time I'd spent with Abbi, the entire day was a fiasco. I rubbed my eyes, trying to think of what to tell Abbigail. I had heard the water running in the shower when I was on the phone. I quickly pulled my boxers and pants on and turned to go talk to her in the bathroom.

But when I spun around, she was standing in the doorway of the bathroom. She looked like every man's perfect dream girl standing there wrapped in a fluffy towel, backlit from the fixtures in the small, steam-filled room behind her.

Except my girl had nothing but utter disappointment on her face, having overheard the conversation I'd just ended with Grant.

She knew I was leaving.

I'd just taken her virginity, and now I was leaving.

Score one for the asshole.

# CONTINUE READING
## THE SHARK'S EDGE SERIES

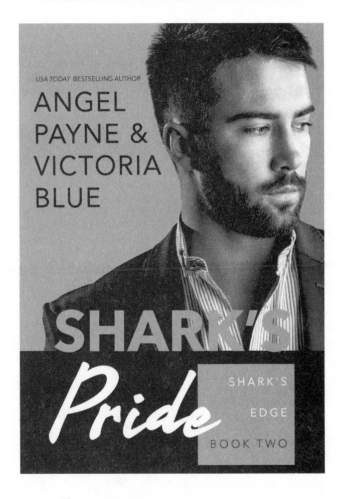

*USA TODAY* BESTSELLING AUTHOR

ANGEL
PAYNE &
VICTORIA
BLUE

SHARK'S
*Pride*

SHARK'S
EDGE

BOOK TWO

*Keep reading for an excerpt!*

# EXCERPT FROM *SHARK'S PRIDE*
## BOOK TWO IN THE SHARK'S EDGE SERIES

Though so many things could be handled electronically in a modern business world, a surprising number of things still weren't. Terryn had several piles neatly separated and labeled for me, coded in order of how they needed to be handled. One pile needed signatures. The next needed to be reviewed and returned to her for corrections. A third stack was all new items, or so the label told me. I knew better. They were problems in disguise.

I moved that last pile off to the side of my desk. Way off. I'd tackle that mess after lunch. At the moment, my brain was only good for blindly scrawling my name on the indicated blank and moving on to the next.

I moved through the stack efficiently until the familiar knock came on my door.

She wasn't a moment too soon. My nerves and my stomach were throwing in the towel, and if Abbigail hadn't shown up when she did, it would've taken three men and a boy to stop me from texting her again.

"In!" I called while resuming my mindless task. No sense changing my habits completely for the woman—or so I kept trying to fool myself. But a man had to keep his balance somewhere, and the woman had already upended me in so many other ways.

"Hey there."

Abbigail said it quietly while scooting her head and shoulders beyond the edge of the door. She gripped the wood like it was a floating panel from the sinking Titanic. I'd never seen anything more adorable.

"Sebastian?"

"Yes?"

"I asked if this was a good time," she prompted. "Are you ready for lunch?"

I swore to God, every answer in my mind sounded over-the-top. Maybe beyond that. But I was helpless to verbalize any of them as I looked all the way up, into her eyes. The world fell away. The minutes stopped mattering. And as soon as she walked over to stand in front of my desk, my balance went to hell too.

God, I'd missed her.

I stood abruptly, knocking my chair back into the now-worn dent in the bookcase.

Abbigail's sharp inhale at my sudden movements just spurred me on more. I rounded my desk to stand directly in front of her, so close that my slacks rustled in the thick canvas of her apron. Her chest dipped with stuttering breaths as she tried to feign calm control.

I slid my index finger beneath her chin and tilted her face up until our eyes locked.

"Hi," I barely whispered.

"Hi."

"You're stunning."

She reached up to nervously toy with her ponytail. I stopped her by cuffing her wrist and directing it back down to her side. "Now you say, 'thank you.'"

A small grin quirked at the corner of her mouth before she said, almost too quietly, "Thank you."

"I'm going to kiss you," I told her, much like I did the first time our mouths met in the park after Vela's soccer game.

"Okay." Her whisper was even softer than before. And a thousand times sexier, if my cock was a correct barometer.

"I'm still not asking, Abbigail." I squinted my eyes playfully—yes, playfully—as I pressed in for a proper hello. Her warm lips welcomed me, yielding beneath mine. I stayed there for a few moments before pulling back, not allowing myself to deepen the kiss...waiting on her to either demand or deny me at this point.

As right as her gorgeous little mewl was, I hesitated to take her mouth again. If I started more, I'd never be able to stop. My cock spoke up loud and clear about that point, as well. I was damn sure if—no, when—I got inside her pussy again, I'd want to spend hours showing her all the ways I had missed what was mine.

*Mine.*

Christ, how right that sounded too.

After stepping back to put even more space between us, I waited for Abbi to look at me again. Instead, she jerked around and started busying herself with my lunch. I cleared my throat in objection—not that she heeded the glaring hint. I got a fast, furtive glance before she continued bustling about.

"Over here?" she asked, all business in her tone. "The usual spot?"

"That's fine."

I waved my hand, not caring if she left the food in her van for the afternoon. I wanted her attention, not her damn sandwich.

And I was damn determined to get it. No matter what that entailed.

*This story continues in*
**Shark's Pride:** *Shark's Edge Book Two!*

# ALSO BY
# ANGEL PAYNE & VICTORIA BLUE

# ALSO BY ANGEL PAYNE

# ALSO BY VICTORIA BLUE

**Misadventures:**
*Misadventures with a Book Boyfriend*
*Misadventures at City Hall*


**For a full list of Angel's & Victoria's other titles,
visit them at AngelPayne.com & VictoriaBlue.com**

# ACKNOWLEDGMENTS

A new series has so many special moments. And by special, I mean both awesome and challenging. I owe the most significant debt of gratitude to the team at Waterhouse Press for enduring the process that birthed this book and this series. Meredith Wild and Scott Saunders specifically—thank you. Thank you for not blocking me on your phones and social media accounts after listening to me whine, complain, and freak out in frustration countless times.

And as always, thank you to the Maniacs sprinting team, Angel and Meredith, for keeping me on track when I'd much rather be shopping online! Thank you, Martha Frantz, for keeping me on track socially and being an excellent sounding board to help me ensure I'm not losing my mind! And lastly, thank you, Amy Bourne, for sharing my love of all things Audible! Because all work and no swoon makes the day really long and tedious!

—Victoria

Incredible thanks and gratitude to so many who helped bring this series into an amazing reality.

Most prominently, I'm thankful to the Creator for blessing me with such an amazing writing partner. Victoria Blue, you are such an epic and exquisite goddess. This story and this world are such a bright entity because of your presence, guidance, voice, and vision. Thank you for helping me get after the sharky bread!

Shannon Hunt, for being our very first beta reader and championing our gorgeous Sebastian from the start. Here he is at last, girl!

Meredith Wild, for leaping off the cliff with us into a new fictional world and for having faith in this work. We're both beyond grateful!

The entire Waterhouse Press team, for taking Bas and Abbi under your wing and into your hearts, and working as hard as we have on perfecting and promoting the work: Jon Mac, Robyn Lee, Jennifer Becker, Haley Byrd, Keli Jo Nida, Kurt Vachon, Yvonne Ellis, Jesse Kench, Amber Maxwell, and Dana Bridges. But most especially, so many thanks to the magnificent Scott Saunders, Editor God on High and human being extraordinaire. Your input and expertise on this one has been "above and beyond," and we are truly grateful!

Martha Frantz, for keeping me organized and on track so many days. I am so appreciative of you!

My writing/publishing world sisters, who are always there with a shoulder and more: Shayla Black, Jenna Jacob, Helen Hardt, Eden Bradley, Regina Wamba, Rebekah Ganiere, and Nelle L'Amour. You ladies have talked me off (and onto!) sooo many ledges—and the ledges and I are thankful!

Every member of the wild, wonderful, crazy, and beautiful Payne Passion nation. No matter where I've connected with you, I am truly blessed for your presence in my world. Thank you for continuing to believe in the stories and supporting the work. Your hearts and souls are so precious and perfect to me. Stay passionate!

—Angel

# ABOUT ANGEL PAYNE

*USA Today* bestselling romance author Angel Payne loves to focus on high-heat romance starring memorable alpha men and the women who love them. She has numerous book series to her credit, including the action-packed Bolt Saga and Honor Bound series, Secrets of Stone series (with Victoria Blue), the intertwined Cimarron and Temptation Court series, the Suited for Sin series, and the Lords of Sin historicals, as well as several standalone titles.

Angel is a native Southern Californian, leading to her love of being in the outdoors, where she often reads and writes. She still lives in Southern California with her soul-mate husband and beautiful daughter, to whom she is a proud cosplay/culture con mom. Her passions also include whisky tasting, shoe shopping, and travel.

Visit her at AngelPayne.com

# ABOUT VICTORIA BLUE

International bestselling author Victoria Blue lives in her own portion of the galaxy known as Southern California. There, she finds the love and life-sustaining power of one amazing sun, two unique and awe-inspiring planets, and four indifferent yet comforting moons. Life is fantastic and challenging and every day brings new adventures to be discovered. She looks forward to seeing what's next!

Visit her at VictoriaBlue.com